A Fiddler and
Fiora Mystery

THE KING

OF

NOTHING

A. E. MAXWELL

HarperPaperbacks
A Division of HarperCollins*Publishers*

This is a work of fiction. The characters, incidents, and dialogues are products of the author's imagination and are not to be construed as real. Any resemblance to actual events or persons, living or dead, is entirely coincidental.

HarperPaperbacks *A Division of* HarperCollins*Publishers*
10 East 53rd Street, New York, N.Y. 10022

A hardcover edition of this book was published in 1992 by Villard Books, a division of Random House, Inc.

Cover illustration by Danilo Ducak

First HarperPaperbacks printing: July 1994

Printed in the United States of America

HarperPaperbacks and colophon are trademarks of HarperCollins*Publishers*

10 9 8 7 6 5 4 3 2 1

Praise for A. E. Maxwell
and
Fiddler and Fiora

"Maxwell is good, really good, able to create believable, engaging, and original characters and set them plausibly into a story of nonstop suspense."   —*Chicago Sun-Times*

"Maxwell's style is sexy and hard-hitting."
—*Publishers Weekly*

"[Maxwell] combines wit, humor, suspense and a believable plot with just the right mix of action and dialogue for a good read."   —*United Press International*

"One of the most interesting and engaging private eyes since Robert Parker's Spenser."   —*Advertising Age*

"Weary of dreary police procedurals, morally ambiguous cold warriors, hypersensitive and much-too-introspective private eyes? Then you may be just the man or woman enough to ride shotgun with A. E. Maxwell's Fiddler."
—*Los Angeles Herald Examiner*

"The most unusual, up-to-date private eye with the hard-boiled characteristics of the legendary Sam Spade."
—*San Antonio Express News*

"Fiddler, growing from book to book, gives Travis McGee a run for his money."   —*Kirkus Reviews*

"Fiddler, like the legendary Philip Marlowe, is one of a kind . . . he tackles each situation with all the restraint of a rampaging bull. A. E. Maxwell, like Raymond Chandler, is a master at creating atmosphere."
—*Saint John Telegraph*

"One of the slickest, most likeable detectives."
—*Mystery News*

Also by A. E. Maxwell

JUST ANOTHER DAY IN PARADISE
THE FROG AND THE SCORPION
GATSBY'S VINEYARD
JUST ENOUGH LIGHT TO KILL
THE ART OF SURVIVAL
MONEY BURNS

Available from HarperPaperbacks

For
LOWELL KING MAXWELL
still on his throne

THE KING OF NOTHING

ONE

Rory Cairns fished for his beloved salmon at the peak of their power, when the fish were balanced on the brink of their bittersweet, majestic journey up the river to death and regeneration. He once told me he hunted, fought, and loved salmon because their strength kept him young.

It must have worked. Had I not known that Rory fought in World War II, I would have guessed his age at less than sixty. A lot less. Only in full sunlight did the few threads of gray show through his thick brown hair. He was six feet two inches, two hundred and ten pounds, as thick through the shoulders as a good Garry oak and as light on his feet as a falling leaf. Scots by birth and American be choice, he still spoke in the Gaelic rhythms of his childhood when he was excited.

"Fish on!" Rory yelled. "Take the wheel up there, Fiddler. This tup is mine!"

I had no doubt of it. That afternoon Rory

seemed ageless as a rock, indestructible as the tide. I was a lot younger myself, that day. I had never thought of Rory as an old man. I had never thought of his death. He was the King of Nothing and he would go on forever, fishing and fiddling, living and enjoying.

Oh, sure, he would die someday—everyone did —but it would be some other day. Not today. Never today. And when he did die, it would be the way the salmon did, a consummation rather than simple annihilation.

It was a nice illusion, and like most illusions it lasted just long enough to break a lot of hearts.

"I'm on the wheel," I called, grabbing it.

Over the stern of the twenty-four-foot power-boat, a fishing rod was bent parallel to the blue ocean. The line ran above the surface for thirty yards, as the reel screamed its adrenaline song of a muscular salmon swimming flat out beneath the sea.

Rory lost seventy-five yards of line before the reel quit screaming. Throughout that first run he kept the rod tip at one o'clock and his right palm cuppped against the reel, taking his own advice: Let the tackle do the work; make the fish do the fighting.

Unlike human beings, fish don't know when they're beaten. that's why they win more often than they lose.

"Snatch that other line," Rory said, without looking toward me. "Be quick, laddie. He's a muckle wan."

I checked the heading, locked the wheel, and slid down the handrails to the stern well. A quick yank on the second rod popped the trolling planer and freed the line. I reeled frantically. Thirty seconds later I had wound in the shocking-pink planer, the leader, and the plug. I stashed the rod where it wouldn't get in the way.

Rory's reel screamed again.

I laughed and wished Fiora were there to share the fun. There is no sound in the world like that of a fine big fish stripping line. But Fiora was more than a thousand miles away, wrestling with corporate devils while she tried to close the biggest deal of her life.

"Soon," she had told me last night on the phone. "Soon we'll both be free. Then we can be the Prince and Princess of Nothing."

The reel was still screaming.

"Next stop Tokyo," I said.

Rory half grinned, half snarled, like my Rhodesian Ridgeback with a mouthful of frayed, knotted sock and me tugging on the other end. Rory and Kwame both regarded hard work as the ultimate fun.

Finally Rory was satisfied with the balance between himself, the line, and his unseen opponent. He raised the tip of his rod experimentally. The tip guide bobbed twice as the salmon tried to throw off the hook.

"Nae, smolt," Rory crooned to the fish. "None of your sly tricks, now. Ye're mine." To me he said, "He's coming up. Out near that big slick."

I started to object. No way could the fish be that far from the boat. But suddenly a fin bigger than my hand appeared in the slick. I felt like a kid in church and uttered my grandmother's favorite oath, "Sweet heavenly days!" And then, "You'll need a dip net the size of a purse seiner to bring that bastard in."

Rory lifted the tip another few inches, then dropped it and reeled in, picking up the slack. The tendons of his elbow and neck were corded beneath his weathered skin. Each time he dipped and reeled he picked up another yard of monofilament. Slowly the salmon was being turned back toward us.

Then I remembered I was supposed to be piloting the boat. A quick 360-degree head check told me we had trouble. The rock wall of the shore was still fifty yards to starboard, but dead ahead, seventy-five yards away, a commercial long-liner was bearing down on us. The fisherman was in his stern well, straightening a tangled cable and preparing to drop his trolling pig over the side. The trolling arms were straight out, parallel to the water. The boat was on autopilot, steering a course that would cut between us and our fish.

"Long-liner!" I yelled to Rory.

He spared the situation one fast look. "Cross his bow. Jump to it, but don't yank this hook!"

I leaped for the wheel, cranked hard to port, and slapped the trottle forward, trying to slip into gear without racing the engine. I could miss the troller's hull easily enough, but the long trolling arms were another matter. They were too low for us to go under, and they reeached out ten yards on either side of his boat. I had a lot of water to cross and not much time to do it.

And I had to drag a tender-mouthed king salmon behind me like a squalling child.

I hit the horn, sending a long blast over the water. The other man looked up, saw what was happening, and went back to his work. He could have given way toward shore a few points without fouling his gear, but there's little love lost between commercial and sport fisherman.

I turned across his bow anyway.

By now we were going too fast for fishing and too slow for comfort. We came so close to the troller that I could read the numbers on both sides of his bow through my port window. His prow made a liquid sound as it sliced through the still water. His throttled-down marine diesel had a muscular growl. I still had the entire length of his trolling arm to travel.

I wasn't going to make it.

The commercial fisherman and I watched one another and the tip of his outrigger. At the last moment, he touched a lever that lifted the arm a few feet, allowing the flying bridge—and me—to remain attached to the rest of Rory's boat.

Somehow Rory had kept the fish on during our careful dash for open water. The line now sliced steeply down through the water and disappeared. The fish was down deep, sulking. The depth sounder showed seventy feet of water beneath the keel.

I pulled the throttle back to neutral and went back to the well in case Rory needed me. Dip and retrieve. Dip and retrieve. Gently, relentlessly, Rory wrapped more line around the reel. The surface of the sea reflected the afternoon sunlight, hiding the depths. I shaded my eyes and looked again.

Fifteen feet down and ten yards off the port quarter, I saw a sleek, muscular shape. I tried to find words to describe the fish but they weren't necessary. Rory already knew what a fish he had tied into. He could feel the monster's power humming back up through his line.

The salmon was coming slowly toward us. His back was the color of a good green olive and his ventral fins were flared like the speed brakes on a 737. Rory lifted the fish's head. The salmon took one look at the boat and bolted, peeling off most of the line Rory had so carefully reclaimed.

Abruptly the line went slack.

"Bugger all!" Rory said, reeling in angrily. "I'm getting old." Then his voice changed. "Throttle! The cunning deil's turned back at us!"

I leaped to the wheel and tapped the throttle. The boat surged a few feet forward before I backed off again.

"Steady," Rory cried. "Just keep the tension up."

My reflexes were still tuned to my Cobra. Boat driving takes a different touch. For the next twenty minutes I steered, oversteered, corrected, and fiddled with the trottle all at once. Rory reeled while he praised me and cursed the fish and vice versa. Usually vice versa.

Most of the time I take orders about as well as a brick wall—just ask Fiora. But with Rory it was different. Watching him was a peak experience. He directed me and the boat, the rod, and the king salmon with the salty tongue and deft strength of the true fisherman.

In the end, he won.

"Out of gear," Rory called. "Get back here where I need you."

I popped the boat out of gear, shook out the big dip net, and got back there. The tip of Rory's rod pointed straight down beside the boat. The fish was seven or eight feet below, resting upright in the water, tired but not wallowing. The net was twenty-eight inches across at the mouth, and he looked too big to fit.

"Fifty pounds, minimum," I said.

Rory grunted.

I set aside the net and reached for a three-foot-long heavy wooden pole with a needle-sharp gaff hook the size of my hand at one end.

"No," Rory said. "No gaff."

I would have challenged anyone but Rory. Instead, I shut up and stood back to learn a new fishing trick.

Rory shifted the reel to his right hand and gently raised it high above his head, keeping tension on the fish and leaning over the gunwale at the same time, drawing the salmon up beside the boat. Scots fisherman and Pacific salmon measured one another.

Broad shoulders, an elegant body, an arching tail so powerful he could catch herring and needle-fish that were faster than hummingbirds—the salmon was magnificent. For me, it would have been the fish of a lifetime, and I suspected it was no different for Rory. Salmon this size are rarely caught by sport fishermen on twenty-pound test line, which was the heaviest Rory ever used.

"Sixty-five pounds, maybe seventy," he said. "Look at the girth of him."

The salmon's gill covers flared and closed rhythmically. He wasn't beaten, just gathering strength. Without a gaff, boating him would be impossible. I waited to see what Rory would do.

He reached into a well beneath the rail and handed me a rusty pair of lineman's wire cutters. I stared at him in disbelief.

"I've got more fish in me," he said, "more days yet to live. This laddie . . . let him go to do what he was born to do. He hasn't much time left."

That was Rory, always the right touch, always the grace to know the right thing to do. As usual he had taught me something, about fishing and about life. Once the adrenaline of the fight faded, the intelligent mind took over. This salmon shouldn't end up as eight-ounce cans of smoked protein to be noshed on by the climax predator known as *Homo sapiens*.

I caught the tight fishing line with my right hand and carefully pulled the salmon toward the side of the boat. Rory backed off a click on the reel, laid the rod aside, and leaned over to watch me cut the line.

When I drew the heavy salmon toward me, sliding the open nippers down the line toward the plug, the fish rolled, revealing the single hook that was holding him. I slid the nippers all the way down and got lucky. Before the salmon could panic, I grabbed the hook. One fast twist, and the barb slipped past the bony ridge at the corner of the fish's mouth, setting him free.

Now, I know fish can't wink.

And I know this one did. Then he gave one flick

of his heavy spotted tail and vanished. Rory laughed with pure pleasure. So did I.

"Breed more of yourself, smolt," Rory called after the salmon. "That's all any of us can do."

It was an odd thing for a man with no children to say, but the subject of life's cycles was clearly on Rory's mind. He was silent the rest of the afternoon, even after we plunged back through the little tidal bore into Arbutus Creek and his boathouse. Nor did he say anything more while he watched me go through my daily workout in the last hot sunlight: running for stamina, some Asian exercises for concentration and coordination, and rope climbing to remind me how much I hated the whole regime.

Rory supervised as I went hand over hand up the rope I'd tied around the center roof beam of his house. He made sure my butt was flat on the ground before I started hauling myself up. He counted, too: ten times up and back. We argued over the last number—I swore I'd already done eleven, but he held firm. So I went up the damn thing again, sweating like a roasting goose and reminding myself every inch of the way that it was better than the alternative, which was to run out of breath, speed, or strength at the wrong time.

That night, after a dinner of Rory's Scottish sushi—salmon and halibut and sticky rice and green mustard—he brought up the subject of death and regeneration again in a roundabout way. We were sitting on the lush lawn that grew between his home and the boathouse at the river's edge.

Rory had his violin out and was playing, trying to tempt me into a lesson in the mystery of the Scottish fiddle.

I enjoyed listening to him play but refused the instrument he held out to me. I hadn't had a violin under my chin for years, not since shortly after Uncle Jake died, taking most of my illusions with him.

"No, thanks," I said. "My hands never were as good as the music I wanted to play."

"Maybe that was the music's fault," he said. "Beethoven and Mozart are for court concerts and drawing room ensembles, but you're of Scots blood, the kind of man who should be sawing away with bent wrist on laments and strathspeys and reels."

I just smiled, shook my head, and took another swallow of red ale.

"Think on it," he urged. "Being a fiddler suits you. Medieval fiddlers were street musicians, not gentry. Hell, sometimes pickpockets and cutpurses took up fiddles as an excuse to prowl the marketplace crowds for victims. Cromwell called fiddlers 'rogues, vagabonds, and sturdy beggars who should be proceeded against and punished accordingly.'"

"How about some Niel Gow?" I said, shaking my head. Gow was the first and most famous of the Scottish fiddlers. I loved his mannered sadness, the echoes of the bagpipe in his songs.

Rory sighed and put the fiddle back under his chin. But when he began to play, the music was the son's, Nathaniel's, not the father's. I recognized the tune instantly—"Caledonia's Wail for Niel Gow

Her Favourite Minstrel.'' The music was rich with the best kind of Scottish sadness, the kind that renews the soul instead of numbing it. When the last notes of the old lament faded, Rory laid his burnished old Hardie fiddle back in its velvet-lined case.

''Wait here, Fiddler. I have something for you.''

It was just as well that he left me for a moment. It gave me time to stare out at the strait and let my eyes dry themselves. While I waited in the crimson light of evening, I watched the river run down to the sea, mingling its fresh water with the vast salt ocean. A pair of mallards flew downstream, passing so close I could hear the hushed, urgent rush of air over their wings. I wished Fiora were here to share the twilight . . . and to share whatever Rory had been trying to say for several days.

He came back out with a small stone crock under his arm and two heavy crystal glasses in one hand. In his other hand he carried a long parcel wrapped in clean cotton cloth and tied with a red silk sash. He set the glasses and the crock of single-malt Scotch between us, then sank back into his chair with the long parcel across his lap. After a moment he reached for the crock.

The cork made a distinct sound as it pulled free. The smell of good Scotch lifted into the twilight. Rory poured two drinks and handed me one. Crystal clinked on crystal in a silent toast. The liquor was warm and smooth and tasted faintly of the ocean. I looked at the label: Lagavulin, an Islay malt, fifteen years old. The Islay whisky makers must have dried their malt with seaweed fires.

For a few minutes we sipped in silence, appreciating the Scotch and the peace of the land. Rory had thirty acres of Pacific Northwest paradise. About twenty were first-growth Douglas fir and cedar, blackberry, and alder thickets. The cleared ground was on a low bench set back from the river valley. His big brick Victorian house had the best view in western Washington. Below the house, right on the bank of the river that marked one side of the property, was a four-room cottage. Nearby was a small freshwater turning basin and a boathouse.

"When I first came here," Rory said, "the land wasn't worth a bucket of fish heads. Neither was I. I was the King of Nothing, and bugger anyone who got in my way."

I grinned, seeing in my mind a younger, defiant Rory coming to the shores of an alien land.

"But that was then. Now shoreline's very dear. Fifty-four acres of bare land down the road sold for half a million dollars last month." Rory glared at me. "That's the doing of all your California equity immigrants."

Like most Washingtonians, Rory loved to regard Californians as the source of all problems. It beat blaming the greed of their friends and neighbors.

"Don't blame us," I said. "We're being driven out by honest cash from the Middle East and Asia and dishonest cash from South America. There's only so much Gold Coast property and way too much money wanting to buy it."

Rory grunted. "Is that what Fiora says?"

"She told me about the honest cash. The dishonest cash I figured out all by myself."

"Well, laddie, I don't know what this thirty acres

is worth now and I don't care. When it comes to weighing and measuring and writing it down in columns, it won't be my problem. It will be yours."

Uh-oh.

"I'm seventy-five and I have no child," Rory said softly.

"You look twenty years younger. You act it too."

Rory's teeth flashed in a twilight smile that faded slowly. "Be that as it may, there is a time for all things. . . . I had a new will drawn up. You're the executor, but I expect you to rely on Fiora. She has more brains than the two of us together."

"Make her the executor," I said quickly.

"She has enough to do. Besides, she'll enjoy watching you add the columns."

"Shit."

Rory laughed. "I subdivided the land last year. The big house and woodlot are in one parcel. The cottage, boathouse, and five acres on the river are in the other. I want you to sell the big parcel and deliver the proceeds to the Wildlife Hostel."

"Is there any special rush?" I asked carefully.

He shook his head. "My doctor tells me I'll live to bury him."

"How old is your doctor?"

"Fifty."

I let out a long breath I hadn't been aware of holding.

He sniffed the Lagavulin again, examined the pale gold whisky in the glass, and continued. "The smaller parcel—the cottage and the boathouse—now belongs to Fiora. I've already registered the transaction at the County Recorder's Office."

I glanced down the slope to the cottage. The

front deck of the little house looked down the river and out onto the strait. Across the channel, almost lost in the gloaming, was Vancouver Island. Behind me the Olympic Coast Range stood out like teeth on a band saw.

"Do you know what Fiora said just before I came up here?" I asked. "She told me the only waterfront property she has ever wanted to own is the piece you just gave her."

Rory nodded as though he had known all along. It wouldn't surprise me if he had. He and Fiora had a special understanding, the kind that doesn't need words to make the details clear.

"The cottage gives her peace," Rory said. He looked at the long, flat package in his lap. "My gift to you isn't peace. But then, like me, you're a belligerent bastard. You've never looked for peace."

Fiora always said that Rory's smile could light the darkest night. But the smile on his face at that moment was comforting rather than illuminating.

"You're the only man I know who understands the purpose for which this was made," he said simply. "Take it."

I recognized the gift even before he placed it in my hands but I studied the parcel for a long moment, letting my emotions sort themselves out. The red silk cord that secured the folded cotton bag felt cool and smooth to my fingertips. It was looped neatly around one end of the package, then secured with an intricate knot. Two polished metal end beads lay perfectly aligned atop the knot. When I pulled, the knot dissolved. I laid back the flap of the bag, exposing the leather-wrapped handle and scarlet-lacquered scabbard of the old Japanese sword.

"Rory . . . ." My voice was still dried up. I knew what the sword meant to him. "You don't have to pay me to be your executor."

"I'm not. I've known for years the sword was yours. Now you know, too."

The scarlet of the scabbard matched the colors in the evening sky. I turned it and drew the sword slowly, savoring its balance, marveling at the graceful arch of the steel. The polished blade glowed redly as it caught the last crimson light. The cloudlike halo pattern that ran the length of the blade along the temper line was more sharply defined than I remembered. It was a beautifully made tool, Rory's souvenir of the second time the whole world went to war.

Like most men who survived both the battlefield and the prison camp, Rory had made his own private, separate peace with his wartime experiences. Sometimes, rarely, he told me about them, but never if someone else was present, even Fiora. Some of the stories he told were brutally funny. Some were dark anecdotes that worked themselves out of his memory like slivers of shrapnel.

"It looks different," I said. "More vivid."

"I took it to a man in Seattle, a Japanese who collects and reconditions swords. I wanted it polished up for you. When it was done, it looked so good he wanted to buy it from me. Wouldn't take no for an answer. I thought I'd have to pry it out of his fingers."

"I'm glad you did. It's worth more than a few

hundred dollars and a spot on some collector's den wall."

"Five thousand."

"What?"

"He offered me five thousand as I was walking out the door. Said the new Japanese monied class is crazy for old swords."

I whistled. "Be damned. Guess land isn't the only thing that's being chased by overseas money. Weak dollars and strong yen. Wonder if Fiora will like this thing any better when she finds out how much it's worth."

"She won't," Rory said flatly. He held out his hand. "May I?"

I held the sword by the back of the blade, edge toward me, and let Rory take it from my hands. He made a small bow, almost an unconscious gesture.

"Before you accept the sword, you should know that the blade is cursed. That's why Fiora hated it from the first time she saw it."

"Fiora, my Scots witch," I muttered, half serious.

"Yes." Rory was wholly serious.

"Hell." I sighed. "So what's the curse, male pattern baldness?"

Rory gave me a dark smile. "Nothing that hard to fix. Each generation that holds the sword has to feed it at least once or it will turn on them and kill them."

"Feed it," I said neutrally.

"Blood."

"No problem. I'll shave with it. That should do the trick."

It didn't, of course.

two

Like firearms, swords are a little too portable, a little too valuable, and much too dangerous to leave lying around. Rory had already rearranged his glass-fronted weapons locker, putting a newly acquired varmint rifle in the sword's old spot. The duffel in the Cobra's truck was the only locked compartment available, so I stowed the sword there on my way out the door the following morning.

Rory and I were headed for Marley Burnside's wildlife sanctuary, just across the road from Rory's place. Marley spent her entire working life as a pediatrics nurse in the country hospital that served most of western Washington. Retired now, she lived on a forty-acre meadow in the middle of the woods. Small and birdlike herself, her mission and pleasure in life was caring for feathered victims of bad luck and human malice.

Even though it was less than a quarter mile to

Marley's place, we took Rory's pickup. The bed was loaded with lumber, chicken wire, and tools. Rory usually spent at least one day a week doing the heavy lifting for Marley. Today's job called for two heavy lifters.

I was happy for the distraction. Fiora hadn't called for two days. I was beginning to think something had gone wrong in the middle of her efforts to sell Pacific Rim. Every human being wants one thing: even. More than anyone I know, except me, Fiora burned with that existential desire. She wanted parity for herself; but more than that, and more fiercely, she wanted parity for her sex. She wanted to prove that women could conduct themselves and their own businesses in a way that was honorable, constructive, and profitable.

As always, I wished Fiora luck but wasn't holding my breath for the announcement of her success. So far as I was concerned, my former wife and present lover was bucking a stacked deck as tall as the Sears Tower. Today's world is controlled by states and nations, corporations and cartels and collectives. People like me—outlaws, loose cannons, free spirits—don't care much for the way the world is structured, but we don't have the inclination or patience to change it. Blow it up, yes. Remake it, no.

Fiora's brilliance lies in understanding that organizations of whatever size are an inevitable result of man's hierarchical tendencies. Instead of ignoring or fighting that urge toward structure, she used it to create something constructive, and she ran it in a way that didn't chew up other, weaker people along the way. Pacific Rim was Fiora's child, her consummation, and her revenge, all in one.

I wanted her to succeed, even if I doubted she would. That was why I wanted so badly for her to call. Maybe I wasn't holding my breath, but my fingers were crossed so hard they ached.

Marley was waiting for us beside a stack of telephone poles. In her hands was a rough blueprint for a flight cage big enough to let eagles exercise. It took me ten minutes to forget about life's uncontrollable intangibles. The telephone poles were about two hundred tangible pounds apiece. The holes they went into were four feet deep. Rory and I could lift the poles, but just barely.

By ten, I had sweated through my shirt. Marley kept a steady flow of lemonade, coffee, and well water running through us. At ten-fifteen, she brought summer sausage sandwiches and homemade peanut-butter cookies. At twelve-thirty, we ate again—cold poached salmon with dill mustard, sourdough rolls, and sliced tomatoes still warm from the sun.

By four, all twelve poles were in place and tamped down. I had splinters in my shoulders, blisters beneath my work gloves, and a farmer's tan from the waist up. Another set of Marley's volunteer conscript laborers was due in on the weekend to stretch screening, so we called it a day.

Back at Rory's place I showered, shaved, and watched the phone. It finally rang just as I was going to say the hell with it and try one of the deep halibut holes on the water in front of the house. Rory was closer to the phone, so he nailed it, assured the caller that he was fine, and held the phone out to me.

"Are you all right?" I asked.

Simultaneously Fiora asked me the same thing.

"I'm fine," I answered.

So did she. Simultaneously.

"Are you sure?" Fiora asked before I could.

"Yes. What's wrong?"

"Nothing. Everything's fine."

"You don't sound like it," I said. "Are you sleeping okay?"

It was our own shorthand. Silence came back to me over the wire. That told me all I needed to know: My Scots witch had been dreaming the kind of dreams that made both of us edgy.

Dreaming is Fiora's curse. Sometimes she'll dream that someone she loves is in danger. Often, that someone is me. But she won't dream about the source of my danger. Hell, no. That might be useful. What she gets is a clear sense of danger that she once described as the sensation of ice forming just beneath her skin.

The first few times it happened, I laughed it off. Then I almost died in Mexico, and Uncle Jake did die, and Fiora knew he was dead and I was alive before I did. And she could prove it. After that I believed her. Unfortunately, that made life harder rather than easier. A Distant Early Warning system, Fiora is not. Her dreaming is erratic. Sometimes there's no warning. Sometimes there's a "sort of" warning.

And sometimes she wakes up shaking. That's when she reaches for me and I hold her and neither one of us says anything because there's nothing to say. What will happen will happen, and all the half-assed dreams in the world won't stop it.

The dreams sure can grate on my nerves, though. And on hers.

"Love?" I asked.

"We agreed not to talk about it, remember?"

Fiora's tone told me she hated the whole business. She is even less comfortable with her curse than I am. With one outstanding exception, she has no patience for things that aren't rational, logical, and predictable. That one exception is me.

"How bad is it?" I asked.

"Don't ask."

I didn't. If she knew anything, she would tell me.

"How goes the sales campaign?" I asked instead.

"Interesting," she said flatly. "The New Yorkers withdrew."

"Why?"

"Damned if I know. They just went sideways, that's all. It happens. If investment banking were easy, I would have lost interest in it long before now."

The hollow connection made it hard for me to catch the emotional inflections in her voice, but I thought I heard more irritation than true anger. That didn't surprise me; I'd often wondered whether she truly wanted to sell off the company that was her child. What did surprise me was my disappointment that the deal had gone south. I badly wanted her off the short leash that executive responsibility entailed.

"Maybe it's just as well," I said. "That company means a lot to you."

"I have another offer."

"A good one?"

"I'll tell you all about it in ninety minutes, when you pick me up at the airport."

"Ninety minutes? I can't make Sea-Tac that fast, even in the Cobra."

"I'm not coming into Sea-Tac. I borrowed a private plane. The pilot said he can drop me wherever is convenient for you. All we need is a five-thousand-foot surfaced runway."

I grinned like a kid who had just figured out how to get Santa Claus to stop twice. "Tell the pilot to check his charts for Port Angeles."

"That's what I figured too," she said. "He's already cleared in there."

"Ninety minutes?"

"Uh-huh. Drive something besides the Cobra if you can."

That surprised me. Fiora had turned over a new leaf on the subject of the Cobra. Now she enjoyed the car damn near as much as I did. At least, she had seemed to.

"Have you decided you don't like muscle cars after all?" I asked.

"I have quite a bit of—er, baggage. I want us to be free to play as long as we can."

Fiora's tone was a promise, a surprise, a mystery. My fingers tingled with a sudden race of blood. At its core, our bond has always been physical. We had been apart nearly two weeks. It felt more like two months.

"I'm on my way," I said.

"Fiddler—"

"I'm always careful," I said, saving her from having to warn me.

She made an odd sound at the back of her throat, laughter or sadness or both. "I love you."

Fiora hung up before I could give back her words. When I looked up, Rory was watching me.

"Trouble?" he asked.

I shrugged. "She's not sleeping well, but I think it's just the stress."

He tossed me a set of keys. "Take my truck."

I was so surprised I missed the pass. "Did Fiora tell you she had baggage?"

Rory shook his head and smiled that odd Scots smile he and Fiora shared back and forth between them. I snatched the keys off the floor and silently thanked all my ancestors who *weren't* fey Celts.

The road from Malahat was two old lanes wide, and it twisted like a timber rattler. The pickup was no Cobra, either. I dodged loaded logging trucks and motor homes with California plates and spent ten miserable minutes behind a Port-a-Potty honey wagon. But I made the Port Angeles airport in eighty-five minutes.

I figured I had time to spare. The only plane in sight was a big Gulfstream IV executive jet on final approach. Fiora had plenty of successful friends, but none so successful they could keep a Gulfstream in the air. Wondering who the new kid on the corporate block was, I parked outside the chain-link fence and stood beside the truck to watch the landing. After a minute or two, a guy in a baseball cap came jogging out of the shack that served as an office for the fixed-base operator.

"You Fiddler?" he asked.

I nodded.

"That's your plane." He pointed at the jet, which had just touched down. "The pilot wants you to bring the truck out to the taxiway."

I looked from the pickup to the snazzy jet. Not for the first time, I wondered whether Fiora really understood what she was doing, trading power and wealth for more time with a man whose future prospects were as shadowed as his past.

While the baseball cap held the gate open, I drove through and out onto the apron, wondering what Fiora was bringing that required a pickup to haul it away. Before I shut off the engine, the executive jet screamed smartly up to the transient parking area.

I got out and stood with my fingers in my ears until the pilot shut off the starboard engine. The turbine was still spooling down when the forward door unhinged, swung in, then opened out. A short stairway came out like a corrugated metal tongue.

Fiora danced down the steps with one end of a leather strap in her hand. The other end was attached somewhere back in the cabin. She pulled once, then again, as though trying to dislodge a stubborn suitcase. Suddenly a big brown-rust streak erupted from the plane and landed in one bound on the hardtop.

"Kwame!" Fiora said, exasperated. "Heel!"

Ignoring her, Kwame N'Krumah lifted his leg against the landing gear of the $10-million jet. His expression was a combination of relief and revenge. Apparently he would have preferred a 747.

An Asian young enough and good-looking

enough to make my hackles rise appeared in the doorway. He wore a tailored black businessman's suit and a perfectly knotted burgundy silk tie. He watched Fiora with an indulgent smile, then set about supervising the off-loading of the rest of her luggage.

Fiora tried to head toward me but Kwame's 130-pound strength stopped her. She tugged once, then dropped the leash and ran to me. An instant later Kwame caught my scent. He hit his running stride in two long bounds. He couldn't believe it when I sidestepped his ecstatic lunge and grabbed Fiora instead.

She's not a big woman, yet the strength of her embrace always surprises me. She hung on to me hard, letting her body say all the things words never quite covered. I lifted her and held her hard in return. The scent and the feel of her body against mine were both familiar and new each time.

"Oh, God, but it's good to see you," Fiora whispered against my neck.

She tilted her head back. Her hazel-green eyes went over me like hands, searching for signs of change, telling me it had seemed like a lot more than two weeks for her, too. Reassured that there were no new scars, she kissed me hard on the lips while I tried to fend off Kwame, who was wanting his share of attention.

I put Fiora's feet back on the taxiway, scooped up Kwame's lead, and reminded him of his manners with one quick word.

"Sit."

Immediately Kwame dropped to his haunches

and waited like the well-trained attack dog he had once been. Solid, muscular, the color of the African lions his ancestors were bred to hunt, Kwame watched while I returned Fiora's kiss with interest.

"How's my favorite wheeler-dealer?" I asked when I released her. "All the ducks in a row yet, or are they still going south on you?"

"Later," she said, under her breath.

Fiora turned to the handsome Japanese, who approached us with her briefcase in his hand. A valet trudged along behind under the weight of two big suitcases and a garment bag. Two body-guards finished out the entourage.

"Ron, this is Fiddler," she said. "Fiddler, this is Roniko Nakamichi. He's CEO of Nakamichi Securities in Tokyo."

That explained the Gulfstream IV. Even a business illiterate like me had heard of the House of Nakamichi. It ranked right up there with the houses of Rothschild and Morgan.

"Hello," he said, holding out his hand. "Call me Ron."

I took the hand that guided several billions of dollars' worth of international finance and waited for him to set the tension. Some Japanese executives use handshakes as tests of strength; others are limp-wristers in the Latin style. Nakamichi was aggressive and he must have worked out. His grip was numbing. I would have returned the favor, but I wasn't certain how much Fiora needed his good wishes.

"Thanks for saving me the trip to Sea-Tac," I said.

"It was my pleasure," he said. "Ms. Flynn has been most gracious."

His English was unaccented and colloquial, as though he had learned it in the United States. His manner was subtly Japanese rather than Japanese-American. Part of it was the way he stood centered over his feet rather than laid back on his heels. Part of it was the way he looked at me without clearly focusing on me. His eyes were alert but not nervous. His glance was restless, like that of a good boxer, a pit boss, or a swordsman.

"Kwame is the one who should say thanks," Fiora said. "If it weren't for the executive shuttle service, he'd be back in California in a kennel."

"Yeah, but he's going to look awfully funny riding back to LA on the luggage rack of the Cobra," I said, bending over and slapping Kwame's muscular barrel with open-handed affection.

Kwame washed my knuckles with a tongue the size of a hand towel. After a few good licks, he looked me in the eye and whined softly, asking to be freed. His glance went to the grass beyond the chain-link fence, then back at me.

"Gotcha," I said, straightening. "Excuse me. Kwame has an appointment with the greenery."

While Kwame enjoyed the grass, the valet put Fiora's bags in the back of the truck and Fiora exchanged a few more words with Nakamichi. They shook hands formally; then the Japanese and his valet and bodyguards climbed back aboard the plane. As soon as the door was secured, the jet taxied quickly toward the fuel stand at the other end of the airport.

By the time we got back, Fiora was up on the

rear bumper of the truck, digging in a compartment of her garment bag. She looked incongrous
against the dusty truck in her Donna Karan suit
and elegant heels, but she didn't plan on staying
that way. She pulled out jeans, a white cotton
shirt, and a pair of boat shoes. When I walked up
behind her, she turned and threw herself into my
arms without even looking.

"I've been worried about you," Fiora whispered. "Are you sure nothing is going on?"

"So far so good."

She let out a long breath. "Okay."

"What about you?" I asked. "What happened?
Who's Nakamichi?"

"A white knight who's setting me free from the
dungeon."

"I thought that was my job."

Fiora laughed softly against my neck. "In this
case, the white knight gets the dungeon and you
get the fair lady."

"Sold."

For a few moments longer Fiora held me. Then
she tilted her head back and looked at me. Despite
the smile and the clarity of her eyes, I sensed her
tension.

"Drop the other shoe," I said.

"Nothing to drop. The New Yorkers started going sideways, Nakamichi entered the bidding, and
we cut a deal for Pacific Rim."

"It's done?"

"All but the paperwork."

"Are you happy with it?" I asked.

"I'm quitting winners. Nobody can ask for more
than that."

I thought about quitting winners while Fiora changed in the ladies' room. I would have felt better if I hadn't known her so well. Normally she hummed with energy, as though she were plugged into some cosmic power source. Not today. Today she was tight, not vibrant.

Maybe all the doing, undoing, and redoing of deals had drained her. Maybe she was just tired. Maybe all she needed was a few weeks of fishing and laughing and loving to take away the shadows I sensed behind her smile.

Maybe.

And maybe she was sad at selling off her child, no matter how difficult and demanding that child had become. I wasn't taking Fiora to see Rory until I knew. Having two fey Scots reading each other's minds and leaving me floundering around in the dark wasn't my favorite way to spend the evening.

"I'm buying dinner," I announced when Fiora reappeared in jeans.

"Now you tell me. I should have stayed in the business armor."

Her choice of words made me smile. "Armor, huh? I always saw it that way, but I didn't know you did."

"I started to." Fiora smiled oddly. "That was the beginning of the end."

"Of what?"

"My love affair with the corporate world."

After that, Fiora seemed content to be silent. She sat very close to me in the truck. If a turn in the road pulled her away, she came back instantly, as though uneasy unless she was in physical contact. That was unlike her. A more independent woman I have never known. It was the source of much of the friction between us, and much of the pleasure, too. Clinging vines give me a rash.

I found a roadhouse at the edge of Port Angeles. The beef was local and well marbled, the russet potatoes were mealy and full of butter, sour cream, and chopped green onions, and the wine was a Washington state Merlot that tasted like ripe red plums as well as grapes. Fiora ate more than I had expected and less than I'd hoped. We wrapped up scraps and bones for Kwame, then drove down a dirt road and walked for a while on the beach. The silver mist and the vague lapping of water against sand gave the place an aura of unearthly peace.

"What happened with the New Yorkers?" I asked finally.

"They knew going in that I wasn't going to stay with the company," Fiora said after a moment. "Suddenly they got nervous about it. They wanted me to stay on for three years. Salary only. No percentage or profit participation. No performance bonuses. No golden parachute. Nothing but the warm glow from a job well done."

"Nice guys."

She shrugged. "I didn't expect nice. Smart, maybe, but not nice."

"What happened when you told them to go shit in their mess kits?"

"They stalled while they ran the top job past some high-priced East Coast types. Once the word of a glitch went out, I started getting calls. One was from Nakamichi. He remembered me from a Tokyo business seminar I gave on women managers and cultural conflict."

"Did you remember him?"

Fiora gave me a sideways look, lifted my hand to her mouth, and bit the base of my thumb in a way that brought my body to full alert.

"He's offering less money than the New York group," she said, "but he's compensating by giving me something money can't buy."

"Don't let me guess."

"I won't. He's offering me a chance to teach Japanese men that women are more than *shokuba no hana*, flowers in the workplace."

"Jesus, you do love to tilt at windmills."

"It's one of the things we have in common," she replied. "But unlike you, I have no use for rusty lances and spavined nags."

"So what do you plan to use, a hammer?"

"The ink brush is mightier than military toys, which is why I'm using a big part of Pacific Rim's sale price to endow a chair at the Harvard Business School. Ron has agreed to endow a similar chair at the University of Tokyo. The occupant of each chair will be a woman. Her brief will be to instruct women in the acquisition and use of power."

I looked at Fiora, impressed. "Son of a bitch."

"Daughter, in my case. Ron wants me to occupy the Tokyo chair for the first year."

"Are you going to do it?"

"I don't know," Fiora said. "Would you come with me?"

"Yes."

"Just like that? No hesitation, no hedging?"

"Just like that."

Her smile was much brighter than the setting sun. She put her arm around my waist and hooked her fingers in the back pocket of my Levi's so deeply I could feel the warmth and pressure of her hand on the muscles of my butt.

"Should I start packing?" I asked.

She shook her head. "It's all verbal. No deal is truly made until dotted lines are signed and the check doesn't bounce."

"When will that be?"

"The papers should be ready in a few days. I can sign them in Ron's Seattle office. With any luck, I'll never again have to enter a door with my name on it."

I slid my fingers beneath the collar of her cotton shirt and felt the soft skin in the hollow of her throat.

"Are you sure it's what you want?" I asked.

Fiora answered without words, holding me very hard.

By the time we got back to Rory's house, it was dark. A light was on in his kitchen, but not in the rest of the house. I was surprised he hadn't waited up to see Fiora, but not too surprised. He had worked hard all day, hard enough to flatten a man half his age.

I hadn't mentioned Rory's bequest, but we always stayed in the cabin. I drove past the house and on down the long driveway to the river. As I turned the wheel, the headlights washed over the long wooden stairway that came down from the lawn to the boathouse.

Rory lay face down at the foot of the stairs.

tHREE

Fiora was out and running by the time I cranked the wheel over hard, bringing the headlights back to Rory. I kicked up the high beams. A swath of hard white light cut the darkness. Rory's body had the slack look of death. He was sprawled head down at the foot of the stairs, as though he had fallen. His face was hidden in the shadow cast by his shoulder.

By the time I set the brake and piled out of the truck, Fiora was kneeling beside him. Her right hand probed his neck, seeking a pulse. Her concentration was as fierce as a falcon's. Later she might scream or cry or shake, but not now.

"He's alive," Fiora said as I ran up. "I can just feel a carotid heartbeat."

Kwame appeared beside me, as silent as the night. He slipped beneath my hand to sniff at the stranger lying on the ground. Then he looked up at me and wagged his tail tentatively, uncertain what game the inscrutable humans were playing. His attitude confirmed that Rory was indeed alive; most animals shy away from fresh death.

Rory made a blurred sound. The thumb of his outflung left hand jerked reflexively. He might not be dead but he wasn't far from it, either.

"Blankets in the cottage," I said to Fiora. "Cover him but don't try to move him."

The nearest phone was in the kitchen of the big house. I took the stairs two and three at a time. The kitchen door was unlocked. I grabbed the phone from the wall beside the door and punched 911.

As the emergency number rang, I noticed for the first time the stench of burned meat. A blue propane flame wavered beneath a frying pan. Pork chops. I stretched the phone cord and turned off the stove. Finally the dispatcher in Malahat answered.

"Nine-one-one, do you have an emergency?"

"Yes. There's—"

"Wait one," she said, cutting me off.

I was on hold.

"Shit!"

I said that and a lot more to the walls. This was the sticks, for Chrissake, not LA. There shouldn't be emergencies stacked up like planes in a landing pattern.

The dispatcher came back on the line. "What kind of help do you need?"

"Medical," I said instantly. "We have a man down, unconscious. Straits Road eight miles southwest of Malahat. It looks as though he fell down a long outdoor flight of stairs. He's alive but just barely."

"Where are you? What's the address?"

I told her and gave the road directions.

"Stand by, sir." Just off the phone, I heard the mechanical yelp of an emergency alarm. "Malahat Bay volunteers, this is a call-up, medical aid, code three."

The dispatcher's voice was calm and controlled. She was talking into a goddam radio. The closest emergency squad was eight miles away and a bunch of half-assed paid-call volunteers in the bargain.

"You have anything closer?" I asked. "This man is over seventy and he's dying."

In the background I heard a voice over a radio squawk box.

"Malahat Bay," the voice said. *"We have a crew at the station. What's the dispatch?"*

The dispatcher read them the address. The volunteer captain came back with *"Ten-four."* In the radio background, I heard a siren start to spool up.

"An EMT team is on the way," the dispatcher said after she had taken my name. "An ambulance will be right behind them. The hospital has been alerted. Is your victim bleeding? Is he in a dangerous location?"

"No."

"Then leave him where he is. Don't move him. Try to keep him warm. Help will be there shortly."

I hit the top of the boathouse stairs running, but the banister stopped me cold. The unpainted two-by-four railing was intended more as a guide than as a support. Something had cracked the wood about five feet from the top. Sharp daggers of broken wood on the underside suggested Rory had fallen against the banister and then gone down the staircase out of control.

I raced down the stairs. Putting together how it had happened could wait. Rory wouldn't.

Fiora had gotten a flashlight and two heavy wool blankets from the cabin. One blanket was draped over Rory's torso and Fiora was adjusting the second over his legs. She looked up, her face pale and spectral in the glare of the headlights.

"It's . . . bad," she said. "Look."

Fiora flashed the light on Rory's face. His eyes were half closed. They didn't respond to light. She moved the beam to the pale skin just below Rory's hairline. A blue line of bruising the width of a pencil showed clearly in the light. I wondered if he had somehow whacked his head on the railing or perhaps on the edge of a stair.

Rory didn't flinch when I slid my fingers up into his hair. I touched the bruised area gently. It was spongy. I didn't need five years of medical school to guess that the skull was fractured.

I took the flashlight from Fiora and aimed it up the long stairs. She could see the broken railing and guess for herself what had happened.

"He hasn't been here too long," I said. I hardly recognized the voice as my own. Too hard. Too controlled. "He was cooking dinner. Food was still on the fire. Burned but not charcoal. He must have come to the head of the stairs for something and slipped."

Rory made another blurred sound and stirred as

though trying to get up. Fiora put her hand on his shoulder and spoke quietly to him.

"Lie still, Rory," she said. "Help is on the way. Just lie still."

The words or the gentle female touch registered somewhere in Rory's brain. His restless stirring subsided.

"Who's coming?" she asked quietly.

"We got lucky. Malahat Bay is a volunteer fire department, but there was a response team hanging around the station. Eight miles, eight minutes, more or less."

I glanced at my watch. Four minutes had gone by since the emergency crew was dispatched. There was nothing to do but wait. It's one of those things I've never done well.

Fiora continued touching Rory very lightly and talking to him as though she expected him to understand. Perhaps he did. Consciousness is a slippery state. No one could be certain how much of Rory was with us.

I knelt beside Fiora, putting my hand next to hers, touching Rory gently.

"You're going to have a lot of explaining to do," I warned him. "Scaring your favorite girl like this."

Fiora took my free hand in hers. "You still owe me a big salmon, forty pounds at least," she said to him softly. "You promised. Remember? You remember, don't you?"

Rory didn't respond but I remembered. We had been fishing far offshore and deep, with sixteen-pound cannonball sinkers and quick-release clips. We had gone hours without a strike. Rory had been grumbling about Scots witches like Fiora who brought him bad luck. Then the port-side pole bent almost double from the force of a hit.

Fiora fought the fish well, fought until her arms were trembling and her hands were weak, fought with every bit of her strength . . . and, a foot from the net, the leader broke. Fiora swore like a man and wept like a girl. The combination entranced Rory. Once he had quit cursing himself for failing to change the leader often enough, he vowed to find her a better fish.

"You'd better hang on, Rory," I said. "She'll haunt you wherever you go if you don't make good on that fish. Remember what you told me? 'A fisherman's promise on the water is like a priest's promise in church.'"

Fiora and I talked to Rory by turns, touching him, coaxing him, luring him, trying to drag him back to the land of the living with our voices because that was all we had. From far off up the road a siren's lament keened in the darkness.

"Stay with him," I said.

Fiora nodded and started talking again, reminding Rory of all that was good in his life. It was a long list. Any man would have been glad to claim it.

I grabbed the flashlight and jogged up to the road. Two sets of headlights and two red light bars came at me out of the night. When they were a hundred yards away, I turned on the flashlight and signaled. The fire truck downshifted and began to slow.

Standing to one side of Rory's driveway, I held the flashlight so hard my hand ached. I practiced waiting while the truck made a snail's progress toward me.

Finally the truck pulled up. The driver had a workingman's beard and eyes that were brightened by the excitement of a highway run. He wore a stained yellow Nomex turnout coat and a helmet that showed the marks of honest use.

"Climb on and show us where," he called to me.

I hooked my arm through a handrail just behind the cab and stepped onto the wide steel running board. There was another fireman in the cab and two more on the rear running board.

The big rig's air brakes wheezed and blew like a killer whale. The driver was still announcing their arrival into the radio mike when the two men piled off the back ledge of the truck and jogged toward Rory, lugging an emergency trunk between them. The second vehicle pulled up. It was a green-and-white patrol car, sheriff or state police.

Fiora took Kwame by the collar and stood aside, watching the men. When she saw that they knew their business, she let out a long breath and visibly relaxed. I got Kwame's leash from the truck and snapped the hank through the ring end of his choke-chain collar. Kwame was quivering a bit with excitement, but at my command he sat perfectly still, watching the strangers and the red lights.

Fiora was shaking a little too, when I put my arm around her shoulder. She put her arm around my waist and hung on.

The response team worked for twenty minutes without quitting. That was the first good sign. The second was that they used the oxygen bag but not the defibrillator. Another, more subtle, was the way they started an IV on the first try, no wincing or flinching, no reluctance to jab human flesh, nothing but the efficient motions of people who have done a job often enough to know how but not so often that they've lost interest.

They fitted Rory with a cervical collar, rolled him over onto a back board, and immobilized him with Velcro straps. He was as white as the headlights. From time to time he groaned, but he didn't respond when they spoke to him.

A private ambulance rolled in, red lights but no siren. The top-heavy vehicle crabbed and edged and groaned in the little turnaround at the end of the driveway. Finally the back of the ambulance pointed toward us. The doors opened and the two crewmen got out. They stood by, chatting in low voices with the cop while they waited for the medics to finish. The officer wore khaki green jeans and a tan shirt, the uniform of the Malahat Sheriff's Department, and carried a .357 Magnum. I could see a Day-Glo orange front sight through the open end of the holster.

Another set of emergency lights appeared at the edge of the lawn above us. After a while a second deputy appeared at the top of the stairs. He signaled his partner. The two of them met at the midpoint in the stairway to confer. The first deputy looked around, caught my eye, and motioned with his head. I gave Fiora a squeeze and put Kwame's leash in her hand.

"You the reporting party?" the deputy asked as I climbed up to him.

"Yes," I said.

"What's your relationship?"

The plastic nameplate on his shirt said his name was Lindstrom. His voice said he didn't care about the questions or the answers. He was in his mid-thirties and had straw-colored hair where he hadn't already gone bald. The line of his mouth said he was disgusted with the world. His eyes no longer gave a damn.

I had seen a lot of small-time, small-town cops like Lindstrom. The only remarkable thing about him was his salt-cracked, calloused hands. Fisherman's hands. He must have been moonlighting on a commercial boat to make ends meet.

"I'm a friend of Rory's," I said. "I've been staying with him for the past two weeks while Fiora wrapped up some business in California."

"Fiora?"

Lindstrom was filling in blanks in his report. He wanted a one-world label for Fiora: wife, mother, sister, aunt, cousin, girlfriend, fiancée.

None of them got the job done. Fiora never fit into a single niche with me. That was the good and the bad of our relationship.

"My ex," I said finally, figuring that was a label the cop would understand.

He did. He grunted and went on. "When she get here?"

"She flew into Port Angeles this afternoon. I picked her up, took her out to dinner, and came back here. Thirty seconds after we hit the driveway I was on the phone to nine-one-one."

The second deputy's nameplate said NORDWIER. He was younger, bigger, and in better shape than Lindstrom. But Nordwier's eyes were blank as beach pebbles. Neither of these guys was bright enough or motivated enough to double his salary by getting on the state highway patrol.

"You know how it happened?" Nordwier asked.

"It looks like Rory fell, probably from the top of the stairs," I said. "You saw the railing."

Neither of the cops replied.

The hair on my neck stirred.

"That your car over there?" Nordwier asked. "The one with them foreign plates?"

"Last time I checked, California was part of the union," I said.

"Why you driving Rory's truck? Your fancy sports car break down?"

I reminded myself that these were public servants, no better and no worse than a lot I'd dealt with.

"Fiora brought the dog and too many suitcases for the Cobra."

"She got that dog up here on an airplane, huh?" Lindstrom was skeptical.

My neck hairs stirred some more.

"Private plane," I said. "A friend dropped her off."

"Uh-huh."

His tone said I was a liar.

"Look," I said. "If you don't like my answers, ask better questions."

Lindstrom gave me the kind of look he must have perfected dragging local drunks out of local bars. If Rory hadn't been dying at the bottom of the stairs, I would have laughed in his face.

"Questions make you nervous?" he asked finally.

"No."

Lindstrom stared at me a while longer. Then, without breaking eye contact, he spoke out of the corner of his mouth. "Show him, Charlie."

"C'mon." Nordwier jerked his thumb up the stairway. His tone said I didn't really have a choice.

The dewy grass slapped wetly against the toes of my shoes. On the lawn, beyond the influence of the flashing lights, the stars were clear in the night sky. The Dipper pointed at the pole star and Orion loomed in the southeast. For a moment, everything seemed unreal, a stage setting left over from a play.

Nordwier was bigger than I am, maybe six-four. But he watched me the way a terrier watches a wolf. He kept his clipboard in his left hand and his right hand close to the square scarred butt of the pistol in his holster. He sent me up the stairs in front of him.

"Inside," he said, when I paused at the kitchen door.

I went inside and stopped. "Now what?"

"You touch anything in here?" he asked.

I pointed at the phone. "I called nine-one-one." Then I caught a whiff of burned pork chops and remembered. "I turned off the stove. But if it's prints you're interested in, you'll find mine all over the house. I've been Rory's guest for two weeks."

Nordwier made a note on the pad on his clipboard. He had a plastic-laminated card beneath the clip, on top of the notepad.

"How about the other room?" he said, nodding toward the living room. "When was the last time you were in there?"

"Last night."

Another note on his pad.

"Take a look, would ya?" he said without looking up. "See if anything's different."

Nordwier had something in mind, so I walked into the living room and looked around. The lamp next to Rory's favorite recliner was on. Its light spread out on the floor, throwing a glitter off the shattered glass from the gun cabinet. The doors of the cabinet stood open. The cabinet itself was empty, a half-dozen guns missing.

For an instant, it seemed as though I was back in the city again. The thought of some dead-end hype, some callow doper, attacking a man like Rory just to steal used guns sent a wave of pure rage through me. For the space of several heartbeats I couldn't speak.

"Was it like this last night?" Nordwier asked.

"Christ!" was all I said.

"You know what was in there?"

"Yes."

"So what's missing?"

I walked over to the cabinet and looked at the empty hooks.

"He had a Purdey over-and-under, a presentation gun, a beauty. The twelve-gauge Remington with the ribbed barrel is missing. So is the thirty-oh-six with the scope, the Marlin Model Ninety-four carbine, and a new bolt-action two twenty-two varmint rifle." As I catalogued the guns, I added their value in my head. The Purdey was worth several thousand; the others several hundred apiece, new. At a pawnshop, the whole bunch might fetch $500.

The deputy watched me carefully, obviously expecting more. I had given him all I knew, a list of the contents of the cabinet as of last night, when I had tucked the sword into the Cobra's trunk. The only other thing that might have been missing was the venerable Colt Woodsman that Rory kept in a drawer with cleaning equipment and ammunition.

I reached for the drawer to check it.

"Don't touch anything," Nordwier snapped. "We're going to look for prints."

"No shit, Sherlock," I said, disgusted. "I've already told you: Mine are all over the place."

Nordwier gave me a hard look. "The sheriff's on his way here. He'll want to talk to you first thing. Now listen up while I read you your rights."

"What?"

He read the Miranda warning off the laminated card on his clipboard.

"Am I under arrest?" I asked through my teeth when he was finished.

"Maybe, maybe not. Depends on how you explain a few things like that key. It also depends on what the sheriff has to say. He'll be along pretty soon, and I know he'll have some questions."

"Key?"

His eyes flicked past me to the open doors of the cabinet for a second. I looked again and saw something that had escaped me the first time I looked, something so obvious that even these dumbshit cops had picked it up. The glass doors of the display cabinet had been smashed, but there was a shiny brass key sticking out of the lock.

Rory hadn't been injured by someone stealing

guns. Someone had stolen the guns to disguise a cold-blooded attempt at murder. The deputy's reading of the litany of St. Miranda suggested he thought I was the guilty party.

fOUR

Fiora met me at the bottom of the stairs. The attendants were lifting the gurney carrying Rory into the ambulance. When they were finished, she turned and looked at me. She didn't have to speak out loud; I read the question in the tilt of her elegant blond head.

"This may turn criminal," I said flatly.

There was nothing else I wanted to say in front of the deputies. Cops have a way of twisting words to support their own preconceptions.

"Somebody hurt Rory on purpose?" Fiora asked.

Her expression said she couldn't believe it. Then she glanced at Nordwier, who had followed me down the stairs like a flat-footed shadow. She sensed Nordwier's edginess as clearly as I had. The pupils of her eyes widened in sudden comprehension, followed immediately by anger.

"Bloody badge-heavy idiots," she said. "They should be sliced into thin strips and used for—"

"Somebody broke into Rory's gun cabinet," I said, interrupting. I know Fiora's opinion of most cops. It's even lower than mine.

"What does that have to do with you?" she asked tightly.

"The key was still in the lock."

Some men are intimidated by intelligent women. I think they're wonderful. At awkward times like this, they save you a lot of explaining.

"The cops think it was staged?" Fiora asked. "By you?"

The edge of disdain in her voice at the second question penetrated even Nordwier's habitual disinterest. He gave her a hard look.

"The deputies want me to talk to the sheriff," I said. "You go ahead with the ambulance. I'll be along in a few minutes. Hurry up, love. They'll be leaving soon."

Fiora started to object, then used her intelligence again. Nordwier wouldn't need much of an excuse to hold her. In fact, he should be holding her, but he was too slow to figure out that if I was involved, so was Fiora.

Without a word she handed me Kwame's leash and headed for the ambulance. The ambulance driver put her up front, which told me they were still working over Rory in back.

No sooner had the ambulance gone than a gray Chevrolet sedan with a red spotlight came down the driveway to where we were. The driver was sixteen or seventeen years old. He stayed in the car. The man who climbed out the passenger door was short and built like a barrel. He wore a short-sleeved white shirt, tan khakis, and Tony Lama boots. He had a Korean War crew cut with white sidewalls and a stump of unsmoked cigar in the corner of his mouth. He worked on the unlit smoke like a cud.

Family: Good ol' boy. Genus: Country sheriff. Species: *Elected cop.*

Better than a rent-a-cop in some ways and worse in others. I wondered if the sheriff had training in anything besides cutting deals and rousting drunks.

Lindstrom read his notes to the sheriff while Nordwier made sure I didn't break for the woods. The emergency medical techs and the volunteer firemen were cleaning up. They accepted my thanks gravely.

"I don't know how much good we did," the driver in the red helmet said. "He's hurt pretty bad. Both legs fractured, probably the hips, too. That skull fracture's depressed." He hesitated. "You his son?"

I shook my head.

"We've got to get in touch with his family."

"He doesn't have any."

The driver muttered something under his breath, then said, "Well, that's a problem. We're going to need permission, one way or another."

"I'm Rory's executor, if that's any help."

Nordwier gave me a look. I ignored him.

"Well, then, you better stand by," the driver said. "I have a feeling you're going to need to make a few decisions sometime tonight."

"What does that mean?"

The driver met my glance, then looked away uneasily. "I'm just a medical technician, not a doctor."

"Give it to me straight," I said.

He shrugged. "His breathing was going downhill. I have a hunch they'll want to put him on life support up at Malahat Regional. Did he leave instructions about that kind of thing?"

The steak and baked potato tried to crawl back up my throat. I've looked at my own death more than once, and Fiora's too. This was different. This wasn't a matter of adrenaline and quick choices. This was a cold-blooded choosing. Should Rory's body be hooked up and forced to breathe indefinitely in the hope of simple survival?

But survival isn't simple. It's as complex as a human brain that might or might not function along with the lungs. We hadn't figured out a way to force a brain to live. What would a seventy-five-year-old man with a serious head injury and fractured hips and legs want? Would he want life, no matter what?

I wouldn't. But I wasn't choosing for myself.

Could I choose for Rory?

"I don't know if he left instructions," I said.

"Well, if I were you, I'd find out right quick. The paper you're looking for is called a power of attorney for health care. Everybody ought to have one, believe me, but most folks don't, leastways not the folks we see, and they're always the ones that need them most."

"I'll do what I can."

Lindstrom and the sheriff walked slowly toward me, still finishing their conversation. The sheriff's driver—probably his son—remained stiffly behind the wheel, barely tall enough to see over it.

At close range the sheriff didn't seem as short as at first glance. He was built like a sandstone county courthouse and had the rolling gait of a seaman. My guess was he probably retired from the criminal branch of the Office of Naval Investigations and was supplementing his pension. He tossed away the badly chewed stump of cigar and fished its other half out of the pocket of his shirt.

"I'm Ray Bolton, the Malahat sheriff," he said. "Your name is Fiddler."

What an investigator. I nodded.

"How's Rory doing?" he asked.

"He was breathing when the ambulance left," I said. "The firemen said he had a depressed skull fracture and two broken hips or legs. In a man his age, that's not good news."

Bolton listened to me carefully, as though trying to catch fear or nervousness in my voice. It was hard to tell what he heard. I was hanging on to what was left of my patience. The strain showed in my voice. It was one of the reasons Fiora had simply handed me the leash and left. Years together had taught her when and when not to crowd me.

"A terrible thing," Bolton said. "Really terrible. You seem awfully calm, to have seen all that."

I bit back my first response, but the look in my eyes must have made him reconsider his first impression.

"If I thought hysterics would help Rory, I'd be screaming down the moon," I said.

The sheriff shifted the fresh cigar stump from one side of his mouth to the other and studied me.

His head bobbed a quarter inch, acknowledging my anger.

"Rory's real popular around Malahat," Bolton said finally. "If that makes any difference."

"It doesn't surprise me. He's one of the few really decent men I've ever known."

Bolton studied me a while longer. His eyes were a little bloodshot. His manner told me I wasn't the first person he had ever interrogated, nor would I be the last.

"Well, then," he said, "if that's true, I expect you won't mind answering a few questions. No need to confer with a lawyer or anything?"

"None."

"Good. Why don't you just show us what happened, walk us through it, from the time you left this afternoon until right now."

As Bolton moved past me to the foot of the stairs, I caught a whiff of alcohol. A drinker, but only off duty. That explained the clothes and the boy driver. No matter. Bolton seemed more competent half drunk than his deputies were stone sober.

I took Kwame off the leash, told him to heel, and headed up the stairway. The deputies gave Kwame a long look, saw that he was well behaved, and followed. I put Kwame in the truck and took the sheriff through my movements, step by step, from the time Fiora called to the moment we pulled in by the boathouse and saw Rory's body.

Then I took the cops across the lawn toward the big house and showed them the kitchen phone and the burned pork chops on the stove. I recalled every detail I could think of, giving them as much material as they needed to corroborate the statement. Nordwier and Lindstrom scribbled notes as fast as they could.

We walked into the living room. The doors of the gun cabinet still stood open. Bolton pulled a Mini-MagLite out of his hip pocket and spotlighted the slivered wood around the broken latch. From there he moved on to the round brass head of the key in the lock. He shifted the cigar stump around.

"That *is* the key for the cabinet, I presume?" he asked.

"I've never used it," I said. "Rory was in the cabinet last evening. He probably forgot to take out the key."

Bolton glanced at me. "Why you suppose the doors got smashed, then, what with the key right there?"

Not too subtle. Or maybe very. Hard to tell with the good ol' boy act.

That's why I use it myself from time to time.

"Whoever did it could have been in a hurry," I said, "or they could have wanted somebody like you to think Rory got hurt during a bungled burglary."

A cold grin bracketed the sheriff's cigar stump. "You're pretty quick, boy. You aren't a cop or anything, are you?"

"Not for a long time. I'm not a boy, either."

With a noncommittal grunt, Bolton went back to studying the cabinet. He didn't touch anything.

"What's missing?" he asked abruptly.

"Three rifles, two shotguns including an expensive English double-barreled piece, and maybe a

Colt Woodsman target pistol. I can't tell about the Colt without getting into the drawer down below.''

''Don't,'' he said. ''State lab is sending a crime-scene technician out.''

Better that than relying on Mutt and Jeff.

''You'll want exemplars from me,'' I said.

He grunted again. ''We'll need a complete list of the missing guns, too. Serial numbers would help, if you have them.''

''I can describe them but that's it.'' My glance fell on Rory's desk. ''Wait a minute. If I don't touch the face of the drawer, can I get in the desk?''

Bolton nodded.

I poked a pencil through the handle of the lower right-hand drawer and found the upright files Rory kept for his personal expenses. The file he had shown to me last night was right where he had left it.

''I handled the file last night,'' I said, and waited.

Bolton glanced at the file header, saw the word WILL, and grunted. ''Why did he show it to you?''

''I'm his executor.''

He grunted again. ''Go ahead.''

I pulled out the file, flipped it open, and found the three-page single-spaced document marked *Last Will and Testament of Rory Cairns*.

''He listed the long guns under personal property,'' I said. ''Serial numbers, too.''

Bolton must have left his reading glasses at home. He took the will and held it out at arm's length, trying to make out the letters and numbers.

''Rory didn't have any family,'' Bolton said. ''Who's the big winner?''

The guns were part of Rory's bequest to me,

which also included "one Japanese steel sword in scabbard and cloth presentation bag," "three double-handed split-bamboo fly rods," *"The King of Nothing,"* and "one violin," which I didn't know if I could even bring myself to look at, much less use, but I wasn't about to drag in extraneous issues like my inheritance. The quicker we got through this farce of an investigation, the sooner I would be at the hospital.

"Most of his estate goes to the Wildlife Hostel. He gave Fiora the cottage down below and the boathouse, along with a couple of acres of waterfront. He left me the boat and a few personal items, three fly rods, and a sword he brought back from the war."

Bolton gave me a careful look, estimating the value of the bequests, trying to decide whether it could serve as a motive for murder.

I shook my head. "Fiora's net worth is probably bigger than the Malahat County budget, and I do mean the entire budget, not just your department."

He scowled at me. "You don't like this much, do you?"

"Not a damn bit. Particularly when I've cooperated."

Bolton's stained teeth bit into the unlit cigar stump a time or two before he removed it from his mouth so he could speak plainly.

"Well, I don't much care what you like and don't like. My badge and the good voters of Malahat County give me that luxury. We don't have many serious crimes here, and they expect me to solve the ones that do happen. So long as

I'm the sheriff, I'm stuck asking unpleasant questions.''

He waited.

So did I.

"As for your alibi," Bolton continued, "it flowed pretty smooth, which leads me to believe it's probably verifiable. That don't mean you're off the hook, though. You're a smart California boy, smart enough to set up an alibi and let somebody else push Rory down the stairs if you needed to."

I looked as disgusted as I felt.

"Personally," he continued, "I doubt that's what happened. But I keep an open mind . . . if you get my drift."

I got it. "Does that mean I can go to the hospital now?"

Bolton put his cigar back in the corner of his mouth. "Sure thing. Just stay in touch, will you?"

"Count on it. I may not be a Malahat voter but I'd like to see this crime solved too . . . if you get my drift."

He did. He didn't like it one damn bit.

That made two of us.

fIVE

It was just after midnight when I drove around the vest-pocket harbor of Malahat and up the hill to the Malahat Regional Hospital. The parking lot was almost empty. I cracked the pickup's windows, rubbed Kwame's spiky ruff, told him he was handsome, and left him to guard the truck. He watched me all the way across the parking lot, then lay down on the blanket I'd left behind.

For the next ten minutes I did the "Are you family?" pas de deux with the hospital admissions woman. Just as I was going to lose my temper, she confessed that Rory had been rushed through the emergency room and straight into surgery. I made a mental note to call Marley as soon as I could. She had spent a lifetime in hospitals. She would know better than I did how to get tight-assed bureaucrats off the dime.

Green arrows on the floor led me through a maze toward the surgery wing. The long hallway was like the inner corridor of a space station: harsh artificial light and stale air scented with chemicals. Hell will be like that, I thought, completely man-made, no green trees, no fresh air, no salmon, no eagles, no escape, just pain and death: a clean, well-lighted prison of the senses.

Alone and lonely, Fiora leaned against a wall. Her arms were crossed in front of her and her head was bowed. I wondered how many childhood prayers she had remembered. I hoped she had done better than I had.

Fiora was so lost in herself she didn't even sense my approach. If there's anything worse than being helpless, Fiora hasn't found it yet. She hates having to depend on anyone or anything, even me.

It took me a long time to learn her strengths and weaknesses, and even longer to appreciate them. We were married once. Then we were divorced. But we never came apart, not completely. We slept together because we couldn't stay away. Finally we understood that the physical bond was unbreakable because it came from something deeper than the flesh. Slowly we came back together, stronger for the fact that we lived together by choice and not necessity.

It has been a long time since either one of us slept with anyone else. It's been even longer since either one of us wanted to.

"Fiora."

When her head came up, her eyes were dry, but they were much too dark. For a moment she stared at me, confused. Then the tears came, all in a flood, surprising us both. An instant later she was in my arms, her face buried against my chest. I held her for a long time before either of us started to breathe evenly again.

After a time I whispered to her, words without meaning except to say I was there. I didn't try to stop her tears. In the past few years, she has finally learned to cry.

And I have finally learned to let her.

For several minutes Fiora shivered in my arms like a child, as she released emotions that had been stifled too long. Gradually her shudders began to subside. She drew a shallow breath, tipped her head back, and looked up at me again. The tears had washed some of the darkness from her eyes.

"Thanks. I'm okay now," she said, taking a deep breath. "I just don't do very well in hospitals. Especially not when I have to look at ghastly modern art."

"What?"

"A full skull series," Fiora said tightly, "complete with the surgeon's learned lectures on the ramifications of this smudge or that. Life or death or, even worse, neither."

She reached up and brushed her fingers along my hairline, touching a scar that a bullet had left there a long time ago. I had forgotten about it, but she had not. I knew then how she had felt while I lay in a hospital neither dead nor quite living.

It didn't comfort me.

"What did the X rays show?" I asked.

"Rory's brain is bleeding. It started to swell. That's why they had to operate right away."

"How bad is it?"

"If the surgeon knows, he isn't saying. His descriptions are clinical and exquisitely precise. It's every doctor's favorite way of avoiding reality."

"Does this guy know what he's doing? We could get Rory to Seattle in an hour on a medevac flight."

Fiora shrugged. "Dr. Cranmer did his residency at Cedars-Sinai."

"How did you find that out?"

"I asked."

I'll just bet she did, and found out where he graduated in his class, too. Fiora is capable of taking on hell with a garden hose, much less a mere brain surgeon. She really doesn't need me to protect her any more than I need her to protect me. Her self-sufficiency used to irritate me. Then I figured out it was better that way.

Now we protect each other.

"You okay?" she asked, touching my cheek. That's her way of suggesting I might *not* be okay.

"So far so good," I said. "Why?"

"You frightened me when I first saw you," she said simply. "For a second you looked . . . lethal. Is something wrong that I don't know about?"

I shook my head. "The waltz with the sheriff was strictly routine. That's the problem. Once the local cops scratch you and me off the list, the only thing they can think of that's left to scratch is their ass. These officers of the law never did their residency at Cedars."

"Could you do better?"

"Kwame could do better."

Fiora closed her eyes for a moment. I could tell she wanted to argue about something, but I couldn't tell what it was.

"Spit it out," I said.

She smiled sadly. "We've done this lap before. We know all the turns, all the markers, all the potholes and straightaways. I dream, and then I'm afraid for you. You don't dream, and you're not afraid for yourself. I love you anyway. You love me anyway. End of lap. So let's just phone it in this time, okay?"

After a moment I took Fiora's hand. She laced her fingers through mine. Slowly we walked down the hall to the room set aside for people who are waiting for a family member to come out of surgery.

"Remember," she said quietly, "we're full partners now. What you do, I do."

I gave her a long look, "I'm not planning anything."

Yet.

But neither of us said it aloud. We just went into the grim little room, closed the door behind us, and sat down to do what I was worst at.

Waiting.

After a few hours Fiora napped fitfully on the couch, her head on my lap, her shoulders covered by a hospital blanket I had rounded up. I couldn't sleep. During the long hours before dawn I got up several times to look out the window or to walk myself and Kwame.

Malahat had the rhythms of a dying small town. The gas station closed at midnight and the two waterfront beer bars shut down at 2 A.M. The only constructive activity was in the little harbor, where a deck crane loaded swinging bundles of peeled logs into the hold of a green-and-cream-colored freighter moored at the Malahat Lumber Company wharf.

Once, just after 3 A.M., Kwame and I walked far out onto the wharf and read the name and home port on the freighter's stern: *Ganjin Maru*, Yokohama. Economic imperialism at work. The sawmill on the flats above the harbor used to cut lumber for the export trade. Now the sawmill had been shut down. Its jobs were being exported too. No surprise that Malahat looked dead. It was. It just hadn't been buried yet.

I wondered if Nakamichi was in the lumber business. It would have explained why he was in such a hurry to get back into the air. Japanese businessmen aren't very popular in the blue-collar towns of the Pacific Northwest. On the other hand, they can exert a lot of influence. Maybe Ron could press Bolton's button.

On the other side of the harbor, twenty longliners and a dozen square-sterned seine boats wallowed side by side at the fish-packer's pier, shut down for the next five days. Commercial fishing was limited to a few days a week to allow the escape of breeding stock and to give sport fishermen a chance.

Rory was missing the best fishing. By the time he got back on his feet, the commercial men would have vacuumed the ocean clean. If he ever got on his feet again.

* * *

Fiora was asleep on my lap, the only way she seemed to be at peace. I was stroking her hair and watching bad color images on a silent television. The surgeon walked in just before six. He looked disoriented for a moment.

"You waiting for word on Rory Cairns?" he asked.

"Yes."

Fiora woke up as Dr. Cranmer pulled off his scrub cap. A bundle of shoulder-length hair held in place by pins started to come undone. He looked young and frankly tired.

He rubbed his face, trying to restore circulation and expression. "Long night," the doctor said.

"How is he?" I asked. "In simple English, please."

Cranmer studied me for a minute before answering. "He tolerated the surgery better than I expected for a man his age. We cleaned out as much of the blood as we could and did some other things to relieve the pressure on the brain."

"And?"

He started to run his fingers through his hair, got caught in bobby pins, and tugged on his ear instead.

"Depressed skull fractures and brain injuries are a real bitch," Cranmer said finally. "Mr. Cairns could wake up today and feel like a million bucks or he could hang on for a week or two and then die. His age is against him. His physical shape is in his favor. We just have to take things as they come."

"What about his hips?"

"They're broken, but we have to get a handle on

the head injury before we let the orthopedic guys have him."

"Can we see Rory?" Fiora asked.

"He's still under anesthesia." Cranmer hesitated and added, "Go and have some breakfast. You could be in for a long wait."

Fiora looked at the surgeon for a few moments, reading between the lines on his young face. Without a word she got up and left the waiting room. I followed her.

There were five logging trucks in front of a café called Pearl's. It was the best recommendation we were likely to get at that hour. We parked and went in.

The loggers weren't used to strange blondes at six in the morning. Fiora got some long looks, even though she was wearing jeans and one of my old flannel shirts. Somehow the clothes emphasized her femininity instead of detracting from it. Fiora didn't even notice the loggers, which was just as well. She never has understood that she's supposed to be flattered by the unsubtle inspections of strange men. Her reaction tends to be as blunt as her raised middle finger.

So does mine, but that's okay. The men understand that. They look at Fiora, look at me, and go back to looking at their food. No problem.

Neither one of us felt much like eating, but we ordered big breakfasts anyway. As the doctor had said, it would be a long wait. After we ate as much as we could manage, we went back to the hospital.

Rory was still under. The intensive-care nurse let Fiora sit in the room with him for a moment, but I saw all I needed from the doorway. Rory's ruddy Scottish complexion was the color of putty. He didn't move. The cardiac monitor on the wall was the only proof he was still alive, and it wasn't very encouraging.

I took in as much as I could, then walked away and stood in the hallway, breathing deeply, trying to get a grip on my rage that someone could do this to a good man and never pay for it. Not really.

And even if I got my hands on the asshole and extracted the last red drop of justice, it wouldn't change what had happened. If Rory lived, he would never regain the physical peak from which he had fallen. He would be not only old but frail. Freedom had been taken from him. Pain had not.

And there wasn't a damn thing I could do about it.

Gradually I realized that Fiora was standing in front of me, watching me with eyes that were both compassionate and wary.

"Go," she said softly. "Do something."

"Like what?"

"Sleep. Fish. Throw rocks. Kick stumps."

"I'd rather kick ass."

"I know. It radiates from you like heat from a fire." She touched my mustache lightly. "At least take Kwame home. He must be as tired of the truck as you are of this waiting room."

I went.

Fiora was right. Kwame was as glad to see me as I was to leave the smell of the hospital behind. I scratched his ears, he gnawed gently on my chin, and neither one of us looked back as I drove away.

Rory had kept a pair of Brittany spaniels until last year. At fourteen, both dogs became more ill than anything but final rest could cure, so he'd given them a swift, gentle death. Other than holding friends' dogs while their owners went on vacation, the run stayed empty. The doghouse was still sound and so was the chain-link fence, despite the jungle of blackberry bushes that had grown through it. I went to work on the bushes with a machete I found in Rory's toolshed, and the exercise released some of the tension in my shoulders. The brambles were a worthy adversary; they stung and drew blood.

Kwame liked them too. He crashed around in the tangled underbrush, barking and yapping like a puppy, forcing his way into the thickest part of the tangle. A moment later, he emerged with something in his mouth. It took me an instant to recognize it.

"Drop!"

Kwame spat out his prize and gave me a pained look. I gave the look right back.

Dogs may be man's best friend, but they aren't human. They don't share human tastes. Kwame, for instance, loves dead things, old dead things, the deader the better. His new treasure was a raccoon, a dead one. I knew he hadn't killed it, or I would have heard the ruckus. Coons fight like tigers. That meant something else had. Kwame didn't mind that, but I did.

Kwame wagged his tail and looked hopefully at the bundle of fur and sinew.

"Sit."

Kwame sat.

"Stay."

He did, but he watched me with great disappointment.

I wondered if age, illness, or a bullet had finished the animal. It lay on its back where Kwame had dropped it. There were no visible wounds or injuries. The pelt was thick and had a good sheen, even now. The ribs were covered with fat. The teeth were unbroken. There was no obvious cause of death.

That worried me. Kwame's shots were up to date, but the thought of him mouthing a diseased corpse was unsettling.

A fleck of white on the raccoon's snarling lips caught my attention. I looked more closely and spotted other bits of white on the coon's pointy muzzle.

"Lice?"

Kwame whined.

"Shit," I muttered at the dog, "the things I put up with for you."

I was tempted just to dig a hole, bury the coon, and get on with the delousing. But before I gave Kwame a kerosene rubdown, I wanted to be sure he needed it.

With no great pleasure I picked up one of the bits of white and peered at it.

"Be damned. It's rice."

Curious, I pried the coon's frozen jaws apart with the blade of my pocketknife. A wad of rice fell out. It was wrapped in what looked like a strip of squid or octopus.

The poor little masked bastard had died with a mouth full of sushi.

SIX

My first impulse was to get Kwame's stomach pumped. But he has been trained never to eat anything that doesn't come from Fiora's hand or mine. Even so, I opened his lion-trap jaws real fast and had a good look inside. No rice. No rice slurry. Nothing but clean white teeth and a lot of them.

"Good boy, Kwame."

He thumped his tail and licked my chin while I petted and praised him and wondered where the poisoned sushi had come from. Maybe Rory had gotten tired of having his garbage cans raided and the rancid contents spread across his lawn every morning. He could have put out some poisoned sushi after I went to get Fiora at the airport.

It was not only possible, it was probable. Rory and I had picked up trash more than once, swearing the whole time. The local raccoons were all too clever about getting into garbage cans, no matter how carefully they were stored.

"Stay."

I began searching the runway. By the time I was finished, I found the hole in the fence the coon had come in through. I also found two more rice balls in the mowed grass at the edge of the run. There was another ball near the blackberry thicket. That made a total of five, including the one that was still in the raccoon's mouth when the one in his stomach killed him.

The most logical assumption was that Rory had fed the coon its last meal of garbage, in such a way that any neighborhood dogs wouldn't happen across the bait and die by mistake. That was what the cops would say, and they might even have been right.

But my friend Benny has another way of putting it: Assumption is the mother of all fuck-ups, and a logical assumption is the greatest mother of all. Benny should know. As the Ice Cream King of Saigon, he had a chance to watch one assumption after another collapse in 1975.

"Heel."

Kwame took up station at my left heel and waited.

Chalk it up to my nasty mind, but I had a feeling someone had been prowling around the grounds. Someone who hadn't known whether there was a dog in residence. Someone who had chucked a few rounds of poisoned sushi over the fence and waited for a pet to gulp and die. Someone who had then come in close, watched, and waited for me to be alone.

Me, not Rory.

In the dark, Rory and I would be hard to tell

apart. We're the same height, the same width in the shoulders, and have the same dark hair.

The thought that I might have been responsible, indirectly, for Rory's pain chilled me. Yet the pieces fit. Someone had been watching last night, had seen the Cobra sitting alone in the driveway, had seen a big man coming out of the house in the twilight, had made the logical assumption.

No wonder Fiora had been dreaming. I was the one to be crippled or killed, not Rory. I had made a lot more enemies in my life than he had. A South American money mover named Don Faustino, for one. A Russian named Volker for another.

There were others, as well. Too many of them. I try to follow Benny's advice and bury my enemies where I find them, but I'm not always successful.

For a long time I studied the woods around Rory's neatly mowed lawn. There was only one place where a watcher could command a view of both house and cottage: the small rise behind the dog run, covered with second-growth forest and surrounded by blackberry thickets.

I put the lead on Kwame and headed for the rise, but I came at it from the road, the way someone would if he didn't want to be noticed. The blackberry thickets were heavy with late fruit. The canes were like razor whips, but some of them were broken. Some of the leaves were crushed. The trail was even clearer to Kwame. Once he understood what I wanted, he crashed through the brush like the African lion hound he was.

At the top of the rise, Kwame stopped, sniffed around, and came back to me for further instructions. The end of the trail looked no different from any other part of the rise. All I could see was brush, brambles, and forest loam. Then I noticed that the soil had been disturbed. Fist-sized hunks of rock and a dead branch had been pushed aside to make room for someone to lie down. What could have been a partial footprint appeared in a stretch of dirt where debris had been scuffed off, revealing the damp ground beneath.

When I hunkered down for a better look at the print, I could see through the bushes to Rory's house. I was only fifty feet from the stairway where he had fallen.

Or been pushed.

Kwame whined, reminding me that I wasn't alone in the brambles. I focused on the bare piece of earth again. The print—if that's what it was— suggested a small shoe size and an unusually soft sole, maybe a moccasin, but there wasn't enough of an outline to be certain.

I looked around until I was sure there was nothing else to be found before I went back down the hill and called the sheriff. If Bolton was glad to hear from me, he kept it to himself. He and his deputies must have just gotten off the phone, corroborating my alibi from the night before.

That wouldn't have been tough. Port Angeles Airport doesn't see too many Gulfstreams. If that wasn't enough, the steak house probably still had the credit-card voucher imprinted with my charge plate.

I told Bolton how I had spent the past hour. He wasn't impressed.

"More than likely it was a load of bad garbage that killed the coon."

"Maybe," I said. My tone said I doubted it.

The sheriff grunted. "Rory wouldn't be the first man to poison a coon, especially with the rabies problems we've had the last couple of summers. But if it will make you feel better, bring one of them little old balls in. I'll mail it off to Olympia, let them take a look at it."

"What about your crime-scene investigator?"

"Come and gone already. His best guess is, it was a burglary. He didn't find any prints, which probably means gloves, which means the burglar probably just smashed the glass for the hell of it. You know how it is. Some burglars crap on the living room floor, some piss on the biggest chair in the room, some sniff everything in the panty drawer. Kind of a calling card."

"You find any other gun burglaries that look like this one?" I asked skeptically.

"Not yet, but I haven't been looking very long. I put out a teletype on the guns just now. We'll see what turns up in the pawnshops over in Seattle."

"Does that mean I'm off your list?"

"I didn't say that, son. I never rule out suspects until sentence is passed and appeals are exhausted."

He chuckled and hung up an instant before I did.

I called the hospital. Nothing new. No change. Less hope of change with every minute.

Kwame watched while I put his ring-tailed trophy in a cardboard box. We went across the road to Marley's place. She had been away last night, but the neighbors had already told her about Rory. Without explanation, I showed her the raccoon.

She found the grains of rice almost as quickly as I had.

"There's more in his mouth and probably some in his stomach, too," I said, showing her the plastic bag that contained the three uneaten balls.

Marley opened the bag, sniffed, and shook her head.

"It's not strychnine or arsenic," she said. "That's what dog poisoners usually use." She stroked the dead raccoon's fur sadly. "He was in his prime. What a shame."

"Could he have died from eating garbage?"

"Doubt it. Whatever got him was so quick he couldn't even swallow what was in his mouth. That's poison, not garbage gut."

"Come again?"

"Garbage gut. Gastroenteritis if you're feeling fancy. A lot of vomiting, ulcers. It's a hard, slow way to die."

"I wish you were the Malahat sheriff," I said.

"Bolton was a navy career man," she said. "He ran the brig at the nuclear submarine station in Bremerton. That's why people around here elected him—to run the jail."

"Is he the best investigator the county has?"

"You could go to the state police, but they won't want to step in without proof of local incompetence. Out here, it's go along and get along. It works pretty well, most of the time."

"Has Bolton been out to interrogate you?" I asked.

"No. Why should he?"

"His list of suspects seems to be limited to burglars and beneficiaries of Rory's will."

Marley looked blank.

"Rory left the cottage, boathouse, and five acres to Fiora," I said. "I'm supposed to sell the rest and give the money to your Wilderness Hostel."

Marley's jaw sagged. Then she removed her glasses, wiped her eyes, and gave me a bittersweet smile.

"He never told me," she said huskily. "I created a trust, put my farm into it already. I told Rory about it. He must have decided the animals were going to need cash too, once we're both dead."

There was the same acceptance of death in Marley's voice that I had heard in Rory's when he gave me the sword. It told me I could ask the question that nobody had wanted to answer.

"You've talked to the hospital?"

She nodded.

"Is Rory going to live?" I asked bluntly.

"I don't know," Marley said. "Neither do they." She looked at me straight. "You're young, Fiddler. You still think death is the worst thing that can happen. But when you get to be my age, or Rory's, and when you've spent your life in hospitals, death becomes . . . well, if not a friend, then at least not an enemy."

"Is that how Rory felt?"

Marley nodded.

"Are you certain?" I asked. "I couldn't find instructions in his files."

"We talked about it when my sister was in a nursing home. It took eleven years for her body to defeat those damned machines. Rory didn't want that. I don't know anyone who does."

Marley looked out over her land for a moment, wiped her eyes again, and replaced her glasses.

"I'll sit with Rory this afternoon," she said briskly. "Take that lovely girl of yours somewhere and make her smile. Rory thinks the world of her, and you."

I kissed Marley's cheek, surprising both of us. Then I went back across the street and cleaned the dog run down to its original gravel bed. I found nothing but dust, weeds, and stones. After I filled a bucket with water for Kwame, fed him, and locked him in the run, I dropped the rice balls and dead raccoon off at Bolton's office, making no friends in the process. Then I headed for the lawyer whose name was on Rory's will.

Small-town lawyers tend to perch around the courthouse square like night herons around a salmon hatchery. Fred Riger was no different. He had a two-office suite on the second floor of a refurbished Victorian mansion across the street from the courthouse and next door to the county public library. The parking slot marked with Riger's name held a big Oldsmobile with a country-club parking permit and a Bush-Quayle sticker on the bumper.

Riger and his partner shared a secretary-receptionist. The girl must have been down the hall because when I walked into the office, it was Riger himself who stuck his head out of the office and asked what I wanted.

I introduced myself.

"Fiddler . . . " he said, blinking. "Oh. Rory's executor."

Riger was clean-shaven and bald. He had the cheerful, pink fleshy look of a Rotarian toastmaster but not the smile. That had vanished as soon as he recognized my name. He came out of his office and offered his hand to me.

"I just heard about Rory," he said. "Terrible thing. What can I do for you?"

"I found a copy of Rory's will, but nothing else. I was wondering if you had helped him make out any other legal documents."

His guard seemed to go up immediately. "Like what?"

"His doctor asked me about something called a power of attorney for health care."

Riger shook his head. "Those things don't have much legal value around here. We're not part of California yet, no matter how many of you move up here."

"How about the U.S.? Are you part of that?"

"You're referring to the Supreme Court decision about the right to die?"

"Bingo."

Riger touched the bridge of his nose as though testing for breaks. "All probate questions in this county go to Judge Harry Stone. The judge has been paying a nursing home two thousand dollars a month for the past two decades to keep his ninety-three-year-old mother clinically alive. He doesn't see why anyone should miss that particular brand of penance, regardless of what the federal courts think. He's one of those men who believes in letting things work themselves out naturally."

"I don't call a respirator and a feeding tube natural. How about you, counselor? Would you be interested in forcing the issue if it comes to that?"

He studied me carefully for a while, then decided. "I might be. Rory did have me draw up the power of attorney for health care, by the way, even though I told him it probably wouldn't do much good. Would you like a copy?"

Without waiting for my answer, Riger turned and went back into his office, talking as he went.

"I've already got two clients who are being kept alive on machines because their families aren't willing to confront death or the legal system."

He waved me into his office and went to a file cabinet in the corner. He opened the top drawer, withdrew a folder, flipped it open, and muttered something.

"What's wrong?" I asked.

He showed me the open folder. It was empty.

"Serves me right for hiring a friend's daughter," Riger muttered. "Apparently they're not teaching the alphabet in our schools anymore."

He turned away and began searching file folders on either side of Rory's.

"Is the will valid even if you can't find it?" I asked.

"Certainly. It's been recorded."

Riger spread apart more files and rifled through the contents.

"Nope. Not here. How can she misplace two copies of a will, the power of attorney for health care, names and addresses of beneficiaries, an appraisal of personal property right down to the fillings in his teeth—"

He frowned, hearing his own words.

"That could be a problem. Rory was close to the six-hundred-thousand-dollar estate-tax threshold. That's why I told him to get everything appraised, and I mean everything. What with federal budget cuts, the IRS has become more savagely stupid than ever."

Riger hunted through a few more file folders, then slammed the file drawer shut in disgust.

"Damn that child! She must have misfiled it. What's wrong with this generation, anyway? Three weeks ago we had some junkie break in and take our computer and petty cash. Now some illiterate high school girl can't keep the alphabet straight."

Riger sighed explosively as he turned back to me.

"I'm sorry. I'll call you as soon as we find the file."

SEVEN

Fiora and Marley sat in chairs beside Rory's bed in the ICU. Two women, calm in the eye of the storm, talking together quietly as the institutionalized business of living and dying went on around them.

Marley must have been used to hospitals, but Fiora amazed me. Twenty-four hours before, she had been dressed to the teeth and negotiating an eight-figure business deal with a leading international financier. Today she was in jeans and a baggy shirt, keeping bedside watch on an old man. If she noticed the difference in occupations, it didn't show. The sadness in her eyes was for Rory's changed circumstances, not for her own.

Rory lay on his back, his legs immobilized so he couldn't do his hips any more damage. His face was chalky. His skin was cool to the touch and oddly brittle. The cardiac monitor was the only proof that his heart still beat, that his lungs still drew air. He seemed to have shrunk inward, all vitality gone, nothing remaining but a husk of what had once been.

I sensed Fiora watching me, but one thought dominated my mind: Rory had lived close to the land and to the sea, and now he was removed from both. He loved life and respected death and had taught me a good deal about them. He deserved a better life—or death—than modern medical hubris and a sour old judge were willing to allow.

I didn't know that Fiora had stood up until I felt her arm slide around me, reminding me that life is warm, supple, vibrant. I drew her even closer and closed my eyes. When I opened them again, Marley gave me a look and a tilt of her head toward the door.

"Come fishing with me," I said to Fiora.

What I didn't say was that we both needed the sun and brine and gentle rhythms of the sea. We needed air that didn't stink of pain and despair. We needed to remember a Rory who wasn't chained between white sheets, not quite dead and not quite alive.

It was early afternoon by the time we got down to the boathouse. There had been no discussion, but both of us headed for the Boston Whaler that Rory kept for lazy fishing. Although *The King of Nothing* was gassed up and ready to go, neither one of us was ready to climb aboard without Rory.

Out on the water a quarter mile from shore, the tide was ebbing and the sun was warm. I could feel some of the rage beginning to burn off like the last effects of an overnight drunk. The calm straits and rocky, forested shores of the Pacific Northwest have that effect on me.

"Rockfish?" I asked.

It was the first thing either one of us had said since the hospital.

Fiora nodded.

The small outboard motor muttered over the calm water, leaving an expanding V behind. The mooching rods jiggled softly against wooden seats, vibrating as though their whippy tips were alive. I might have raked for herring but it seemed too much trouble. Rory always kept a block or two of frozen bait. One was slowly thawing in half a bucket of water between Fiora's feet. By the time we reached the deeply submerged rocks of Scotsman's Reef, the herring strips would be flexible enough to thread on the hooks. Frozen bait wasn't likely to fetch us up a salmon, but rockfish never seemed to mind.

I guessed at the location of the east end of the reef, cut the motor, and felt silence fall like a benediction over the sea and the little boat. A bit more of my buried anger dissolved, making room for deeper breaths.

By the time I had tied on a pencil-thick sinker with a fisherman's knot, Fiora had her bait in the water and was stripping off line. Thirty seconds later the tip of her rod bounced once, hard. Then it settled down and stayed arched like a stallion's neck.

Classic rockfish. Hit hard once and then sulk.

I smiled and went back to rigging my own line. More than once Rory had tried to teach me the true names of the many varieties of rockfish that abounded along the coast. I had resisted. Let the Ph.D. types exercise their brains dividing finer and finer hairs—or scales, in this case. If you catch it near a rock reef, it's a rockfish. Same goes for birds. If you see them wading along the shore, they're shorebirds.

Rockfish are the blue-collar fish of the ocean. They lack the slashing speed and fierce strength of salmon, and they don't yield the big, meaty fillets of halibut or ling cod. Rockfish are bony, ugly, sullen, and without guile.

They are also perfectly edible, even tasty, if you coat them with potato-chip crumbs and fry them in butter.

Most sport fishermen avoid rockfish but Rory was different, and Rory had imparted his wisdom to me. He regarded rockfish as tasty, reliable, high-protein, low-fat easy meals. Like clams, rockfish were always there for the taking, a bounty that reminded man what Eden must have been like, a lifetime of food at your fingertips so long as you don't screw it up with purse seiners and dragnets.

Rockfish don't require anything fancy in the way of fishing equipment. You start with ten- or twelve-pound monofilament line—because you never know when a salmon might be lurking nearby—tie a pencil sinker on, add ten feet of leader and a hook, put a frozen herring on the hook, and drop the lot over the side of the boat. The sinker finds bottom and the herring floats a few feet above, tossed by the currents like a wounded baitfish until some reef dweller flashes out of nowhere for what looks like a fishy version of fast food. Not much sport but endless reward, and two nice firm white-fleshed fillets on every fish you keep.

Fishing rewards hope more often than most things we do in this life. Even if you never get a bite, you get back in touch with the sea, and once you've done that, getting in touch with your soul isn't far behind.

Rory's words echoed in my mind as I stopped fussing over my rod and watched Fiora reel in her fish. The sad brackets on either side of her mouth had vanished as soon as the fish hit. There was nothing in her world at the moment but the fish at the end of her line. She whooped and reeled and called the fish amazing names when it headed under the boat.

Actually, the boat drifted over the fish. Bottom fish aren't quick or canny. They strike, can't get free, and sulk with spiny fins flared, creating an unreasonable amount of drag for the size they turn out to be.

"Ready?" I asked after a time.

"Almost. See him?"

"Yeah."

The fish was a shadow under the deep green sea. With another few seconds and few feet of line reeled in, Fiora's prize was revealed as deep red and ugly, with a gaping mouth that looked big enough to swallow a football. The spines on his fins were fully spread, thicker than darning needles and every bit as sharp. The poison in the spines wasn't dangerous, but it was damned painful.

"Nice size," I said. "Want to keep him?"

"Waste not, want not." My ever-practical woman.

"Fillet of rockfish, coming right up."

I pulled on a leather glove, grabbed the fish by

the corner of the mouth, and lifted him into the boat.

"Good job," I said, hefting the ugly prize. "Must be close to six pounds."

Holding the needle-nose pliers in one hand and the fish in the other, I put the jaws on the shank of the hook, jerked, and retrieved it from the fishy gullet. While Fiora baited up again, I groped beneath the seat for the fish cosh, found it, thumped the rockfish's pea-sized brain to jelly, and dumped dinner into the holding tub.

Just as I reached for my own rod, Fiora hooked into another fish. Under other circumstances I would have baited up and let her bring in her own fish. It's important to observe the democracy of the fishing boat.

But not today. Democracy be hanged. Today I was pleased just to see the light come back into Fiora's eyes.

After I had dispatched the second rockfish—a remarkably ugly beast the color of a canary caught in seaweed—I leaned back against the gunwale and crossed my arms over my chest, content to watch Fiora fish with her unique blend of womanly grace and hair-raising pragmatism.

She was wearing a wool Dodgers cap, Number 15 sunscreen, and a pair of Ray-Ban Wayfarers. Without looking at me, she knew I was watching her. When the bait was all the way at the bottom, she glanced at me. My eyes were hidden behind sunglasses but she could read my expression.

"Want to talk about it yet?" Fiora asked.

"About what?"

"How you spent the morning."

"You're having fun fishing," I said, not wanting to see the sad lines come back to her face.

"I can fish and listen at the same time."

So I told her what I had found, rice and a dead raccoon and no more. Just the facts and none of the maybes.

I should have known better. Fiora got to the bottom line faster than I had.

"It was supposed to be you, wasn't it," she said, more certainty than question in her voice.

I didn't answer.

She didn't ask again. She simply pumped her rod to set the bait dancing and stared at the point where the line disappeared into the water.

Apparently Fiora had caught the most aggressive fish on the reef, for things calmed down. The rocking of the boat, the warmth of the sun, and a night without sleep hit me like a falling mountain. I stretched out on my back across the seat, braced my feet against the gunwale, and watched the cloud-scattered sky.

The next thing I knew, Fiora was calling to me, her voice rippling with excitement.

"Fish on!"

"Bite your tongue," I muttered. "You're only supposed to say that for salmon."

"This *is* a salmon."

I opened one eye. Fiora's rod was bent in a wicked bow. She lifted the tip of the rod with a swift movement, setting the hook. The rod remained bent, quivering.

"Rockfish," I said. "He's lying doggo on the bottom."

The tip of the rod pumped twice, just to prove

me a liar. Fiora tried to pick up line but the fish moved away, making the reel sing a slow little song. She grunted and tightened the drag a bit. The line kept sliding away.

"Doesn't feel like a rockfish," Fiora said, grabbing the rod with both hands and keeping the tip up, just like Rory had taught her.

"Dogfish, then," I said.

"Ugh."

Fiora didn't like the ugly reddish sharks any better than the local fishermen did.

Smiling slightly, I closed my eyes, settled my spine more comfortably against the wooden seat, and slid back toward sleep.

"Aren't you going to help?" she asked after a moment.

"You're doing fine. Just bring him up until you know what you have. If it's a shark, cut the line. If it's a rockfish, the cosh is underneath my seat and the glove is in the tackle box."

"But—"

"Wake me up when you're ready to head back to shore," I interrupted, yawning, almost falling asleep as I spoke.

The reel screamed softly.

"Tighten the drag and take off the damn clicker," I said. "You're keeping me awake."

Fiora muttered something I chose not to hear, but she took off the clicker. For a few minutes she fought the stubborn fish in silence. The small sounds she made as she worked weren't enough to keep me awake . . . but her startled cry and the sudden distinct splash of a leaping fish brought me bolt upright.

"Dogfish my ass," Fiora said. "That's a salmon!"

"Reel, woman, and put the clicker on! How can you tell what's happening if the clicker is off?"

Though the voice was mine, the words and exasperated cadences were those of Rory Cairns teaching two fumble-fingered Californians the protocols of dealing with the crown prince of the Pacific Ocean. Fiora laughed and blinked away tears and put the clicker on, letting the reel sing to us of muscular salmon and mysteries as deep as the sea.

Every new salmon is an adventure. This one was perfectly proportioned, clean and bright as a silver dollar skipping across the green surface of the water.

"Coho," I shouted, and then I laughed.

Coho are like hooking up with eight pounds of joy. They leap, they dance, they walk on water, they race across the surface, and all the while the reel sings.

Fiora fought the fish and barked contradictory orders to me and laughed, all in one glorious, exuberant tangle. Finally we managed to get the net and the salmon in the same place at the same time. I hoisted the flashing silver fish aboard. Full of life, the vivid coho lay tangled in the green netting on the bottom of the boat. I slid my index finger in under his gill cover and anchored him.

The coho's skin was as cold as the deep ocean. The teeth along his lower lip were sharp as a woodworker's rasp. He nicked me once, drawing a few bright drops of blood from my finger.

I picked up the cosh but hesitated. The coho was such a beautiful spark of life, a glittering bit spun off the driving wheel of the universe.

"Don't you dare throw him back," Fiora said. "He's Rory's gift to me."

I looked up. She smiled despite the tears that magnified her eyes.

"You may have eaten fresh salmon for two weeks, but I just got here," she said. "Rory promised me a salmon. This is it."

I killed the coho the way Rory had taught me, with a single swift blow just behind the eyes. Fiora watched without flinching. Raised by poor ranchers in Montana, she has always known how meat gets to the table.

After I laid the coho with the other fish, Fiora ran her fingertip down the salmon's small silver scales. Next to the coarse scales of the mottled red rockfish and his canary cousin, the salmon seemed hewn from a block of fresh-cast aluminum, then polished with a buffing wheel. The sunlight cast a mother-of-pearl rainbow on his hard gill cover.

"Dinner tonight, poached the way Rory liked it," she said. "Then as salmon salad tomorrow, on crackers with fresh lemon juice squeezed over it."

She took in a long breath and let it out slowly. Once again her fingertips traced the length of the fish, silently admiring its power and perfection.

"You forget how strong life is," Fiora said, "and how fragile. Someday we'll be ashes on the sea and the salmon will eat us."

She looked at me with eyes that were a deeper green than the water beneath the keel of the boat.

"Rory's dead," she whispered.

eIGHT

I don't like being threatened.

In the midst of the second day of probate and cremation arrangements for Rory Cairns, I was even less likely to tolerate an anonymous phone call giving me instructions about how to protect my own "health and well-being."

"You want to say that again, slowly?"

The quality of my voice brought Fiora to full alert. She looked up from the kitchen table in Rory's house. Since Rory died, the table had been doubling as her work desk. The cottage didn't have a telephone, and she had needed to stay in touch with Nakamichi about the thousand details of the Pacific Rim deal while I attended to the more painful details of wrapping up Rory's estate. Between the two tasks, neither of us had gotten more than an hour's sleep the night before.

"It is very simple," the voice on the other end of the line said. "Mr. Cairns was warned that the sword carried a curse. He was offered a chance to relieve himself of the curse. He did not. He died. When Mr. Cairns bequeathed you the samurai sword, he bequeathed you death."

"Shit happens."

"It need not. Think about it, Mr. Fiddler. You have other, safer mementos of your friend."

"Drop off, asshole."

I hung up with emphasis and glared at the tangle of cords and switching box that Fiora had plugged into the telephone's wall jack. For someone who swore she wanted to disentangle herself from the high-pressure world of high finance, Fiora was acting remarkably like a vacationing executive, with a laptop computer, modem, fax, and all the other electronic leashes beloved of power brokers.

"Friend of yours?" Fiora asked.

"Just someone trying to come up with an offer I couldn't refuse."

"For what?"

"Rory's Japanese sword."

"Sell it," she said instantly, turning back to the paperwork. At the moment it consisted of an investment strategy for Marley's Wildlife Hostel and a pile of hospital bills that so far averaged out to one thousand dollars an hour for the nineteen hours Rory had been incarcerated. "If no one is stupid enough to buy the damn thing, give it away."

"I like the sword."

"I don't," she said, revulsion clear in her voice. "There's something *wrong* about it."

"Rory told me the sword was cursed."

"I believe him. Get rid of it."

"Not a chance. I'll live with a Scots witch, but I'm goddamned if I'll believe in Japanese curses."

Fiora ignored me.

I kept talking. "If the worst thing that sword did to Rory was let him live a healthy, productive life until age seventy-five and then strike him down before he knew what was happening—I'll take it."

"That's why Rory gave the bloody thing to you," she muttered.

Something nagged at me, something about the sword and Rory's death and the offer to buy it, but I couldn't figure out what. Every time I thought of Rory, I started thinking about things I hadn't said to him that I should have, things I hadn't thanked him for that I wished I had, things I . . . just things.

I went to Rory's desk and pulled out the file marked WILL, looking for something that might reveal the name of the man in Seattle who had tried to buy the sword from Rory.

The phone rang.

"I'll get it," Fiora called.

"If it's that vulture again—" I began, then stopped when I heard her first words. It was Nakamichi's secretary.

"Hello, Constance. Don't tell me those papers are finally ready!" Fiora paused. "Good. I have the fax hooked up. Go ahead and send."

I got to the kitchen just in time for the blinking light and shrill warning of an incoming fax. The electronic slave began regurgitating paper. I glanced at the words, sank beneath a dense barrage of legalese regarding Nakamichi and Pacific Rim, and struggled back to the surface again before I went down for the last time.

Fiora ripped the first sheet and began reading. The rest of the world ceased to exist for her, including me. As the sheets came in, she ripped and added them to the growing pile.

After the impossible English from Nakamichi, Inc., the various appraisals in the folder seemed simplistic: a straightforward description of the goods, followed by an estimate of worth. I rifled through quickly, looking for the paper dealing with Rory's sword.

There were two papers stapled together. The first was a letter that was two months old. It was handwritten on plain paper and addressed merely to *Mr. Cairns.* Whoever had written the letter was obviously born speaking a language other than English.

The blad now ready. Small pieces of rot before the tsuba I remove. Metal I burnish, now fierce bright. Blade is fine and worthy. Please care for better in future.

I show blade to friend. He like it much. You want sell? He want buy. His letter with mine. Call if you sell. If no, sword wait for you return.

The letter was signed in an uncertain hand by one Itaro Hinaga.

The second sheet had the formality of two cultures behind it. There was an ornate letterhead composed of beautifully executed Japanese ideographs across the top. Across the bottom were several elegantly printed lines in English that identified Mark Oshima as a member of the Asian-American Art Association and an associate of the International Association of Art Appraisers.

The letter itself was addressed not to Rory but to Itaro Hinaga.

I have examined the iron sword with red-lacquered wooden scabbard. I find it appears to be a reasonably good specimen of the sort that dates back to the New Sword Period or perhaps slightly before. The workmanship and tang markings are consistent with that analysis, although it must be remembered that a number of such blades were counterfeited in the late nineteenth century.

The blade is in considerably less than museum condition, as though it has not been properly cleaned and oiled for some time. Its provenance is also badly clouded, as is often the case with such blades recovered here in the United States.

Without a definitive metallurgical examination, it is impossible to date the sword properly. However, it is an interesting piece of the sort that is in some demand in Japan. Therefore I am able to say it is worth at least $5,000, and I am willing to offer that amount for it.

The letter was signed with a quick set of chicken scratches that were identified beneath as the signature of Mark Oshima. I wondered if it was Oshima or the gentleman from the old country who had decided to take advantage of a bogus curse and buy an old sword cheap.

In the kitchen, the fax kept vomiting paper and Fiora kept reading it and making notes on a yellow legal pad. Long after I fell asleep, she kept working. I was tempted to drag her to bed, but I didn't; everyone grieves in his or her own way. While Fiora was crunching numbers, she wasn't making a long list of might-have-beens and if-onlys.

I envied her.

We were up hours before dawn to make the overland trek from Malahat in Rory's truck. It could have been the Cobra—I had a rain bonnet for it—but I was cultivating a different look from the one you get with a Concourse-quality vintage automobile. Whoever had made that call needed to be taught a lesson about the difference between appearance and reality. Rory might have appeared to be an unlettered fisherman, but he wasn't. Nor was his death the opportunity for a little sharp dealing for a sword he had chosen not to sell.

Sometime during the night, I had decided to approach Oshima first. His address was on his letterhead; the sword polisher's wasn't.

Nobody had prowled the grounds in the time since Rory's death. Nobody followed us from Rory's house. Fiora was tense, but she wasn't dreaming about danger. I wasn't either—because I hadn't slept well enough to dream.

Neither Fiora nor I had much to say as we crossed the bridge onto Bainbridge Island near Seabold and drove through the chilly fog to Winslow. She was reviewing her notes. I was looking forward to venting a little anger. The thought of Rory dying because some thug couldn't tell the difference between us in the dark still burned at me like battery acid.

The 6:45 A.M. Winslow ferry was loaded with stockbrokers, bank executives, and other young semiurban professionals headed for an early day in downtown Seattle. Several of the more energetic types jogged laps around the deck for forty minutes, all the way to Elliott Bay, getting their endorphins on line for a day in the belly of the beast.

Fiora hadn't done any laps, but she fit right in with the executive set. She was already dressed for her first meeting with Ron Nakamichi: dark wool suit, pale silk blouse, and black pumps. She sat in the sun lounge, drinking coffee, studying faxes of the proposed sales agreement, and making more notes on a legal pad.

The ease with which she had slipped back into money shuffling irritated me. I knew my reaction wasn't useful, so I went outside and stood on the signal deck. I was alone except for the sea gulls who kept me company in the gray light of morning. An outbound Norwegian freighter and five pleasure boats rocked in the gentle swells off Duwamish Head.

The small craft were trolling in tight circles around a kelp bed, trying to snag the odd king salmon from the shelter of the weeds. Not far beyond, the hammerhead cranes and container derricks of the freight terminal at Elliott Bay rose up out of the early mists. I looked back at the little boats crammed with rods and people and wondered who would bother to meat-fish in waters so close to a thousand outfalls and open sewers.

Then I sensed someone behind me: Fiora. She walked toward me, watching me with shadowed gray-green eyes. She had pulled her Gore-Tex jacket over the chalk stripes and silk. The financial papers were safely tucked away in a soft-sided Eddie Bauer nylon bag.

"You look like those schizo New York brokers who wear business suits and running shoes," I said.

There was more acid in my voice than I liked. Fiora looked at my blue jeans, work boots, and denim shirt.

"And you look like you're fresh in from East Bumblefart with a load of cucumbers," she said. "Quite a pair we make."

I grunted.

"What's wrong?" Fiora asked.

"I was going to ask you the same question. You've been in full money-shuffling mode since that fax started spitting up paper. Is the deal with Nakamichi going south on you?"

She made a sour face, then shrugged. "Not really. The contracts are just incomplete. It's not the quality of legal work I'd expect from Nakamichi's organization."

"Has Ron decided he doesn't want you corrupting the minds of young Japanese women?"

"No, the endowments are all spelled out. So is the no-competition clause. You'll be pleased to know I am specifically forbidden to engage in any business that would compete with Nakamichi for the next five years."

I shouldn't have been pleased, but I was. It showed. Fiora smiled slightly. It lasted only a moment.

"So what's bugging you about the contract?" I asked.

"There's nothing about compensation for the people I'm leaving in place. In fact, there are five different areas that should have been spelled out and weren't. That means a lot of paperwork to take care of today."

"You want me to tag along? Maybe look intimidating? I can run Oshima to ground later."

"Uh-uh," she said. "You'd scare Ron to death. Besides, it's no big deal. Just a lot more paperwork. Ron apologized and offered us one of the Nakamichi condominiums for the night, or as many nights as we want."

"Seattle is a nice city, but I want to catch salmon that haven't been sucking sewer water."

Fiora pulled my arm close, so I could feel her all along it. "I'll bet Ron's condo has silk sheets."

"Well . . ." Never take the first offer.

"I'll let you sleep on the dry side."

"Sold."

She smiled, then her expression changed, back to tight intensity. It shouldn't have irritated me, but it did. "Now let me see the appraisal you've been gnawing on like Kwame with a new bone."

"You've got more important things to think about."

She held out her hand.

After a moment I reached into my jacket pocket and handed the two letters over. Fiora read both of them quickly but not lightly. Her expression told me she was giving the papers the same full-power concentration she had given her pending deal with Nakamichi. When she was finished, she looked at me oddly.

"No wonder you're so touchy," she said. "That's a very slippery piece of paper."

"I'm just a country boy from Malahat, Washington, ma'am," I drawled. "It looks real impressive to me."

"Oh, Jesus. Spare me the shit-kicking act."

"I'll save it for Oshima if you'll tell me what's wrong with the letter."

Fiora shrugged. "Just what you think. An appraisal has to describe a particular item with great precision and then estimate its value within certain limits. This does neither."

"What about the five thousand bucks?"

"Read it again."

"I've read it several times. It's as ambiguous as hell. A lot of swords come in red lacquer cases and have bits of corrosion on the blade. But five thousand isn't bad for something Rory lifted off the body of a prison-camp commandant on V-J Day."

"Prison camp?"

"He spent five years in one during World War Two."

Fiora's eyes widened. "I see. Well, in any case, the appraisal isn't precise. All it says is that the sword is worth at least five thousand dollars. So is the *Mona Lisa*."

"You have a nasty mind, woman."

"Thank you. It's one of the other reasons we get along so well."

"You think this guy Oshima is a phony?"

"More likely he's an opportunist who saw a chance to buy low and sell high," she said. "In any case, you can't trust him. Certified appraisers aren't supposed to bid on items they have been asked to evaluate. It puts them in a clear conflict of interest. But Oshima does exactly that."

Frowning, Fiora looked the letter over again.

"It's quite a balancing act. If you look closely, this isn't a certified appraisal. All these fancy words across the bottom of the page might make you think so, but in reality this letter is nothing more than an offer to buy."

"Would a cop be interested in talking to Oshima about fraud?"

"No. The letter is misleading, but I doubt if it's legally actionable."

I smiled. "Good. I prefer other kinds of action."

INE

I found an all-day parking lot just off Western Avenue, stashed everything of value out of sight under the seat, and locked the truck. Fiora and I walked north past the fireboat dock. Some of the old hump-backed wharf buildings looked pretty much like they did the day in 1897 when the steamer *Portland* docked with the first of the returning Klondike princes. Two tons of placer gold on that ship set off one of the most absurd, tragic, and magnificent gold rushes in history.

Money does the damnedest things to people. In 1897, it turned a hundred thousand otherwise rational human beings into a mob. Yet Fiora was waiting for a paycheck from Nakamichi that was probably equivalent to the modern value of the *Portland*'s cargo, and she was calm and solid as a rock. Her ability to make money was as natural as my ability to put ten rapid-fire rounds in the black at twenty meters.

The wind off the Pacific had an edge to it. The weather had gone from sunny late summer to the first day of autumn, damp and cold. People were seeking shelter in the public market at the end of Pike Place. The market is something special and has been for the last century, a kind of open-air shop for folks who love fresh food of all kinds. Fish, shellfish, meat, poultry, cheese. Fruit, vegetables, herbs, and spices. Bread, pasta, cakes, pies. Wine and beer, coffee and tea.

The seasons change, and so does the produce. Strawberries in early summer, then raspberries, blueberries, and gooseberries, in sequence. Early Elberta peaches, then gigantic Red Tops, then late white Indians. New varieties of apples every two weeks from late July until the end of October. Acorn squash and butternut squash and finally pumpkins. There are line-caught halibut and king salmon almost any time of year, pinks during their Fraser and Columbia River runs, chum salmon and rockfish when there's nothing else around.

The tastes and trends have changed subtly over the years. There's more pasta now, and less pastry. White French bread has given way to sourdough. The Scandinavian stalls used to sell potato lefsen, but somewhere along the way bagels and pitas and tortillas crept in too. Swedish needlework and hardanger lace has been replaced by Lao Hmong *pan dao* and Save-the-Whale T-shirts. But the making and marketing of simple high-quality fresh food remains the heart of the Pike Place Market. It may be the best urban spot in the country. It certainly is one of the best in the world.

Pike Place has its downside, of course. There's a

nasty undercurrent in the urban stream that flows around it. First Avenue has sidewalk gangs of Marielitos, Fidel Castro's savage gift to the American underworld. The Skid Road—what other cities call Skid Row—still exists within half a dozen blocks of the market, where shot-and-a-beer bars, peep shows, and "adult" bookstores mix uneasily with native American art, espresso bars, and trendy microbreweries.

I walked Fiora two blocks down and one block over, to the quiet streets where Nakamichi had two floors in a fifty-story building. Oshima's art gallery was nearby, so on the way back I did a fast recon.

Post Alley is a little footpath that runs for several blocks just uphill of the market. The gallery was on a corner, shoehorned into a little mall between a shop that sold French kitchen utensils and a boutique that specialized in custom-fitted sweats and aerobics costumes. The gallery was dark. The window held some routine Asian watercolors, some okay pieces of Japanese furniture, and some brightly painted masks that looked like K mart specials.

Nothing there to write home about. Oshima must be scrambling to meet the upscale rent payment. That didn't surprise me. Anyone who sends out "appraisals" like the one on Rory's sword was a hustler barely out of the gutter.

I bought a cup of Starbuck's best and a five-day-old copy of the Sunday *New York Times* and looked for a place to wait comfortably for the gallery to open. One of Seattle's homeless had appropriated the closest bench. I found another spot fifty feet away with an unscreened view of Post Alley and settled in.

Panhandlers hit on me three times in the next hour, but I came out ahead; five passersby dropped pocket change into my Styrofoam coffee cup after I'd emptied it. I had the "look" down pat.

The sun broke through a bit before nine. Gulls pumped along just overhead on glistening white wings. The sounds of their cries bounced off the fronts of the high-priced condos and mid-rise office buildings, giving the city a lonely feel.

At a few minutes past ten, a tiny Eurasian girl stalked past my bench with fit, hard-bodied confidence. Her loose, straight hair hung like a shiny curtain to her waist. She wore tight jeans and an oversized University of Hawaii sweatshirt pulled down over her hips. The leather portfolio under her arm could have contained anything from contracts worth thousands to a bologna sandwich. Artist, maybe; model, more likely. She had the kind of face a camera could love, and her eyes had been surgically westernized.

She bought coffee and a slice of carrot cake at Starbuck's, then walked the short block uphill to the mouth of Post Alley. With the ease that comes of long practice, she set her leather purse on the sidewalk by the front door of the gallery, balanced the cake on top of the coffee cup, fished a ring of keys out of her purse with one hand, unlocked the door, then scooped up her purse with her free hand and hurried inside like a person counting off seconds in her head.

So I counted too.

Fifteen seconds later she reappeared and turned

the CLOSED sign to OPEN. Her movements were relaxed again, casual.

Oshima must be doing better than the stuff in the window suggested. The girl's tightly choreographed entrance betrayed an alarm system with a ten-second delay. Rattle the door, and you've got ten seconds to get inside and push the right buttons. If you don't, the system screams like a banshee.

I waited five minutes before I got up and prowled Post Alley, looking nonchalant. The girl was seated at a table toward the back of the gallery, talking on a telephone. She didn't even look up when I walked by.

In the kitchenware store I found a good oyster knife and a prawn peeler. There was a Calphalon fish poacher big enough to handle a twenty-pound king. It was a work of art in its own right, certainly better balanced and made than anything in Oshima's gallery. If Fiora's deal ever closed, I was going to need a little gift for her. The poacher went on the short list.

A few doors away, I found a florist. I bought a mixture of iris and yellow roses as long as the sword. The counter girl wrapped and boxed them. While she was writing up the sale, a young Asian man walked past and turned in next door at the gallery. He was wearing a dark-green soft-shouldered double-breasted suit, fashionably rumpled white shirt, and string-thin tie. His longish dark hair was slicked straight back. The ultimate Post-Modernist, an Asian-American in an Italian suit. Very dap, very sharp.

"Was that Mark Oshima?" I asked.

"His name is Mark," she said. "I don't know his last name."

"Can you put these in a second box? I don't want anything to soak through."

"Sure."

When she was finished, I hiked back to the parking lot, retrieved the sword, and put it in the extra box. Ten minutes later I was back in Post Alley. Just before I pushed into the gallery, I shrugged a little farther into my windbreaker, trying to look like a plumber in a bank lobby full of suits.

It wasn't hard to play the bumpkin for the gallery girl. She had shucked out of her loose sweatshirt to reveal a figure that gave me a lot to be slack-jawed about: a tiny waist, heart-shaped hips, and breasts built—and aimed—like SLAM missiles. She reminded me of Madonna without the steel C-cups.

I couldn't tell whether she was bright enough to use her body to distract men in a business setting or if she simply liked being looked at. But since she had gone to a lot of trouble to get everything in shape and put it on display, I gave her body a thorough inspection.

She liked it.

"Can I help you?" she asked with a smooth, cold smile.

"Uh, yeah, maybe. Somebody told me you buy Japanese stuff."

She glanced at the long narrow box under my arm. I passed on the unsubtle invitation to show it to her.

"Well, sometimes," she said. "What do you have?"

"Some kinda sword from World War Two."

The box stayed under my arm.

She wrinkled her nose in distaste. "We're an art gallery. We don't buy war souvenirs."

Her mouth was heart-shaped too, lips so full they might have been bee-stung or collagened.

"You might try a war surplus store," she offered. "Or maybe the Central Gun Exchange down on First Avenue."

I frowned to show that thinking was an effort. Then I shook my head. "Guy I got it off of said it was couple hundred years old."

That got her. She narrowed her eyes, then finally smiled a little, as if talking to a child. I decided she liked being looked at *and* used her looks as a weapon.

"Could I see the sword?" she asked.

I looked her up and down again. "You the buyer?"

Her dark eyes went as cold as metal buttons. "Just a moment. I'll get the owner."

She moved like an angry dancer. The beaded curtain clicked as she slid through it, leaving me to wait alone.

I gave the gallery a more thorough appraisal than I had given the clerk. The place was . . . odd. It was as though someone had set it up to discourage new business. There was junk in the window, but the pieces toward the back were quality. Most striking were a pair of red- and yellow-lacquered temple dogs as big as Kwame, and a dark-blue silk kimono with a fierce red, yellow, and green dragon on the back. For all their stylized execution, the dogs and the dragon seemed alive. So did the red-crested gray cranes in the triptych painting that nearly filled one wall.

There was also an artfully lighted vertical display case filled with ivory, wood, and brass netsuke. An ivory dwarf thrust his oversized penis through the folds of his kimono; the price tag face up beside him suggested somebody thought the pose was quite clever. Another case held a display of fili-greed bronze disks with a broad slit in the center. Each one was a piece of art. It took me a moment to realize they were sword guards like the one on the sword in the box.

When Mark Oshima brushed through the beaded curtain, I spotted the control panel for the alarm system. It was on the wall just inside the back room.

"What is it?" Oshima demanded, impatient at the interruption.

He was handsome in a sexless way: well formed regular features, clear skin, and soft eyes. He still wore his double-breasted coat, as though he was the kind of man who could sit at a desk all day without wrinkling.

His green suede shoes almost broke me up. I looked around while I got my smile under control.

"I heard you bought old Japanese stuff here," I said after a moment. "Maybe I was wrong. I don't see any swords or anything."

"We do buy a few very fine pieces for export to Japan," Oshima said. "Let me see what you have."

I set the box on the long desk but did not open it. "You pay cash?"

He sighed in exasperation. "Only if I buy, and I don't buy without looking."

"Oh. Yeah."

I slipped the top off the box and let him see the sword bag.

If Oshima recognized it, he didn't show it.

To tease him, I fumbled with the tasseled cords. Finally I undid the careful knot, unfolded the top of the bag, and took it off the scarlet-and-gold scabbard with one motion.

Facial expressions are easy to control, but it's impossible to dampen the autonomic nervous system that controls the workings of the eye. Surprise shows itself in pupil dilation and involuntary blinks.

Oshima's eyes told me he was surprised, very interested, or both.

I laid the bag on the desk and put the sword on top of it with the curved edge toward him.

"Go ahead," I suggested. "You're the expert."

He didn't give me another look at his eyes, but he handled the sword without hesitation. He took the scabbard in his left hand and drew enough steel to see the cloud pattern of the temper line. Then he slid the blade home and laid it back down.

"Where did you get this?" he asked bluntly.

"From a guy."

"Who? When?"

"Hey, man, it's not stolen."

"I didn't suggest that it was," he said blandly.

Like hell he hadn't.

"I just need to know where you got it," Oshima added.

"I inherited it," I said.

"From a dead man?"

Oshima was looking at my eyes now as intently as I had watched his. I couldn't tell whether he was wary by nature or merely smelled a trap.

"That's usually how you inherit things," I said. "From a dead man."

"How did he die? Was it an accident?"

There was a quality to Oshima's voice and to the questions themselves that made the primitive, reptilian part of my brain come to full alert. There was danger here. I didn't know how, I didn't know why; I only knew it was there.

Then my unconscious put it together and I called myself nine kinds of fool.

"Who cares?" I said, looking at the sword. "He died. The sword's mine. You interested or not?"

"Are the police interested?"

"Forget it, man. I'll take the sword down to the Central Gun Exchange. I hear they buy war stuff."

Oddly, Oshima relaxed, as though he was happier buying items from thieves or murderers than he was from legitimate owners. It didn't make the nasty, suspicious, reptilian part of my brain one bit happier.

"This isn't 'war stuff,'" Oshima said disdainfully. "I can show you a real Japanese officer's sword from World War Two. It looks nothing like this."

I shrugged. "My friend told me he swiped it from a dead Jap."

"How much do you want for it?"

I scratched my chin and thought for a moment, then shook my head. "Make me an offer."

Oshima almost took the bait. But instead, he

picked up the scabbard, edge and curve upward, and pulled the sword all the way out. He laid the scabbard aside and studied the blade, handling it with a kind of veiled reverence.

"Tara," he said without looking up, "get the *uchiko* box from my desk."

Tara came back through the beaded curtain with a plain wooden box the size of a cigar box. She set it on the desk and lifted the lid. One section of the box contained a small gourd-shaped device. The bulb was coated with a white powder. Another section of the box contained a stoppered bottle full of oil, sheets of an odd coarse paper, and several small tools.

Oshima took a sheet of the paper, wiped the oiled blade from one end to the other, and tilted the blade until the light from the window danced along the clouded temper mark. Then he rested the tip of the blade on the bag and used one of the tools to punch the two handmade studs out of the handle. With a touch of ceremony, he tapped the hilt against the back of his free hand before he took the back of the blade in another sheet of clean paper and lifted it out of its hilt.

The tang of the blade was unfinished. The rough, dull metal contrasted sharply with the tempered, polished blade. I glimpsed a set of ideographs on the tang, perhaps the signature of its maker. Oshima looked too, for only a moment. Then his eye's met Tara's and an unspoken message passed between them. She melted through the beaded curtain into the back room.

"Come," Oshima said. "Let's talk about this

sword over some tea. Or perhaps something stronger?''

"You got a beer?''

"Certainly. I'll be right back.''

He stepped through the curtain of beads. There came the sounds of crockery and glass and, just beneath it, a soft conversation between Oshima and his girl. A moment later, Oshima returned carrying a tray with a teapot, several small cups, a bottle of Kirin, and a tall clean pilsner glass. He offered the tray to me.

Normally I love watching beer seethe gently in a proper glass, but it would have been out of character for me at the moment. I took the bottle, saluted Oshima, and drank a long draft.

Oshima set the tray aside and returned to the sword, slipping the marked tang into the handle and replacing the hand-wrought pegs.

"It's a decent piece,'' he said, "and it's been cared for reasonably well. So many we see have lain in some attic somewhere for almost fifty years now. They're covered with rust and worth almost nothing.''

"You mean there are lots of these swords around?''

"Quite a few, yes. They were very popular with Japanese officers and many of them were, shall we say, 'liberated' by GIs at the end of the war. Of course, most of them were mass-produced junk, stamped out of inferior metal and badly finished.''

I looked at the sword. "Don't look like junk to me.''

"No, it doesn't. It's different.''

Oshima still held the blade. He tipped it, dropping the point and enjoying the play of light along the edge.

"How different?" I asked. "Did those marks under the handle make it worth more money?"

He looked at me sharply, as though surprised I had noticed the marks.

"They can be important," he said, shrugging, "if there is a suggestion of fraud."

I took another drink of beer. It was warmish and sweet.

"There are many counterfeit blades circulating in Japan," Oshima continued. "Occasionally someone tries to slip one by us here, knowing we pay good money for swords."

He waited for my reaction to the implication that I was conning him.

I smiled, belched fragrantly, and asked, "What do you do with them? Sell them in Japan?"

"That's where the market is." Oshima lifted the sword with two hands and admired its full length. "Americans don't understand the mystique of the blade. Cold steel makes most of us uncomfortable. But in Japan, the sword is an important cultural symbol, as well as a weapon."

He let the tip of the sword drop a few inches, toward my eye, as though testing whether I would flinch. I ignored him and took another swig of beer.

"Like a gun in America, huh? The Great Equalizer." I put down the bottle and stared at Oshima through the triangular point of the sword.

"No. Not like a gun in America. Just the reverse," he said. "The Japanese don't think much of equality. They're hierarchical. They admire structure. That's why firearms were banned by royal decree for three hundred years. Guns were too easy to use. A stupid peasant with a pistol became the equal of a skilled and disciplined samurai who had devoted his entire life to the way of the sword.''

"No wonder Japan lost the war," I said. "Hot lead tops cold steel every time."

"Another beer?" Oshima asked, smiling despite the too-rapid pulse visible in his neck.

I shook my head. "What about it? You interested in buying this cultural symbol or not?"

He hesitated, thinking it over. "There is a client in Japan who might be interested," he said finally. "I'd be taking a chance, buying this without speaking with him first, but I could offer you five hundred, right now."

I finished the beer and set the bottle down with a bang. "No sale, pal. It's worth more than that."

He shrugged elegantly. "One thousand. That's my final offer."

I reached over and took the sword from Oshima. I held it in two hands, right hand forward, left hand at the end of the hilt, as Oshima had done. The position looked awkward but it did something extraordinary to the sword's balance. The sword came alive in my hands. I pointed it at him, as he had done to me.

"I'll try some other places," I said.

"You won't get a better offer."

"Maybe. Maybe not. Somebody in Seattle offered my friend five grand for it."

The figure touched a nerve in Oshima. He

looked past me as though waiting for someone to appear at the door to the gallery.

No one was there.

"Come in the back room," he said. "We'll talk."

tEN

I have many moral failings, but the biggest may be my unabashed willingness to lie to liars. So I followed Oshima into the back room. To keep the bait in front of him I laid the sword on his glass and chrome desk. He steepled his fingers, hid his mouth behind them, and watched me. His eyes were blank, neutral. I had figured him to be somewhere in his late twenties, but the more I studied him, the older he got. He only dressed like a kid.

"You keep five thousand in cash here?" I asked.

"I haven't offered you five thousand," Oshima countered. "I wouldn't do so without a careful metallurgical analysis, as well as a thorough historical investigation. But if the sword is what I think it is, five thousand is a good price for you."

"What do you think the sword is?"

"A fake."

"A fake, huh? Then why pay five grand?"

"Because I can sell it for eight thousand, perhaps even ten."

I picked up the sword again and pointed it in his general direction. "Why should I give you that extra five grand for—what, maybe an hour's work?"

Oshima took the thin porcelain cup from the desk in front of him and tasted the tea with care.

"You don't speak Japanese; I do," he said, sipping and enjoying the tea in the noisy Japanese style. "You don't understand the culture; I do. You don't have any contacts in Japan; I do. I make my living by acquiring World War Two souvenirs in America and reselling them in Tokyo. I've done so for twenty years. You're paying for my expertise, not my time."

I shrugged. "I still don't see five grand in it for you."

"There are a few other American dealers who specialize in swords," Oshima said indifferently. "I can give you their names. They'll offer you no more than a few hundred dollars. They're the dealers who rush through the countryside, advertising in small-town newspapers, buying every piece of *showa* junk they can lay their hands on, and then dumping it at wholesale prices in Japan."

Oshima looked over my shoulder toward the gallery door. I turned in time to see the dancer pass some sort of signal to her boss.

"I do things quite differently," he said as though nothing had happened. "I buy only quality material, and I make it my business to know the other end of the market, the collectors. I understand their tastes as well as the strengths and weaknesses of their collections."

"Five grand for you is still too much."

"Do you think you can do better somewhere else?"

"Better than you'll do without this sword," I shot back.

Oshima sighed. "The sword is a fake, a late nineteenth-century copy of the work of a fairly famous fourteenth-century sword maker named Muramasa. I happen to know a minor industrialist in Osaka who enjoys just such copies. He has counterfeits of swords by the most famous smiths in Japanese history, but he's lacking a Muramasa."

Either Oshima was a world-class liar or Rory's sword was a marvelously executed fraud. I really didn't care which. What was bothering me was the feeling that a lot more than a lousy hundred-percent profit was riding on this for Oshima.

"Mister, I don't care if you call half the folks in Osaka by their first names. Five grand is still too much for you."

Oshima steepled his fingers again and stared at me over them. "You have a sword. It's value is real but limited. I have a market for that sword. I'm willing to consider taking less of a commission. . . ."

He lowered his hands and placed them palm down on the glass desk top.

"How much less?" I asked.

"It depends. You'll have to leave the sword with me so that I can conduct some tests."

"What's to test? It's a fake, right?"

Oshima was quick, I'll give him that. He didn't even blink before he launched into another lecture.

"The sword has to be the right kind of fake to support my estimate of its value. My collector is only interested in older fakes. If this one turns out to be recent, say ten or twenty years old, it will be worth a good deal less. I need to core a metal sample from your sword in order to be certain of its age."

"It's almost fifty years old," I said. "My friend got it off a dead prison guard in World War Two."

"That's what you were told. Unfortunately, in my business, words mean less than laboratory tests."

"What'd you say this guy's name was, the one you think might want the sword?"

Oshima showed me his teeth in the kind of smile that gives rise to ethnic stereotyping. "I didn't say. For obvious reasons."

I tried to look like they weren't obvious to me. "Uh, how long would all this take?"

"A few days, perhaps a week. I use a research laboratory in Los Angeles."

I didn't bother to ask for the lab's name, for obvious reasons.

"I don't like all this waiting around," I said. "How about you give me seven grand right now?"

Oshima's reaction surprised me. If he had been as crooked as I suspected, he would have grabbed the deal in a New York minute. But he didn't. He thought about it a while, then shook his head.

"I can't operate on that small a margin. Six thousand is as high as I can go. But I could have that for you in half an hour. In cash."

I picked up the sword, drew an inch of steel

from the scabbard, then thrust it home again. "I'll think about seven."

"Leave the sword with me. If the tests come back as I think they will, you have nothing to lose."

"No."

"Why?"

"For obvious reasons," I said.

I picked up the silk bag and started to stuff the sword into it. My actions seemed somehow to pain Oshima. He got up and held out his hand.

"May I?" he asked.

When I handed him the sword and bag, he turned the edge of the blade upward, carefully slid the sword and scabbard into the bag, then laid the bag on the desk and whipped the tasseled cords around the folded end of the bag. In ten seconds, he had secured the sword with an intricate, elaborate, mouse-eared knot that left the two weighted tassels perfectly aligned. He handed the sword to me.

"The knot is called *cho mushi*," he said. "It's the way such things are supposed to be done."

I took the sword and put it in the box.

Oshima glanced at his watch. It was as thin as a semiconductor.

"How can I contact you?" he asked. "My collector will be asleep now. I can't speak with him until evening."

The smile I gave him was all teeth. "No problem, pal. I have your number."

Oshima's smile told me he had mine, too.

I suspected we were both right.

When I got outside, the bird dog Oshima had

sicced on me was lounging around an empty *Seattle Times* news box at the stub end of Post Alley. He was a thin Caucasian in his middle twenties with wild Brillo-pad hair. His faded jeans and flannel shirt looked right at home in the mix of First Avenue street hustlers and tourists. He watched Oshima's window until I came out the front door of the gallery. Oshima must have given him some kind of high sign, because the bird dog looked in my direction and nodded.

Just to be certain, I stalled for a minute, looking up and down the street as though I hadn't figured out where to go next. The bird dog made a production out of lighting a cigarette as he waited for me to decide where to go. Not once did he look away from me.

This was not a world-class surveillance expert. He'd have eaten a pocket full of poisoned rice balls himself. But then again. . . .

I headed for a pay phone.

Benny Speidel, the New Zealander who was once a spy known as the Ice Cream King of Saigon, answered his phone on the twenty-third ring. Not a record for him, but not bad.

"G'day, Fiddler," Benny said, knowing I was the only one in the world who would outwait him on the phone.

"Rory's dead," I said.

"Ballocks. I'm sorry for you, mate. What happened?"

"At first I thought someone mistook him for me and pushed him down the stairs. Now I'm not so sure."

"What do you need to be sure?"

I gave him Oshima's name, gallery address, and general description and listened to the hollow plastic *clack* of computer keys.

Benny is what some folks call "handicapped," although never to his face. Thanks to a stray round of friendly fire in Vietnam, his spinal cord consists of two halves that do not communicate. Actually, Benny's wheelchair may be a blessing. He's so damned quick that somebody would probably have shot him by now out of sheer frustration. He can cover more ground from in front of a computer keyboard than most people can in the Concorde. I leave the electronics in my life entirely to Benny, just as I leave the money shuffling to Fiora.

I stood on the street, receiver in hand, listening to Benny hum and whistle and grunt and argue with himself over the proper pathways to enlightenment. The tourists and office workers on early lunch crowded into the market area, taking it back for a few hours from the street people. Nearby a blind fiddler played "Mister Bojangles" in front of an EARTH: LOVE IT OR LEAVE IT banner. Japanese tourists went by like a covey of quail, calling to one another in rising tones. The smell of freshly baked bread competed with that of urine from the alley.

"Incoming," Benny said after a time. "You want it verbal, or are you near a fax?"

"Verbal."

"Thirty-nine, U.S. citizen, no wants, no warrants, no convictions, no record at all. Recent IRS challenge of some of his appraisals was a draw; they gave and he gave. Nothing unusual except his background. His father was born in Japan. The old man was a captain in the Japanese navy and a spy, assigned to infiltrate the U.S. before World War Two. Came to Bainbridge Island. Married. Counted departing destroyers and Boeing bombers until the family was interned in Manzanar."

"A spy? A real honest-to-god spy?"

"That's what it says in my file," Benny replied offhandedly.

"Did Junior follow in his father's footsteps?" I asked.

"If he did, no one's caught him at it," Benny said. "He was raised in the old style, learned the difference between a *katana* and a *tanto* before he learned about curve balls and sliders. Speaks Japanese. Went to school there for a year. Studied the sword discipline of *iai-do* but was too westernized to dedicate himself to anything but chasing money."

"That's our guy, all right. Where the hell do you get this information? Or should I ask?"

"Proprietary data bases, mate," he said. "I checked DMV in Sacramento, but the rest of it comes right out of a profile in the *Wall Street Journal*, the text of which I just got from Lexus-Nexus. It seems your little pal is a bit of an international celebrity. The *Journal* classifies him as one of the new Japanese-American entrepreneurs who are getting rich by acting as cultural mediators."

"They got one thing right," I said. "He's very much into edged weapons. He's trying to buy the one Rory left me."

"How much?" Benny asked.

"Seven thousand and still rising."

"Not bad. You selling?"

"No, but I'm considering giving a few inches of it to him."

"Has he earned it?"

"That's what I'm trying to find out."

Benny read me the entire text of the newspaper piece. It clarified Oshima's background but little else. For the past twenty years, he had made a good living in the WW II souvenir trade.

I listened and listened hard, but I didn't hear anything between the lines that suggested Oshima had a taste for pushing old men downstairs. On the other hand, he had sicced a bird dog on me. An inept one, granted, but it's the thought that counts.

"That's it," Benny said. "Want me to keep looking? There are a couple of data bases that specialize in arts and antiquities. Japanese steel probably gets mentioned."

"Go ahead, if it doesn't get in the way of anything important."

"No worries." Benny paused. "If you need more than information, I can be up there in five hours."

"I'll keep it in mind."

As usual, Benny disconnected without saying good-bye.

I punched in the number of Nakamichi Securities. They had high-quality help. One of them put me through to Fiora in less than ten seconds.

"Hi, how goes the battle?" I asked.

"Fine," she said.

"Is that fine as in frog's hair?" I said.

"Not really."

"Fine as in the abrasion index on a rat-tailed file?"

"Something like that," she said cheerily.

Her tone told me Ron Nakamichi was within earshot, probably with half a dozen of his minions, eager to fetch, carry, and eavesdrop.

"You need some help? Maybe I could rough somebody up?"

"I've already taken care of that," she said smoothly. "But I do appreciate the offer. Are we still on for lunch?"

We hadn't mentioned lunch.

"Sure," I said, "if you want." I glanced at my watch and then turned just enough to catch a glimpse of the bird dog. He was camped out fifty feet away in the market, pretending to be fascinated by a bin of iced sheepshead. Maybe he was.

"McCormick and Schmick," I said. "Have Ron's office get us a quiet booth in back. But give me an hour. I have to see a man about a dog."

"Are you having fun yet?"

I read between Fiora's lines; she reads between mine.

'I'm working on it," I said.

eLEVEN

After I hung up, I did my best imitation of a country boy in the big city for a good time. I poked along amid the buskers and sidewalk scammers at the entrance of the market. I dropped a buck on a blanket in front of the blind fiddler playing "Mister Bojangles" and hunted through a display of Guatemalan cotton shirts. The embroidery was beautiful, in a sinister way, but their idea of "extra large" would have been snug on Fiora.

Moving along slowly, edging toward one of the many exits, I cadged a sample of somebody's alder-smoked salmon and another sample from a Whidbey Island farmer who had a table loaded with baskets of late blueberries. The bird dog lay back in the thin shade under an awning across the street. When I turned into the market proper, he crossed over quickly and fell in behind.

There was a display of New Age handicrafts: rings made from sterling-silver spoon handles,

Athabascan beadwork earrings, and cholla cactus jewelry racks. The goods were okay but it was the mirror I needed. I used it to inspect the tail. He was pop-eyed, and he had a space between his big front teeth, kind of like a Norway rat. His rough woolly hair stuck out every which way, and he hadn't shaved in a few days. I wondered whether Tara had told him to steal the sword or just to find out where I took it.

The market crowd got heavy in front of the fish stalls. Gutted salmon the size of shoats lay on clean crushed ice next to pale squid and pink spotted prawns. Climax ocean predator and prey species alike, all arrayed for the pleasure of the most inventive predator of them all. I stopped to admire the display. There is a clean, inevitable symmetry to life and death. Not nice, not gentle, simply . . . clean.

I wondered if the bird dog would appreciate that symmetry when I brought it forcefully to his attention. But it was hard to administer that kind of education in public.

My first impulse was to head for the Underground. Seattle is really two cities. The earlier one was built on the tidal flats at the edge of the coastal hills. But the flats stank and there were a few other problems. For instance, the toilets flushed the wrong way at high tide. So when serendipity struck and the original downtown burned to the ground, the city fathers took the tops off the nearby hills and filled in the flats where the old buildings still stood. As a result, some of the biggest buildings in town have more floors below ground than above.

I've always thought the Underground was the world's most overrated basement, but it offered some dark alcoves where I could chat up the bird dog without worrying about interference from misguided urban samaritans.

A quick check told me Mr. Brillo was still with me, but he was looking overanxious. He probably lacked the nerve or brains to track me into the Underground. Ah, well. There's always Plan B. I headed for the doorway marked GENTS.

The market is a jigsaw puzzle of half floors and stairways. The rest rooms are on the half floors between the long arcades. The men's room smelled like it hadn't been cleaned for a week. Two young Anglos in Grateful Dead concert tour T-shirts and black Levi's lounged around the sinks, hustling blow jobs or waiting to score some dope.

"Seattle Vice," I said. "Fly or die."

They flew.

The rest room had old-fashioned casement windows with frosted glass. One window was propped open with a three-foot length of steel reinforcement rod. I removed the rod. The window slipped a few inches before it hung up.

The rod already had the start of a bend in it. I laid it across the grimy sink and threw a few more degrees of arc into the bend. Then I went into one of the filthy stalls and closed the door behind me.

The sword slid smoothly out of its cloth bag. The rebar rod was a little lighter but would do nicely as a substitute. Its rough surface snagged on the fine silk as I slid the bar into the bag. I did a fast imitation of Oshima's fancy ceremonial knot and put the bag back in the florist's box. Then I set the box on the stinking piss-stained floor and nudged it until it stuck under the partition into the adjacent stall.

The toilet was barely fit to use, much less to sit on. Holding the sword, I crouched as if sitting on an invisible chair. I hoped Mr. Brillo didn't get lost on the way to the head, because the position was uncomfortable as hell. Fiora tells me females everywhere use it rather than trust their fannies to public toilet seats.

A pair of New Balance 676s came into the rest room. I ducked down far enough to see that the pants cuffs above the shoes were khaki. The bird dog was wearing jeans. I waited while some tourist grumbled about the condition of the facilities, like maybe all the public johns in Idaho had toilets you could drink out of. He mouth-breathed while he used the urinal and then stalked out muttering something about animals.

A pair of scuffed, water-marked leather work shoes walked in. The blue jeans were right but I couldn't see anything else. The work shoes went over to the sink, hesitated a moment, then settled in. The guy ran some water, turned it off, and headed back toward the stalls.

Somebody who washes his hands *before* he goes to the bathroom? Not likely. The guy was just killing time to be sure we were alone.

I tensed my aching thighs and waited, thinking of all those delicate-looking women whose thighs must be like rebar after a lifetime of this crouching.

A work shoe nudged the end of the florist box.

"Sorry," he mumbled.

I doubted it.

There was a rustling noise. The box stirred a little, as though he was making certain I wasn't holding onto the other end.

The box jerked and vanished.

I did my part. "Hey, what the hell!" I yelled, throwing a lot of bass into it.

I counted five, like I was zipping my pants, then shot the sliding latch on the door and yelled again, just for effect. I should have saved my breath. He was long gone.

The bird dog must have been moving fast when he hit the cement steps. A heavyset tourist in a straw hat and a Space Needle T-shirt blocked the stairway as he tried to pick himself up. He had been pushed, he was outraged, and he was about the size and speed of a dying elephant. I had to yank him to his feet to get past.

When I reached the top I glimpsed the heel of one work shoe disappearing down a side aisle. As I ran, I stripped off my windbreaker and wrapped it around the sword to disguise its distinctive outline as much as possible.

The side aisle led to First Street. I stayed in the shadows of the entrance and looked back up First in the direction of Post Alley and Oshima's gallery. This guy was so unprofessional he'd probably run straight back to his master.

No sight of him. I stuck my head out and looked down First toward Pioneer Square. The unusual shape of the florist's box caught my eye. He had it under his arm and was crossing over to the uphill side of the street toward the new entrance to Shorey's Books a block away.

The level sidewalks were clotted with people

catching the southbound First Avenue buses. I stayed close to the store-fronts, letting the crowds screen me as I went down the street, matching the bird dog's pace. He cradled the box in his arms, shielding it from me with his body.

Then he started uphill. Those sidewalks weren't crowded. He would have stuck out clearly, even if he hadn't glanced back over his shoulder every ten or fifteen steps. My sidewalk cover began to thin out in the middle of the second block. I ducked into the doorway of a travel agency and kept an eye on him through the glass.

An articulated trolley bus pulled up at the stop in front of me. I waited until the bus started to move, then slipped out onto the sidewalk and jogged beside it for a block to the next stop, using it as a screen. As the bus slowed, I ducked back into another doorway.

Mr. Brillo was less than a block ahead. To kill time I admired the baguettes and croissants in the window of the upscale boulangerie. Two Marielitos argued in gutter Spanish over a cigarette. Gentrification is not always a smooth process.

The bird dog crossed back to my side of the street at Spring, right in front of the restaurant where I was to meet Fiora. He seemed to be relaxing now. He no longer watched his back trail like a hunted animal.

When he turned the corner and headed down Spring toward the waterfront, I jogged ahead and saw him turn onto Western Avenue, headed for Yesler, the old Skid Road. At one time, the area had teemed with hard men and high rollers. Every scrap of fur trapped in Alaska and the Northwest

Territories passed through an exchange on Western Avenue at Spring. Now it's ristorantes and antiques, continental furniture and twelve-dollar taco plates.

I slowed down. The bird dog would be easy to track here. He didn't belong in the sidewalk crowds of wool pinstripes, starched oxford cloth, and silk blouses the colors of an Impressionist's palette. Taking a chance, I jogged the alley between Spring and Madison and stood there in the alley mouth, waiting for him to show up on the street below me.

He was still out of sight after thirty seconds so I started to get nervous. I waited another fifteen seconds, then ducked down to Western.

The bird dog had vanished.

After the first instant of shock, I remembered Benny's advice: Everybody's got to be somewhere. I started eliminating the alleys and places where he *wasn't*. He wasn't in the alleys off Western south of Madison. He hadn't doubled back up toward First on Cherry. Jefferson was a block of blank walls with no place to hide.

When I got to Yesler and turned uphill, I saw a foot sticking out of a dumpster at the far end of an alley. The shoe on the foot looked familiar.

I took time to make sure nobody was watching, then ducked into the alley and approached the dumpster. I rapped the sole of the scuffed work shoe once, hard, with the butt of the sword. The foot twitched.

I tucked the sword underneath the dumpster, then hauled the bird dog out for a better look. When I stretched him out on the dirty ground, he was barely conscious. Blood welled up darkly from a long wound just in back of the corner of his left eye, as though he had been lashed across the side of the face. For a second I thought of Rory's depressed skull fracture.

He groaned heavily and struggled up to whatever twilight state his brain thought of as consciousness.

"Ma fuu. . . ." he groaned. "Aw, shee. . . ."

"What happened, man?" I asked.

"Ol' Jaa. . . ."

The noises he was making degenerated into wordless groans. I sat him upright against the dumpster. Slowly he slumped over, like a sack of mud. The wound on the side of his face had ragged edges and was so recent the blood hadn't begun to coagulate.

The dumpster was half full of trash but no florist's box.

The alley was L-shaped. The short leg stubbed off on First Avenue. I grabbed the sword, ran to the busy street, and looked both ways. No help in sight. The sidewalks were filling up with lunch crowds, but nobody carried a long florist's box.

The odds were dead even, so I turned right. I went a block at a run, watching the crowds in front of me. Nobody looked back furtively. Nobody sprinted for cover when they saw me coming on fast.

Just as I was beginning to curse my luck at choosing the wrong direction, I saw a medium-size thick-bodied man on the opposite side of the street. He wore a cloth cap, a black jacket, and gray trousers. He hurried along the sidewalk like someone with an important errand, but that wasn't what caught my eye. It was his odd, stiff gait.

I had to look twice to pick up a corner of the florist's box. He was carrying it lengthwise, tucked tightly along his side. I got a few paces ahead of him and looked again. This time he glanced in my direction. He looked not at me but through me. His face told me what the bird dog had been trying to say.

Mr. Brillo had been mugged by the nicest old Japanese gentleman you ever saw.

As I watched, the stoutly built old man joined up with one of the overrated Underground tours and disappeared down a long flight of stairs into the netherworld.

To hell with subtle surveillance. I hit my full stride in three bounds. A northbound First Avenue bus tried to tag me, but I got to the stairway ten or twelve seconds behind the old man.

A tour group blocked the dimly lit passageway. Their guide was babbling with programmed enthusiasm about the granite blocks in the foundation of the Victorian business quarter. I muscled through without apology.

The old man was a shadow, just turning a corner a hundred feet ahead. The farther in I got, the more the air smelled like a tidal flat that had fermented in darkness for a century of nights. The discarded florist's box lay in the dark shadows at the entrance to the side gallery. I slowed to a more cautious pace. When I stepped into the passage, the far end was visible in the dim, yellowish glow of an old light bulb. There was nothing but a wall.

The old thief was nowhere in sight, but it didn't matter. He had walked into a dead end.

"Let's talk," I suggested.

No response.

Behind me the sounds of the tour group faded away as they moved in the opposite direction, leaving us alone. I wasn't particularly worried. I had a sword, at least three decades, and about a hundred pounds on the old man. An unequal contest, unless he had a gun.

When I walked a few steps down the dead end, a shadow moved across the reflective glass in what had once been a harness maker's display window. Adrenaline spurted in the instant before I recognized the shadow as a reflection of myself. I was jumpy. Old man or not, he had at least one weapon, the piece of bent rebar that had been in the flower box. I've seen men killed with less.

"Drop the rebar and come out," I said quietly.

Silence, except for the steady *drip-drip-drap* of water in the distance behind me.

I unwrapped the sword from my jacket and drew the steel. It felt oddly alive in my hand. Maybe the Japanese were on to something after all. With the scabbard in my left hand and the drawn sword in my right, I advanced down the cul-de-sac, checking recessed doorways. As I moved, I kept my left hand free. It has a quicker, harder punch than my right. The doorways along the left-hand side were clearly visible, but there were deep shadows beside the timber braces on the right.

"I'm not a cop," I said matter-of-factly. "I don't care what you did to that skinny dude in the trash can. Just step out where we can see each other while we talk.''

He must have been beside me, just to my right, but I never really saw him. I sensed a quick, silent movement, like my own shadow against glass except no glass was there. A faint hiss was followed by a sudden shock of pain in my right wrist.

It was like being struck by a hammer. My wrist went numb and the sword spun away. The steel blade rang like a bell on the pavement. Something jerked me toward the shadows. The old man materialized a few feet from my elbow.

This time I saw what happened. He made a circular motion with his right hand and suddenly my wrist was free. When he started to slip past me, I cuffed him behind the ear with the fist that held the scabbard. It wasn't much of a blow, but he wasn't a very big man.

He staggered and stumbled to one side long enough for me to grab the sword and step back. Suddenly he found his balance. He straightened up and faced me in a single fluid motion, holding his hands in front of himself in what could have been a gesture of supplication.

The light from behind me fell on his face. His eyes were hooded and he was clean-shaven. For a man old enough to have liver spots on his face and the backs of his hands, he had moved with uncanny speed.

''Nice trick,'' I said, meaning it. ''Don't try it again.''

His eyes narrowed and his head tilted, as though he didn't understand my words.

I showed him the tip of the sword, figuring the

weapon was self-explanatory. He stared at the sword, understood my threat . . . and then he looked right past the sword to me. He may have felt fear, but he showed none, not in his eyes, not in his face, not in his fragile, suspended hands.

The hair on my neck stirred. Whoever this man was, he wasn't some kid's kindly old grandfather.

"The sword. Mine," the old man said.

The words were correct but his accent was heavy and glottal, as though he seldom used English.

"Wrong," I said distinctly. "The sword is mine, but it's for sale. Make me a better offer than Oshima did."

"How much?"

"A life for Rory's death."

The old man didn't understand me.

"How much?" he asked again.

"The previous owner was murdered," I said flatly. "Whoever killed him was after the sword. I want the killer."

The kindly grandfather expression vanished. What might have been a smile passed over his face —but if that was a smile, I never wanted to see this guy laugh.

"Sword killed," he said carefully.

I mistook his words. "No," I said. "My friend died in a fall. I think he was pushed."

"Sword," he insisted. "Sword cursed. Very dangerous."

"Dangerous for you," I said, bringing up the sword tip so that he couldn't look past it, "but not for me. Tell me your name."

The odd expression passed over the man's face

again. It seemed a lot less like a smile this time. He opened his left hand slowly and moved it away from his body. It was a theatrical gesture, the kind a magician uses to distract you from his real purpose. I kept my eyes on his other hand.

Without warning the old man opened his right hand and flung an odd weapon at me, a ball and chain. I had seen its handiwork already, on the bird dog and perhaps on Rory. One end of the chain was weighted with a small lump of lead, like the knot on the end of a spring-loaded sap. The old man held the other end between his fingers. The weighted end flew at my left eye, trailing chain behind like the guide wires on a TOW missile.

The gambit would have worked, but for my reflexes and his fear of damaging the sword. I ducked to one side and flicked at the chain with the tip of the sword. The chain caught, changing the trajectory of the weight. It whistled to a stop a few inches from my head. Instantly I dropped the sword tip to avoid tangling it in the chain.

He was as fast as a lightning stroke. He retrieved the chain and flung it again before I could get out of range. The ball whacked across my knuckles. The sword guard caught the weight and turned it aside. He retrieved the weight, stepped inside the tip of the blade, and lashed out with his left hand, catching me with the chain just below the breastbone.

The blow staggered me. For a second I couldn't breathe. I tried to loop my left arm around the old man, but he slid under my grasp. Then he danced back a step and lashed out again with the doubled chain. It wrapped around my wrist, burning like hell. I grabbed the chain in my hand before he could retrieve it. He had both ends and I had the middle but he no longer had enough chain to use the weapon against me.

The world was gray and out of focus. I still couldn't breathe. I jerked the old man toward me. He came like a falling leaf, light and fluttering. He got off a round kick at the side of my knee that buckled my leg. I jerked again. All I got for my efforts was off balance.

The old man dropped the chain I held and walked away with the unhurried stride of a man who knew he would not be followed. He was right. I leaned against a cold limestone-block wall, trying to keep my balance on my good leg and at the same time drag a little air into my lungs. After a moment, the stars and gray clouds went away.

Half my size and twice my age, and he had man-handled me like a sack of oats. At least he didn't get the sword. And I had the chain. Hell, it was a clean victory, right? I'd even gotten the florist's box back.

Maybe I could fill it with pansies.

tWELVE

I reemerged from the netherworld into a symphony of sirens. Someone had called 911 about the guy face down in front of the dumpster; a paramedic unit and a blue-and-white squad car were parked in the alley. I joined the little crowd of busybodies just as the medics were loading him onto a gurney. He sort of rolled his eyes in my direction, but he looked like a club fighter who'd taken one too many combinations.

Seattle beat cops are throwbacks and proud of it. They still wear tin-star badges and carry hickory-stick batons. A lot of them have hair to their collars, like old-time timber beasts or tugboat deckhands. One of them between the crowd and the action was twirling the tips of his heavily waxed mustache.

"What happened?" I asked.

"Guy tripped and fell," he said. "No big deal."

"Tourist?"

The cop made a face. "Just some street guy. Name's Carlton. He hangs out around here."

Then the cop realized he was answering questions instead of asking them. That made him unhappy. He gave me a long dark stare. He missed the welts on my wrist because I had my sleeve pulled down, but he must have smelled the residue of battle on me.

"You know something about this?" he asked.

"Me? Naw. I'm from LA," I said, as though that explained everything.

He tried to figure out what LA had to do with anything, but by then I had wandered off, just one more tourist. The florist's box with the sword in it made me feel as conspicuous as a naked nun. I turned a couple of square blocks on Western, just out of paranoia, but I hadn't collected any shadows. I hiked uphill to First and cut around toward Spring.

My midsection was still tender and my wrist felt like somebody had stamped on it with a caulk boot, but I had quit limping by the time I got to the restaurant. Fiora wasn't there yet, so I soaked the wrist in a basin of cold water for a while in the rest room, doing deep knee bends on the bad knee to keep it from stiffening up.

Fiora was waiting by the reservations desk when I came out. Ron Nakamichi was with her. One of his bodyguards was standing two paces back. The other was waiting at the door of a private dining room. We ignored one another.

"What happened?" Fiora said instantly, looking at my leg.

"Nothing," I said.

She spotted the red welts beneath my sleeve. When she reached for my arm to examine it, I tried to pull back.

"Fiddler," she said.

It was a warning and we both knew it. I could submit to an exam or I could wrestle with her over it.

"Christ," I said under my breath.

Fiora was too busy looking at my wrist to answer.

Nakamichi stood to one side, looking faintly amused. He had just sat through a whole morning of the Royal Fiora. He seemed to enjoy watching somebody else get the treatment.

More gently than I had expected, Fiora pulled the sleeve back into place when she was finished.

"Busy morning?" she asked, smiling, but there was nothing cheerful about her eyes.

"I tripped. You know how I am about stairs."

She made the connection between stairs and Rory and dropped the subject.

The maître d' appeared with the speed of a hummingbird teleporting to a feeder. Fiora and I might have gotten a quiet booth in the back of the restaurant, but I'd have had to lay twenty bucks on him. Just by asking nicely, Nakamichi got a small private dining room with velvet curtains, real crystal, bone china, and our very own waiter. Iced platters of oysters, clams, mussels, shrimp, and sushi were already spread on the table. As we sat down, the wine steward popped the cork on a bottle of Cristal.

From an Underground ninja to jet-set luxury in five minutes. Culture shock must have made me dizzy. I misjudged the width of the flower box when I set it on the chair next to me. The box hit the floor and came apart, dumping the sword at Nakamichi's feet. The half-assed knot I'd tied came unraveled, and the brilliant lacquer scabbard gleamed like a gem. Nakamichi looked from the gold-and-scarlet scabbard to me with something close to shock.

"Sorry," I said, bending to retrieve the sword.

"Permit me," he said simultaneously.

Whether I was going to permit him or not, he was already reaching. I must have made some noise, because he looked at me again.

"Forgive me," he said, withdrawing immediately. "I didn't realize you were a collector of swords. My father, too, is quite—ah, careful who handles his samurai treasures."

The way Nakamichi said collector made it sound like another word for fanatic.

"I'm not a collector," I said. "I just inherited this sword from an old friend. I brought it to Seattle for an appraisal."

Nakamichi nodded and looked away, making it very clear that he wasn't going to intrude on whatever mystical relationship I might have with my inheritance.

In the face of all those good manners, I had no choice but to be a prince myself and let him see it. Besides, there was something about the sword that kind of grew on me. I liked looking at it, savoring its weight and fine balance, and following the unique signature of the cloud temper line with my fingertips.

The sword was becoming an old friend in my

hand by now. It came to me almost eagerly. As I drew the blade from its scabbard I sensed Fiora's distaste, an inner withdrawal that was both intangible and very real.

Rory had been right; my Scots witch hated the sword. Fiora was a creature of light. The blade was not.

"If your father collected swords," I said to Nakamichi, "maybe you can tell me something about this one. I spent the morning with an appraiser of old Japanese swords, but I'm not sure I trust his opinion."

He handled the weapon like most men handle a baby, hesitant to take hold of it. He almost knocked over twelve bucks' worth of Cristal with one end of the scabbard, then made a pass at a platter of Quinault oysters on the half shell with the tip. I rescued the oysters before they ended up face down on the floor.

"What did this appraiser tell you?" Nakamichi asked, ignoring the oysters.

"He said it was a nineteenth-century copy of an earlier blade."

Nakamichi tilted the sword. The temper line seemed to shift and coil like smoke in a draft. He grunted.

I tried one of the oysters I had rescued. It tasted salty and a little rank. Some Pacific Northwest shellfish are like Seattle's Underground, overrated.

"If it is a copy," Nakamichi said, looking up from the sword, "I think it is a very good one. Of course, I am no expert in such things."

"Would this one be worth ten thousand dollars?"

"Is that what you were offered?" Nakamichi asked, surprised.

"No." I tasted the Cristal. Cold and clean and golden, like winter sunlight and fresh bread. "He said he figured it might be worth ten, tops, in Japan."

Nakamichi thought it over while he looked at the blade some more. Then he shook his head.

"I must defer to his expertise," Nakamichi said, "yet few handmade blades are worth *less* than ten thousand American dollars in Japan."

"Even forgeries?" Fiora asked.

He nodded. "My countrymen hold swords in the same kind of reverence Europeans hold fine paintings or illuminated manuscripts.

"For men such as my father," Nakamichi continued, "the Sacred Mirror, the Comma-shaped Bead, and the Sword are the benchmarks of our culture, the three national art treasures of Japan. Of them, the sword is the most varied and the most collected."

With care, Nakamichi handed the sword back to me. When I took it, he added, "In Japan, swords regularly sell for millions of yen, hundreds of thousands of dollars. If you wish to sell, I will ask my father to recommend a more—er, generous dealer than the one you found. I suspect his bid is very low."

Fiora looked at the sword and then quickly at the food. She took a sourdough roll and broke it in half.

"Would you mind putting that thing away?" she asked finally, dropping half the roll on my butter plate. "It's a bit unwieldy as a butter knife."

I slid the blade into the scabbard, the scabbard into the silk, and knotted the long silk cord. It looked a lot better when Oshima had done it.

"It's not likely the sword is worth much," Fiora muttered. "Rory kept it as a souvenir, the same way he kept old photos."

"My father told me many times that there are more important Japanese swords in America than there are in Japan, thanks to the war and to your General MacArthur," Nakamichi said.

He picked up a pair of chopsticks and sampled the sushi—flakes of pearly blue raw halibut and greenling the color of apple jade, all wrapped in seaweed. He nodded approvingly and moved the platter to a place where Fiora and I could reach it easily.

"The occupation forces melted down hundreds of thousands of blades," Nakamichi said simply. "No exceptions were made for art treasures. Swords were weapons, to be confiscated and destroyed. It was a cultural tragedy for Japan. The remaining swords are considered of inestimable value. That is why even fakes command a high price."

The raw halibut had a clean taste, like salt water from a thousand miles offshore. I suddenly wished I were back on the *King of Nothing* with Rory, a thousand salmon ahead of us and no regrets behind.

Beneath the table Fiora's hand rested lightly on my thigh, telling me that she too was remembering. When she moved her hand to resume eating, she brushed over the odd weapon I had put in my jacket pocket. She looked at me, a question clear in her hazel-green eyes.

I took the old man's flail from my jacket pocket and let its chain coil up like a snake in my hand. For all its efficiency, the weapon was crudely made. The chain was lightweight, the sort you can buy by the foot in a hardware store. The weights were soft malleable metal, melted and hand formed from lead ingots of the sort fishermen use to manufacture sinkers.

"Another souvenir?" Nakamichi asked.

"After a fashion." I dumped it on the table between us. "You know anything about these weapons?"

He poked at the chain and weights with a delicate forefinger. "I do not know what it is called, but it is a tool of the martial arts. I have seen such things in bad samurai movies. Is this also part of your inheritance?"

"The old man I got it from was alive the last time I saw him. He told me he owned the sword."

Fiora gave me a sharp look. I ignored it.

Nakamichi raised the champagne flute to his lips and drank half of it in a long mouthful, swallowing without tasting. Absently he took two whole prawns the size of mice from the iced platter. He held one between his fingers and shucked it skillfully with his chopsticks, then waved the naked crustacean through the sauce. He ate the prawn, head and all, chewing slowly with his mouth open, as though he lost his occidental manners when he picked up chopsticks.

While Nakamichi peeled the second prawn with offhand deftness, the waiter brought two big crockery bowls of steamer clams. He refilled everyone's champagne glasses, dropped another loaf of bread and fresh salted butter on the table, and vanished.

"Fascinating," Nakamichi said finally, snapping back from his inner meditation on prawns. "You seem to have an affinity for Japanese weapons."

Fiora gave me another look. I reached for the steamers.

The waiter reappeared just as Nakamichi selected a large, well-marked butter clam from one of the bowls, extracted the orangish-brown flesh with his sticks, and then tipped the broth from the empty shell onto his tongue. The waiter bent low, murmured something, and withdrew. Nakamichi wiped his fingers thoroughly on the clean linen napkin and stood.

"Excuse me. A matter has come up. I regret, but—"

"Of course," Fiora said briskly.

"The new drafts should be complete by two o'clock," he said.

She nodded and reached for a clam. "I have other things to take care of, but I'll try to get by before you close. If that's not possible, I'll come by tomorrow sometime."

She sounded as if she were making arrangements to have her tires rotated, not closing an important deal. The lady was well and truly pissed off at Mr. Roniko Nakamichi.

Nakamichi inclined his head a half inch and then turned to me. "It has been a pleasure. If you wish the name of a competent appraiser, Fiora has my number."

That she did. She didn't like it, either.

When Nakamichi was out of sight, Fiora dropped the empty clamshell onto her plate. She didn't reach for another. So far she had eaten only one clam, one oyster, and one prawn. That amounted to about 150 calories of energy. Apparently she thought that was enough. She cleared her palate with Cristal and dropped her napkin on the plate.

I selected an unusually large manila clam, fished the ugly orange morsel out of the shell with a fork, and held it out.

"Open up," I said.

Automatically Fiora opened her mouth, took the clam, and began chewing. It must have tasted good because she picked up her napkin and put it back on her lap. She was still radiating anger on a wavelength only I seemed to pick up, but she was looking at the bowl of steamers as though she had just realized they were there. I handed her the oyster fork. As she took it I touched the back of her hand.

"Rough morning?" I asked.

"No visible bruises, unlike you," Fiora said, drawing the clam bowl closer. "Things are just moving slower than I expected and I'm more impatient than I should be, that's all."

I made an encouraging noise. She wasn't expecting me to solve her problem; she just needed to describe it.

Fiora ate her way through the bowl of clams as she talked, discarding empty shells like an aggressive sea otter. Most of the terms she used had more meaning for her than for me—indemnification clauses and cross-collateralization and employment contracts, the radar chaff and radio static of modern corporate life. Fiora and Nakamichi had an agreement, a handshake deal. But all such arrangements suffer when they're translated into bureaucratese and legalese.

"Part of the problem is trying to reconcile two corporate cultures," Fiora concluded after a few minutes. "I tend to operate with very little structure. But Nakamichi Securities isn't a stand-alone corporation; it's a *zaibatsu*, a financial clique. There isn't just one sales contract to negotiate, there are about a dozen formal and informal treaties with related corporations. Then there are all these quasi-personal relationships that have to be observed."

Clamshells clattered as Fiora made a sound of disgust.

"God, give me a nice straightforward English garden maze to negotiate blindfolded at midnight. It would be a piece of cake."

Shellfish are all right, but Fiora needed more. The brain uses 40 percent of the body's energy, and her brain had been working hard all morning. I buttered a piece of roll and put it on the small plate between us. She hit the bread the way a cutthroat trout hits a Deadly Dick. Then she went back to the clams.

"Arguing with a Japanese corporation is like kicking a tar baby," she continued. "You just never get unstuck. Throw in a few American lawyers and you've got the Tar Baby from Hell."

She looked at me.

"One of Ron's five-hundred-dollar-an-hour American barristers actually proposed a clause this morning that mentioned 'all rights in the universe both known and unknown.'"

I blinked. "Unknown?"

"Yeah."

Fiora smiled for the first time since I had limped into sight. Then she tossed the last shell on the mound in front of her and went fishing through the cloudy broth for clams that might have escaped her fork.

"You think he's trying to back out?" I asked.

Fiora let the waiter pour the last mouthful of Cristal from the bottle into her glass before she answered.

"No," she said as the waiter walked away. "Ron's too busy to waste time going sideways on me. I was surprised it took ten minutes for the waiter to interrupt with a call."

She took half of the remaining mouthful of champagne and handed the glass to me. The warmth of her hand had released the yeasty smell of the liquid. I inhaled, tasted a little, and inhaled again.

Fiora looked from my fingers on the glass to my mouth and then back to my hand. She drew the first deep breath she had taken since we sat down. It did interesting things to the fit of her blouse.

"What really happened to you?" Fiora asked. "How did you hurt your leg?"

"I was mugged by an old man."

"Fiddler, I'm serious."

"So am I."

She didn't believe me at first, but she did by the time we finished lunch and walked to Nakamichi's condominium. The condo was on the eleventh floor of a building that overlooked the Alaska Way Viaduct. The truck traffic was faintly audible from the balcony. That was the apartment's only flaw; the rest was as perfect as any urban living space I've ever seen: a 270-degree view—Hurricane Ridge and the Cascades in the distance, Elliott Bay and Puget Sound in mid-range, and the working waterfront in close.

Around the corner, the cityscape loomed like a prosperous banker in a three-piece suit. At night the lights would be spectacular. Four blocks to the local market—Pike Place—a dozen eating and drinking places within easy crawl, and all the free entertainment in the world, what with the fire-boats, the ferry docks, the freight terminal, and, overhead, the outbound traffic patterns of Boeing Field and Sea-Tac.

I opened the sliding doors to let the afternoon breezes flow through the room. A Boeing 747 popped up from behind the Kingdome, climbing on a long diagonal. The outbound Alaska State Ferry blasted a salute as it left its berth, headed for Haines Junction.

Fiora came back from the kitchen with a big bottle of sparkling water. While I drank, she took off her jacket and stood in a patch of bright sunlight in the living room, eyes closed, face turned up to the warmth. She stretched the tight muscles between her shoulder blades like a cat. The cream silk of her blouse and the neutral silk of her bra became translucent over the dark rose tips of her breasts.

Suddenly it felt like I hadn't touched her in a week.

She opened her eyes and looked at me. Then

she closed them and stretched again. The tips of her breasts had begun to swell as though I had caressed them.

"It's funny," she said in a low voice. "I always feel it when you look at me that way, even if I can't see your eyes."

"Do you like it when I look at you that way?"

"The way iron filings like a magnet."

Her lashes lifted, showing me the hunger in her eyes. She came over and stood in my shadow. Slowly, very slowly, she eased forward until our bodies touched at the one spot where both of us ached.

"What about the phone calls you had to make?" I asked.

"I'm returning the only important call right now."

As Fiora closed her eyes, her mouth took on the quiet, interior smile that she sometimes gets when she is most relaxed and sexy. She rotated her hips ever so slightly.

Gravity doubled. I reached for the top button of her blouse. The clear, soft skin of her face and neck had taken a bit of sun while we were fishing the other day. The tan came to a point on the pale skin above her breastbone. I undid the second button and saw that her bra closed in front. I let my knuckles brush the swells of her breasts as I toyed with the catch.

"I know how much the Nakamichi deal means to you," I said. "I don't want to distract you."

Fiora smiled lazily and moved, enjoying the sexual hunger spreading through my body. Then she lifted her hands to undo the catch of the bra. I caught her fingers and held them.

"I'll let you know if I need any help," I said.

She left her hands over mine as I undid the catch and slid the cups away. When I stopped to admire her, she guided my fingers inside the blouse to the dark points of flesh that needed stroking.

"You may not need help," she said huskily, "but I do. Help me, love."

thirteen

The phone woke us an hour later. Fiora picked it up before I could. Her tone told me she was back on the leash again and hard at work. I got up and went out to the kitchen, looking for something substantial to eat. Whoever said oysters are all a man needs had never been to bed with a woman like Fiora.

Nakamichi's housekeeper must not have known about the new tenants. She let herself in the maid's door while I was building cheddar, salami, and cracker sandwiches on the butcher's block in the center of the kitchen. Her eyes got as big as overcoat buttons when she saw me. The butcher's block between us was high enough for modesty's sake but just barely. She shut her eyes, mumbled something in Japanese, and backed out in a hurry.

The door closed behind her with emphasis and locked automatically. I tried the front door key on the lock, saw that they were different, and shot the inside bolt to prevent embarrassing the little old lady again.

After I showered and dressed, I left Fiora to the thousand details already drawing frown lines on her face and walked out onto Western Avenue with the florist's box tucked under my arm. The sunshine was warm and silky, but a haze had begun to gather out over the water, like a smudge on your Ray-Bans.

I turned some square blocks looking for shadows. When I was certain I was alone, I went to the Central Gun Exchange.

The lanky, bearded black man behind the counter put down the Walther P-38 he had been cleaning and looked at me. There was no curiosity in his glance; guys walked into his store carrying long packages all the time. He wore a black Harley-Davidson T-shirt and black 501s. His biceps were the size of Virginia hams. His general air of physical competence suggested he had not taken the Special Forces buckle on his belt in pawn but had earned it.

I laid the battered florist's box on the glass counter and lifted the cover. The sword lay on top of the silk bag. The guy's eyebrows lifted a bit when he saw the sword.

"Nice piece," he said. "You selling?"

"Pawn. What'll you give?"

He wiped his hands thoroughly on an oil rag before he pulled the sword from its scabbard and inspected the steel.

"Looks old," he said.

"Some expert told me it was a copy. I don't know one way or the other."

"I'll go three," he said after a moment.

I looked past him to the heavy steel vault door. Inside were rows of long guns and wall pegs loaded with pistols. A lot of hunters pawn their guns in December and don't redeem them until hunting season, just to avoid the hassle of storing the weapons at home.

"Does pawned stuff go in the vault?" I asked.

He nodded.

"Good," I said. "I'd hate to have the sword on public display."

He gave me a look as hard as the steel of the blade. Pawnshops have to be as discreet as confessionals and more secure than museums.

"If it's stolen I don't want it," he said bluntly.

"Some guys I know come in here," I explained. "I'd hate for them to recognize the sword and figure I have a few hundred bucks in my jeans, if you get my drift."

The guy's face relaxed. He got it.

I hiked back to the market three hundred dollars richer and with both hands free.

At the market I bought a couple of late Red Top peaches the size of slow-pitch softballs and found a vacant bench in a crowded vest-pocket park. The bench gave me a filtered view of Oshima's gallery. I watched the tourists come and go from Post Alley for twenty minutes. It looked like the last hot afternoon of the summer, and everybody was more interested in sun than they were in art.

An Indian kid sat in a chemically induced trance at the base of a ten-foot totem, staring at me. I remembered him from that morning, one of the local street people. He was still wearing a filthy white T-shirt and a pair of blue jeans old and dirty enough to stand by themselves in the corner.

I took a bite from a peach, more from boredom than hunger. The fruit was so ripe it almost exploded in my hand.

The kid's eyes were glassy, but they stayed on the peach as I brought it to my mouth again. I took the second peach from the paper bag and held it out. Slowly, his eyes began to focus. He looked at me. I nodded.

It took him three tries, but he got his feet under him and shuffled over. I moved aside to make room on the bench and handed him the peach. He sat down and studied the fruit for a few seconds, as though waiting for it to ferment into something with more kick. Finally the sweet smell got through the fuzz in his brain. He took a tentative bite, then attacked the peach with a speed that spoke of real hunger.

"You live around here?" I asked.

The kid looked puzzled for several seconds, then shook his head. "Up island."

He had that flat Canadian accent, like a file on soft metal. He took a noisy bite of the peach.

"But you stay around here," I said.

He nodded and pointed with his chin toward the grass beneath the totem pole. "There."

"You know a guy named Carlton?" I asked. "He hangs around here too."

The hazy look came back. With a week's growth of sparse beard, flat face, and almond-shaped eyes, he looked more Asian than Indian. A land-bridge refugee, marooned in a world not of his own making.

"Huh," he said.

It wasn't a question. It wasn't an answer, either.

"Carlton," I repeated. "Tall skinny kid, hair like a Brillo pad. I saw him over in Post Alley this morning."

Bingo.

The Indian lowered the peach from his mouth. A look of baffled anger spread across his face.

"That sumbitch, he run me off one day, just for sleeping there. Bastard. He don't own the sidewalk."

"Which sidewalk?"

"In front of that Jap art place," he said, pointing at Oshima's. "He works there. Good money. Scores enough shit for three dudes, but he don't share none. Sumbitch."

"Well, ol' Carlton's probably going to miss a few days of work," I said.

"Eh?"

Definitely Canadian. Flat, almost atonal.

"Somebody cracked him on the head, down by Pioneer Square," I explained.

"Good," the Indian said. "Sumbitch has it coming. Hope he dies. Never shared nothing' with me."

"Paramedics took him, so he'll probably live. You know where they take street people?"

The kid worked on the peach some more. His stomach must have been dead empty. The fructose hit him like a shot of adrenaline. He looked brighter, less fuzzed out. When I repeated my question, he licked his lips and thought about it.

"I fell on a bottle, cut hell out of my leg," he said finally, hiking his pants leg to show me.

A half-moon scab as big as my fist smiled up from his calf.

"They took me to a hospital on First," he said. "They do a lot of detox there."

"Did you detox?"

"Nah."

He patted the hip pocket of his jeans, then fished a folded sheet of paper out and handed it to me. It was an outpatient referral form from Harborview Hospital. He handled it with an odd care, a ticket to a world he wasn't sure he wanted to visit—and not sure he didn't want to visit, either.

"Harborview," he said. "That's the place."

"Next time you go by there, try detox."

"What for, dude?"

"Summer's winding down. It's going to start raining again pretty soon. You'll need a warm place to go."

He sucked on the peach pit and nodded slowly. "Yeah," he said. "Mebbe."

"You have some other place to stay? A job maybe?"

He stared off toward Elliott Bay, a little lost and suddenly ten years younger, a child.

"My mom lives in Campbell River," he said, as though just remembering. "I got fired off a seine boat in Victoria for drinking. I don't even remember how I got here."

Campbell River was a Canadian fishing and pulp-mill town halfway up Vancouver Island. The town was only a hundred and fifty miles north, but it might as well have been on the moon. He looked at me as though he knew this was the last day of summer.

"You want to go home?" I asked.

Glancing away, he ducked his head in a nod that said he wanted to be anywhere but where he was.

"What's your name?" I asked.

He didn't have to think, this time. "Sammy. Sammy Nanoose."

"Sammy, how much does a room cost around here?"

"I know a flophouse out toward Queen Anne that gets twelve but only if you're sober."

"You think you can hack that for one night?"

He thought a while before he said slowly, "Mebbe. If I had some food. . . ."

He wasn't cadging cash or sympathy. He was just trying to put things together in his mind.

The pawnshop had paid me in twenties. I peeled off one and held it where Sammy could see it.

"Make you a deal," I said. "I'll give you this for food and flop. You come back to this bench tomorrow with twenty bucks' worth of receipts, not one of them for a bottle, and I'll buy you a ticket on the *Princess Marguerite.*"

He mulled through that for a while. "The *Marguerite*, yeah, that's how I got here, ain't it?"

The *Marguerite* is an old steamship that makes a round trip from Victoria to Seattle once a day in the summertime. It probably was the way he got here. Other than swimming, it was the cheapest way from here to there.

"Take the *Marguerite* home, Sammy. Cities aren't good for you."

For a moment there was someone home behind his bloodshot black eyes. "Yeah, I know."

He looked at the twenty-dollar bill. It was

enough to kill him, if he spent it the wrong place. He seemed to understand that.

"Why you doing this?" he asked, focusing on me for the first time.

"Cities aren't good for me, either. I always get in trouble, sooner or later." I handed him the twenty. "Meet me here in the morning. We'll walk over to the pier together. If you're not here by seven-thirty, I'll know you aren't coming. Got it?"

Slowly he blinked, trying to assimilate what I'd said. He nodded gravely and stood up. I could see him planning his route to the flop already. Then he looked at me and offered a hand that hadn't been washed in a week.

I shook it.

"You be careful, dude," Sammy said. "Something's happening. There's cops hanging around."

"There usually are."

"Not like these. Suits. A man and a woman."

He pointed a scarred thumb at a four-door Plymouth parked a block above Post Alley. The angle wasn't great, but by leaning out so far I almost fell, I could see two figures in the front and maybe a third in the back.

Like Sammy said. Suits.

"We all thought they was narcs," he said.

"How do you know I'm not?"

"Don't matter." Sammy grinned and shoved the twenty in his pocket. "Your money's good, either way."

I laughed. "See you," I said, hoping I would.

He waved and headed off toward First Avenue to catch the free bus.

I settled back to watch the gallery, and the car watching the gallery.

Nothing happened for another twenty minutes, so I took a roundabout stroll that let me study the Plymouth from several angles without being studied in return. The car had civilian plates but sported a little pigtail antenna that could have worked for a cellular phone or a radio.

The trio inside was odd. Really odd. The guy behind the wheel had that Irishman's suntan: pale skin and a flush of burst capillaries on his cheeks and across his nose. Too much whisky, too many cigarettes. He wore a dark suit, white shirt, and dark necktie that screamed "fed." He also had the relaxed, hard-eyed look that comes from sitting for hours at a time on a busy city street, waiting for something ugly to happen.

The woman was softer. She wore business clothes and light makeup. Her eyes were alert, intelligent. She looked out of place on the street, too nervous to be a lady cop. Maybe an attorney, maybe even a reporter, but not a cop. A gun would have made her flinch.

The little guy in the backseat was a civilian too. Lots of law enforcement agencies are recruiting Asians, but nobody ever qualified on the pistol range squinting through glasses that thick.

I made one run directly past them, trying to catch a bit of their conversation through their open windows. They weren't talking. Silently they watched Oshima's place. Their expressions made it clear that nobody was having a good time.

No surprise. There was nothing to see. The lights were on in Oshima's office, and that was it. The gallery itself was dead quiet. A few tourists wandered in, looked around, and shot outside again as though afraid the atmosphere might be contagious.

The market crowds began to thin out by four o'clock. I had to move around a bit to keep a screen between myself and the surveillance. I read every label on every overpriced bottle of Washington chardonnay and Oregon pinot noir in the upscale bottle shop on the corner. Finally I selected a mixed case and had it delivered to the condo. Then I admired displays of ground coffee and fresh bagels and cream cheese and fruit. I skimmed the latest edition of the *Post-Intelligencer* and did map coordinates on every good catch from the fishing report in the sports section.

And all the while I was trying to make sense out of the tableau of people watching people.

Nothing clicked.

At four-thirty a lively young redhead in a halter top bounced by cheerfully, saluting the world with a long paper bag that contained a fresh épée from the bread stall in the market annex. The length of the bread made me think of the sword.

On a hunch, I went over to the stall and had the girl there pick out the longest loaf she could find. It was too long for a single bag, so she slid a second bag over the exposed end of the loaf.

As I walked back into the street crowds, I tucked the bread under my arm, carrying it like I had the sword. When I turned the corner past the wine shop and moved up the street in full view of the Plymouth, I slowed to a saunter. I wanted to give the suits time for a good look before I turned into Oshima's gallery.

I shouldn't have worried. All three suits piled out of the car and trotted down the steep hill toward me within ten seconds. The woman had a tough time keeping the pace with her high heels. Surprisingly, the small Asian was leading the charge, with the Irishman right behind.

It was an effort, but I pretended not to notice them. I pushed open the door of Oshima's place and went inside, the long parcel still tucked under my arm. Tara slipped through the beaded curtain. Her polite, bored gallery-girl smile dissolved into a glare when she saw me.

"What do you want?"

Just then the gallery door swung open behind me. The Asian rushed in, winded from his downhill run.

"Stop!" he commanded. "Don't move!"

His voice lacked authority but the cop's didn't.

"Hold it right there," the cop said loudly. "We want to talk to you."

"What about?" I asked.

"About whatever it is you're carrying. Put it down on the counter. Please."

His tone made it something more forceful than a request. So did his body language. His coat was open and his hand was resting on the butt of a pistol.

fOURTEEN

I carefully laid the long parcel on the counter and showed the cop my empty hands. His own hand didn't leave his pistol butt.

"Show us what's in the bag," the cop said. "Please."

I hoped he had a sense of humor, but I doubted it. I slid the paper bag off the short end of the épée.

"Anybody else hungry?" I asked.

No one was, so I broke off the crusty tip of the loaf and ate it myself. While I was chewing, Oshima came through the beaded curtains, saw the bread on the counter, and looked confused.

"You have any salami back there?" I asked, breaking off another hunk of the bread. "No? How about a serving of crow?"

Oshima looked like he had just sat down on a halibut jig with treble hooks. The white-collar cop took over. He was a lot more relaxed now that he knew I wasn't armed.

"Mr. Oshima," he said, "is this the man who offered you the sword this morning?"

Oshima looked at me and thought about lying. When I didn't give him a clue, he decided the truth was safer. I looked forward to the change in his tactics. Up to now he had shown no great fervor for truth.

"Yes, that's him." Oshima nodded for emphasis, then turned toward me. "Where's the sword?"

I brushed bread crumbs from the counter. "Does that mean you're upping the ante to ten thousand?"

"Where sword?" the little Asian in the glasses demanded. "National art treasure. Matter of highest interest Japan government!"

I let my left eyebrow climb in a manner that drives Fiora nuts. "An international incident, no less. Oshima, baby, you astonish me."

Oshima looked like he wanted to disappear, but only after he throttled me.

"You sly devil," I continued. "You never told me your collector was the Emperor of Japan. What has the world come to, when emperors are reduced to collecting fakes?"

The frail man in the glasses burst into speech. I don't know any Japanese, but I doubt that he was singing any praises.

The woman stepped forward. "Let me handle this, Mr. Sato. You are here as an observer only."

Unwillingly he subsided, probably because she was five inches taller than he was and her voice was like a razor blade.

"Where is the sword?" she asked me.

"Who are you?" I asked through a mouthful of bread.

"Nan Decker. I'm with the State Department. We have reason to believe the sword was illegally obtained and improperly imported. We intend to confiscate it."

I looked at the cop. "Who are you, the culture police?"

"Don't get in the way, mister," he warned. "You could be a hero, or you could be in deep kimchi."

"FBI, right?" I said.

He produced his buzzer with a smooth experienced motion. The ID card said he was Supervisory Special Agent Francis X. Claherty, Federal Bureau of Investigation.

"Betcha five bucks I know what the *X* stands for," I said.

He wasn't a gambler. "Where's the sword?"

I jerked a thumb toward Oshima. "Ask the expert."

"Me? I don't have it," the gallery owner objected.

His voice was a little shrill, as though he wasn't entirely sure his disclaimer would fly. He looked at me unhappily, asking for help. I let him dangle there for a moment, a small repayment for siccing the bird dog on me.

"It's been stolen," I said to Claherty.

Sato's squeal sounded like Japanese for "Holy shit!" Nan Decker tried to soothe him in his own language. Claherty stood there looking like he had just tumbled down the white rabbit's hole.

"You're trying to tell us the sword's gone missing?" he finally asked.

"Bingo. Somebody snatched it in the market."

I watched Oshima as I spoke, but he didn't even twitch an eyelid. No surprise there. Good liars are better actors.

"Balls," Claherty muttered. "Why did you come back here if you don't have the sword?"

Uh-oh. A thinker.

I shrugged. "I thought Oshima might know something. The guy who stole it matches the description of a local dude called Carlton. He spends a lot of time here in Post Alley."

Oshima swallowed and looked at me hard. It had begun to dawn on him that I wasn't from East Bumblefart after all. Like the gifted liar he was, he adjusted instantly to the new scenario.

"I have a part-time employee named Carlton," he said to Claherty, "but I'm sure he's not a thief."

"Get him out here and let's ask him," Claherty said.

Oshima looked distressed. "He didn't show up for work today."

I snorted audibly.

"It's true," Oshima insisted. "Ask Tara. Carlton hasn't been in the shop all day, has he, dear?"

Tara was leaning against the far end of the counter as though needing its support. She nodded instant agreement, but she looked scared. She was treading deep water and getting tired already.

"Do you know there's a law against lying to a federal agent?" I asked Tara idly. "If I were you, I'd make Mr. Claherty read you your Miranda rights before you say anything else."

"That's not necessary," Claherty said.

"Don't bet on it," I said. "A missing sword is one thing. Murder is another."

Funny how one little word like "murder" can throw a hush across a whole room. Suddenly I could hear the ship rats rustling in the dumpster behind the fancy nouvelle cuisine place across the street.

Claherty recovered first, probably because he was more used to violent death than the others were.

"So you *are* the guy from Malahat," he said.

My estimation of the FBI went up, but I saw no need to pass out compliments. This was a damned inconvenient time to run across a shining example of interagency cooperation.

"How's old Sheriff What's-his-name?" I asked.

"Sheriff Bolton is a lot brighter than you are if you think you'll throw us off stride with this murder crap."

"Sheriff Bolton is just bright enough to worry about me ruining his crime stats by proving Rory was murdered," I said. "You know how touchy these cow-county cops are."

"Calling it murder doesn't prove a thing," Claherty retorted. "Right now everybody's more interested in the sword."

"Yeah, I noticed." I looked at Oshima.

Claherty caught the look. Ever hopeful of dividing and conquering, he did his best to dismantle whatever trust Oshima and I might have.

"Mr. Oshima has been very helpful," Claherty said. "He gave us Mr. Cairns's name. When nobody answered Mr. Cairns's number, I called the locals. They filled us in real quick."

Nan Decker stepped in, trying to seize the initiative from the FBI. I wished her luck. A lot of folks have tried it. Not many succeed.

"Mr. Sato is assistant curator at the Imperial Museum in Tokyo," Decker said. "He believes the sword you lost is one of the most important cultural artifacts in Japanese history. Rumors of its rediscovery have been circulating in his country for several weeks."

That would be about the time Rory brought the sword in to be appraised. Oshima was a real prince.

"Ten thousand, huh?" I asked, giving him a look.

Sato nodded excitedly. "Very important. National art treasure. Very, very important."

"Does Japan want the sword enough to kill for it?" I asked.

Sato looked curiously at Decker, as though the nuance of the question eluded him. Decker's translation must have been very good. She even had managed to impart the silent accusation.

Sato scowled and tried to mow me down with a burst of invective.

I waited for the translation, watching Decker at work. She was tall and plump, a little hippy and trying to disguise it. Maybe by the time she was thirty-five, she would figure out that thin thighs aren't what make some women sexy.

"Mr. Sato says he rejects any suggestion that his government would act improperly," Decker said carefully.

I wasn't impressed.

"He says he has traveled a long way and has

observed every propriety. He says my presence here is a sign of that."

Decker translated in a flat, verbatim monotone that told me her choice of words was correct and precise.

"Everybody thinks the CIA hires killers," I said. "Why should Japan's secret service be any different?" She started to translate but I broke in. "And anyway, why should the State Department care? Your words, Ms. Decker, not Sato's."

For an instant she looked young and a little uncertain. This was probably her first important assignment.

"I work for the Cultural Recoveries Office," Decker said evenly. "We help other nations locate and repatriate stolen antiquities and art."

"Greek statutes, Mayan gold, those things I can understand, but a war trophy? That's getting a little picky, isn't it?"

"The GI from Texas who stole ten million dollars' worth of altar paintings from a German church felt the same way," she shot back.

I shrugged. "I'll let you and Mr. Sato debate the international laws on looting. I'm interested in the sword for one reason only. It will lead me to whoever killed my friend."

I looked at Sato.

"You help me find Mr. Cairns's killer and I'll do everything I can to return the sword to its place of honor. Otherwise, get the hell out of my way."

He looked puzzled.

"Translate," I said to Decker without looking away. "And don't polish it, lady."

Decker translated. Sato listened.

He wasn't as foolish as he looked on first impression. When she finished, he took off his thick glasses, rubbed them with the tip of his tie, and put them back on his nose. Then he spoke in Japanese.

Decker translated. "Mr. Sato says death is tragic any time, by any means, but some things are worse than the death of a single man."

"Murder, not death. There's a difference."

"My translation was precise."

I didn't doubt it. She was young, but she was bright. I looked back at Oshima.

"Guess this deal is turning into a dead loss all around," I said.

"I told you the truth," he said quickly. "Until these people approached me, I had no idea the sword was anything but a well-executed fake. That's why I sent it back to Mr. Cairns after appraising it. If I had thought the sword was real, it would never have left my possession."

That I believed.

"Well, it's gone now," I said.

"I don't believe you," Oshima said angrily. "You wouldn't be careless enough to let Carlton steal it. He's a weakling, a fool, and a drug user."

"Really? Then why did you hire him?"

Oshima bristled but kept his temper.

"Where is your trusted employee?" I asked.

"I haven't the faintest idea."

"In that case, I'm gone," I said. "Unless you three secret agents have some objection?"

The two diplomats looked at the special agent. Diplomats may hate cops, but they're always the first to yell for one when things go sour.

Claherty shrugged and shook his head, as

though he could think of no reason to detain me.
That was technically true, but such small matters
don't usually bother federal agents. He could have
gotten me booked into a local mental ward on a
seventy-two-hour hold, if he thought it was worth
the paperwork.

I left, but Claherty caught up before I had taken
three steps down the sidewalk.

"Slow down, Fiddler." He fell in beside me.
"You didn't report the sword's theft to the cops, did
you?"

I shook my head.

"Now how do you suppose I know that?" he
asked.

"Because you think it wasn't stolen."

We turned the corner heading back into the
market. The last of the vendors was packing up.
The meat and cheese and fish cases were empty.

Claherty stopped walking. I stopped too, because his hand was on my arm.

"That's part of it," he said, "but I mostly know
the sword wasn't stolen because you're the kind of
character who likes to take the law into his own
hands."

"Soundex strikes again."

He nodded. "Yeah, I ran your name on Soundex
and all the others. Interesting file. I also called a
guy named Mike Innes. Maybe you remember
him? He sends his regards, by the way. He's retired
over in Tucson now, but he still does consulting for
private industry."

Innes was the FBI counterintelligence specialist
who had twice gotten between me and a man
whose continued existence threatened me—and,

more importantly, Fiora. Both times, Innes had duly noted my presence in the FBI's internal record system.

"That's the problem with jerking the Bureau around," Claherty continued easily. "It's kind of like jerking the Jesuits. We both have lots of people and real long memories."

"A threat," I said, "nicely disguised behind a genial smile and a gentle historical allusion. But a threat just the same."

"Naw," Claherty said. "Just a bit of information. I thought if you knew the players, you might line up on our team."

I jerked a thumb over my shoulder in the direction of the gallery. "I've got the State Department after me, plus the full force and majesty of the Japanese government. What makes you think the FBI is going to scare me any more or less?"

"Those two are kids in pinstripes." He dismissed Sato and Decker with a wave of his hand. "They'll do a top dance and call you bad names, but they won't do a damn thing that hurts. It's guys like me that will make you hurt if you don't do the right thing."

I looked around, but there was no dumpster handy. It was probably just as well. I'm not good at resisting certain kinds of temptation.

"You were smart, warning that poor little girl," he continued affably. "She's the weak link. I'm going to go back in there, take her aside, and break her down. It shouldn't take me much more than half an hour."

"Always nice to meet a man who enjoys his work."

He laughed. It wasn't a nice sound.

"Listen, cowboy," Claherty said. "I drew the ticket on this case, which means I'm responsible for how it comes out. That means how you come out too, because you're part of it. You make me feel good, I make you feel good."

Francis Xavier Claherty should have been an Irish politician, an actor, or a priest. Not only did he love talking, his raspy voice commanded attention even when the words didn't.

"Innes tells me you're a wise guy," Claherty continued. "You know how things work. That's why I took you aside to ask you, man to man, to tell the truth."

I've been hard-assed from time to time in my life, but usually by a duo, one playing good cop and the other playing bad cop. Claherty was trying to fill both roles. It made for some fast emotional shifts, but his voice was up to it. So was his technique: Simple and direct as a wrecking ball, good or bad, and nothing in between to confuse the suspect.

Claherty gave me a few beats to think over his offer.

I already knew the answer, but I waited, not wanting to disturb the flow of his performance.

"Last chance," he warned. "If I find out you've been lying to me, for whatever reason, I'll grind you and your blond lady friend into tiny little pieces and sell you for crab bait."

I looked at my watch.

"You'll be audited," Claherty said in a deftly rising voice.

"You'll be skin-searched every time you cross a

border. You'll fail every driver's test you take from now until the day you die."

"What if I'm telling you the truth about the sword?"

"Then everything will turn out just like it's supposed to," he said. "The bad guys will be punished and the good guys will be rewarded, just like Judgment Day."

"Then I'll see you in hell," I said. "It was invented for guys like you and me."

I walked away without looking back. It wouldn't have done any good, one way or the other.

fIFTEEN

I knew what I had to do, but it took me forty-five minutes and three beers to secure the props. First, I had to find the right kind of bar. This one was on Second Avenue. Between the first and the second beers, I called Fiora. She sounded cool and confident, like she was beginning to wear the bastards down. She promised to be back at the condo by seven-thirty. I told her I might be a few minutes late.

During the second beer, I started goofing around with the other guys along the bar—the white pimp with acne scars who drank vodka, the two bikers doing tequila slammers, and the emphysemic old man in the straw fedora who was gulping air and seven-sevens with equal desperation. The talk was mostly baseball and bullshit.

I was the long-haul trucker from LA, and I thought the Mariners were going to finish dead last. But I also thought Chuck Knox was the best coach in the NFL, so it was cool.

I bought a round with my third beer and peeled two twenties off my roll. I laid them side by side on the dark wood. The barkeep was fat and bald. He kept a short beer under the bar, right next to the sawed-off butt of a pool cue with a leather thong through it. When he finished serving the round and came by to collect, I leaned forward a bit.

"I could use something to keep me awake between here and Redding, some blow, maybe," I said quietly.

The bartender didn't even look up. When he turned away, the second twenty still lay on the counter next to a handful of change from the first.

I got up and went to the john. When I came back, the second twenty was gone and there was a matchbook lying between my change and my beer. I drank half the beer, picked up the change and the matches, and put them in my pocket.

"See you guys next turnaround," I said and walked out.

I bought two hard-packs of Marlboros in a drugstore and hiked First Hill to get rid of the buzz. It felt good to sweat and breathe smokeless air again.

The fountains in Freeway Park danced, and the leaves on some of the trees had begun the color shift from dark green to autumn gold. I felt a little autumnal myself. The feeling didn't improve as I walked into the emergency room at Harborview. The place smelled of pain and dying. It was too much like the place I had last seen Rory.

A nurse whose faded green scrubs matched her eyes examined me carefully.

"I'm okay," I said. "I'm just looking for a friend. A guy named Carlton."

"Is that his first name or his last?"

"Dunno."

The look she gave me said she didn't think I was the kind of guy whose friends only had one name. I guess I was too clean. On the other hand, she smelled the barfly cigarette smoke on me. I got close enough to give her a blast of the stale beer on my breath. Her good impression changed fast. I became one of "them," another urban casualty, one of the walking wounded in a high-stress society.

I showed her the two packs of cigarettes. "Look, I know Carlton's gonna be hurting."

The nurse sympathized even as she disapproved. "What time did he come in?"

I told her and she checked the ER log.

"Carlton Stevens," she said after a time. "He gave an address on Pine."

"That's him. How's he doing?"

"Compared to what?"

She gave me a room number.

The nursing station was empty. Harborview is a University of Washington teaching hospital, which means it has good people but not enough of them. Nobody saw me walk into the three-bed ward.

Carlton was in the last bed, closest to the window. His forty-yard stare was focused somewhere behind the television set bolted to the wall opposite his bed.

"Hey, Carlton, how ya doing, dude?" I said, drawing the privacy curtain between us and the black man in the next bed.

The cut on the side of Carlton's face had been

sutured. His left eye was swollen halfway shut. Even after he managed to focus on me, it took him several seconds to remember where he had seen me last. And why.

His eyes got big and his mouth sucked air.

I held my finger to my lips and said softly, "Be cool and you'll be okay. I didn't bring the cops—this time."

He clamped his mouth shut.

I smiled. It didn't reassure him. I leaned over and turned up the volume on the television speaker that hung on the rail beside him.

"How'd ya. . . ."

Words were hard for him to form. He had taken a pretty bad shot to the head.

"How did I find you?" I asked.

He nodded, winced, and lay still.

"The same way I'll find you again unless you tell me the truth," I said flatly. "Except if I have to come looking again, I'm going to be pissed off. You don't want to piss me off, Carlton."

"Wh—What ya want?" he said.

"The sword."

"I ain't got it."

"Yeah? Who does?"

His good eye rolled around in fear. His lips worked but nothing happened. It was hard to decide whether he was holding out or simply unable to put his sad story in words.

"Listen up, pal." I leaned forward. "Two phone calls and you're in shit up to your stitches. The first call would be to nine-one-one. The second would be to Oshima."

"I ain't got the sword," he said, flinching. "Sumbitch stole it."

"Someone stole it?" I managed to look surprised. "From you?"

"Yeah."

I thought it over and allowed myself to be convinced.

"Who took it?" I asked.

There was a patch of raw red skin on Carlton's right cheek, as if it had been buffed with extra-coarse sandpaper. His nervous fingers sought the raw spot and picked at it. He didn't know whether to fear me or Oshima more.

I took the matchbook from my pocket and unfolded it. There were two thin paper bindles behind the back row of matches. Light grams, ten bucks a pop. I still didn't know which of the five men in the bar had been the supplier. Probably the old man in the straw fedora. He was the most desperate, the closest to the end of his string. I showed Carlton the bindles.

"Nerves getting you?" I asked softly. "Skin started to crawl yet? They don't give you much painkiller when you have a head injury. Bet you could use a little jolt, huh? One for now and one for later."

His right eye recognized the bindles instantly, two letters from home. His fingers twitched with the desire to take the matchbook. I pulled my hand back a few inches, just out of his reach. A tear formed in the corner of his swollen eye.

It would have been less unpleasant to beat the truth out of him, but I didn't have the luxury of choice.

"Words, Carlton. Give me some words. And they better make sense."

"Oshima . . . he just wanted you followed," Carlton said in a rush, never looking away from the bindles. "Some old Jap took the sword. Tried to kill me."

I doubted it. That old man had known exactly what he was doing. If he had wanted Carlton dead, Carlton would have come to Harborview DOA.

"An old man, huh? What's his name?" I asked.

"Dunno."

"Bullshit." I pulled the matchbook farther back. "You expect me to believe someone just walked by and decided to grab the sword from you?"

"I didn't say that. Just said I dunno who done it," Carlton said.

There was a definite whine to his voice, and beneath that a dope hunger that made him forget he was afraid of Oshima. But not of me. I held the keys to the magic kingdom.

"Tell me all of it," I said. "And I mean *all* of it."

Carlton looked at the matchbook, licked his lips painfully, and began talking fast, telling the truth because he didn't have the brains or strength right then to lie.

"Old dude stopped me on the street one day like he knew me," Carlton said. "He handed me half a C-note and told me to meet him that night in the Underground if I wanted the other half."

"Keep talking."

"I went. Guy said he'd give me a grand if I got the sword for him."

"When was that?"

"A week, ten days ago."

"And he already knew about the sword?"

"Yeah. Called it a funny name." Carlton frowned. "The Thousand-Year Sword. That dude was a real flake."

"How did you know what sword he meant?"

"Oshima had it a while."

"When?" I asked.

"Dunno. Month. Maybe more. Can't remember."

"Did Oshima think the sword was worth a lot then?"

"Nah. A few weeks ago he started getting calls from Japan." Carlton smiled, cracking one of the scabs on his lips. "Oshima was pissed off."

"Why?"

"He'd given the sword back already. It belonged to some dude from Malahat."

"Did the old Japanese ever tell you how he found out about the sword?"

Carlton shook his head, grimaced with pain, and said, "He don't speak English too good. Didn't have much to say. Just wanted the sword."

"What did he offer?"

"A grand. Gave me a number to call if I got the sword. I called right after Tara woke me up this morning. The old man called back a few minutes later."

"Go on," I said, pulling the matchbook back just a bit. "I want all of it."

Carlton's dry, coated tongue went futilely over his lips. I thought he was going to get mulish on me, but his reluctance melted at the sight of the dope.

"He told me to get the sword and meet him down on Yesler," Carlton said painfully.

"And then you tried to hold him up for more money."

The quick shift of Carlton's good eye told me I was right. An easy guess. This was a kid who wasn't bright enough to be a good crook. He probably never even realized I had stiffed him with a piece of bent rebar.

"You gonna tell Oshima?" he asked.

"Maybe. How long will you be in here?"

"Three days." Carlton licked his lips and looked at the bindles again. "I'm still so dizzy I can't stand up."

"What number did the old man give you?"

"It's in my jeans."

I went through the steel locker where Carlton's belongings had been stashed. His clothes were so bad the staff had put them in a garbage bag. After a few tries I found a grubby bit of paper with a number on it.

"This it?" I asked, going back to the bed.

"Yeah."

"How long did it take for him to call you back?"

" 'Bout five minutes. Funny, though. It sounded the same."

"What did?" I asked.

"The noise."

"In the background?"

"Yeah."

"If Oshima comes here, you never saw me."

Carlton nodded.

I put the matchbook by his pillow, tossed the cigarettes on the bedside table, and left.

The nearest pay phone was in the hospital lobby. The calling card worked just fine, but Benny's connection was a machine.

"Rack off, mate. I'm out. If it's an emergency, try the Beach Ball. If it's the fair lady with bad taste in men, wait for the tone and speak to me."

I waited for the tone.

"Nice try, Benny, but the fair lady is too busy to kiss any long-distance frogs." I read off the phone number from Carlton's jeans and asked Benny to match it to an address. I left Nakamichi's condo as my call-back number.

For a while I cruised the district around Oshima's gallery, hoping to pick up the old man. Nothing doing. I quartered the Underground. Nobody home but tourists. Finally I gave up and went back to the condo.

Fiora was already there. She had changed into light cotton sweats and was sitting on the couch in the twilight, counting the lighted windows in the White building. She had a glass of the Washington chardonnay, so flinty she had had to put ice in it. I tried the wine and decided on beer.

A platter next to Fiora held the rest of the cheddar, some cold prawns, a chub of summer sausage, crackers, mustard, and a mound of sliced bell peppers. It was hard to tell about the peppers, but the rest of the food looked untouched.

Fiora said hello when I walked in, but she wasn't really there. I had seen her like this before, when she was juggling too many things and dancing on oiled marbles at the same time.

I drank the beer for my thirst, then poured another glass of wine and cut a chunk of sausage. The garlic was so pungent I cut a second slice and offered it to Fiora as prophylaxis. She took it without looking away from the urban view. Way off in the gloaming, almost hidden by the Kingdome, was the pale pink cone of Mount Rainier.

I sat down and put away a few more rounds of sausage. When I started crunching on the fragrant golden bell peppers, Fiora slid over and elbowed my bicep, a sign she wanted in. I put my arm across her shoulders and she snuggled close.

"So how's it going?" I asked after she finished counting the lighted windows.

"Don't ask. How about you?"

"Let's put it this way. Michael Innes sends greetings."

That got Fiora's full attention. "How did the FBI get involved in this?"

"Rory's sword is a Japanese national treasure."

She looked at me. "Tell me you're joking."

"Nope. You've convinced me that it's a waste of time to lie to a Scots witch."

"I'm listening."

And she was. That's the amazing thing about Fiora. She has the kind of concentration that can make mountains get up and walk. I told her what I'd done, and she summarized the results in one sentence.

"In other words, you're still on your belly hunting rattlesnakes bare-handed in the dark."

"I prefer to think of it as investigating," I said.

For a moment I tried to balance the wineglass on my knee so I could reach for a piece of cheddar and a cracker without letting go of Fiora. She read my mind, made two cracker sandwiches out of cheese, sausage, and Dijon, and fed me one of them.

"Did Benny call?" I asked when my mouth was empty enough.

"No. Was he supposed to?"

"I wanted him to crisscross the old ninja's phone number and get me an address."

"You really think that old man killed Rory?"

I shrugged. "He's a player. I'm just trying to figure where he fits on the scorecard."

"Call Benny again," she said. "He'll pick up your second call."

"Doubt it. He's probably checking out the wheelchair access at the Beach Ball."

"Dear God, not again."

The Beach Ball is the only rough bar in Newport Beach. A waterfront dive a block north of the Newport pier, it has steadfastly refused to be gentrified.

Benny shouldn't drink to excess in any bar. He doesn't do it well, which he blames on his spinal-cord injury. Normally, Benny acknowledges his limitations, sticks to a few beers, and avoids places like the Ball, where abalone hunters with wicked curved knives wrestle regular tag-team matches against ex-Navy SEALs who teach diving to the rich and uncoordinated.

When Benny goes to the Ball, though, he knows exactly what he's getting into. He rolls around like a loose cannon, picking fights with the bouncers or the bartenders, usually by testing the bar's compliance with wheelchair-access regulations. If the ramps are stacked with cases of empty long-necks, he breaks them. If the rest-room stall doors aren't wide enough, he breaks those, too.

In other words, Benny goes to the Beach Ball when he's feeling lonesome.

"I should have left Kwame with him," Fiora said.

"That dog doesn't need any more lessons in how to drink beer from a bottle."

Fiora ate another strip of pepper, sighed, and muttered, "Where *is* the damn sword?"

"I'll never tell."

"Neither will I," she retorted.

"I know."

"What's that supposed to mean?"

"Simple. I know you won't tell because you don't know."

She gave me the kind of look I gave Kwame's dead raccoon.

"It's for your own good," I said. "This way you can look the FBI and the State Department right in the eye and tell them you are blissfully unaware. Then you'll be free to go out and hire a lawyer for me when a federal judge orders me to turn the sword over and I refuse."

"Will it come to that?"

"Wouldn't surprise me. Everything else about this has gone from sugar to shit. What about your deal?"

"It's gone through a color shift too."

"What happened?"

Fiora didn't answer.

I pulled her a little closer. The warmth of her body came through the cotton. So did the tension in the bunched muscles of her neck and shoulders.

"What are you going to do?" I asked.

She shrugged. "I was thinking about the New

York sharks Nakamichi preempted a few weeks ago. I could probably revive the deal."

"They'd know Nakamichi washed out," I said. "You'd take a beating."

She shrugged again.

I put the wineglass on the table and then shifted Fiora around so I could work on her neck. It was a good neck, just too damned tight. I worked for a while with a light touch, then started applying the Thumbs of Death.

It took me fifteen minutes to break the tension: a new record, and not one I'd been after. Whatever had happened at Nakamichi's office had gone clear to the bone with Fiora.

"Honey?" I asked. "Do you want to talk about it?"

"Not yet."

Her tone said, *Not ever.*

SIXTEEN

Fiora was still asleep when I pulled on my running clothes and jogged down to the vest-pocket park at the end of the market. I could see the *Princess Marguerite* on the waterfront, but Sammy was nowhere in sight. I did turns around the block to keep a sweat, half convinced I was on a fool's errand. I was wrong.

Sammy turned up at 7:29 wearing clean clothes and carrying a fistful of receipts. We walked down to the waterfront. I bought him a ticket, gave him another twenty for the up-island bus, and got off the ferry just as the big engines were beginning to turn over. I made the run back to the condo as though it were all downhill.

After a fast shower, I called Benny's number. Still no answer, but it only took four rings for the machine to kick in.

"Not this time, Benny," I muttered, punching in the access code that overrode the message. "Yo, home boy!" I yelled into the phone. "Wakey, wakey!"

There was a loud noise, the clattering of a dropped receiver, and the kind of language the FCC doesn't like to hear on telephone lines.

"Aw, does Benny have a hangover?" I asked.

He switched to Urdu, which told me he was really hurting.

"No sympathy here," I said. "Anyone who takes on a load and goes out to play Wheeled Avenger with the boys at the Beach Ball deserves whatever happens to him."

"I hadn't been in the Beach Ball for almost six months," Benny muttered. "They were due for inspection. And tonight I'm going to go back and see if they cleared up their violations."

"You want to come up and go fishing instead?"

"Sod it all, I can't," he grumbled. "Got this job that has to go out by the end of next week."

"It must be awful to have to work for a living."

"Not work, boyo. This is a freebie and a pure pleasure."

"Freebie, huh?" I asked, impressed. Benny only does freebies for friends, and he has damn few of those.

"Yeah. Some guys I know from the Middle East need a miniaturized radio beacon, something that can be tuned to the frequencies of smart bombs."

"Sound like somebody has compromised Saddam Hussein's bootmaker."

Benny chuckled maliciously. "Always trying to leave the world a better place than I found it, mate."

"So am I."

"Would an address on that phone number help the process?" he asked.

"I hope so."

Benny read me an address somewhere between the Kingdome and the freeway.

"It's a pay phone," he said. "I can get you a list of recent toll calls on it, if you want. My pals in the security office don't mind invading the privacy of a public phone. It's sort of like defending the honor of the village whore."

"If I need it, I'll get back to you," I said. "In the meantime, get Saddam's ham radio done."

"How is Fiora's deal going?"

"Don't ask."

"Then don't piss me off."

Benny meant it. He thinks one of his primary purposes in life is to make sure I take good care of my ex-wife.

"As she so delicately put it, the Nakamichi deal has undergone a color shift."

"White to brown?"

"Yeah."

"How's she taking it?"

"She's thinking."

"Bloody hell. I'll be up there real quick."

"You do that. If she gets the bit in her teeth, it'll take both of us to get it back."

I hung up, left Fiora a note, and headed for Seattle's International District. It was just behind the part of the city where the Kingdome squats like an overturned soup plate. Not exactly the high-rolling end of town.

No surprise. Seattle doesn't have a great record on race relations. Labor organizers and jingoists

forcibly expelled the city's entire Chinese popula-
tion in 1886. In 1941, thousands of Japanese were
packed up and shipped to Idaho and Manzanar.
Filipinos have always provided the skilled labor for
the fish-canning industry, but they've never been
integrated into the city's power structure. Everybody who isn't Northern European still tends to get
shunted off into the International District up behind the Kingdome.

On the street I stood out like a piece of popcorn
in a bowl of peanuts. The phone number came
back to a storefront a block west of Interstate 5.
The faded gold-leaf lettering on the heavily soaped
window said the place had once been an Italian
grocery. Now a hand-painted sign said it was a club
for the practice of ken-jutsu and iai-jutsu.

Swordplay.

The place looked deserted, but the sound of atonal Asian music came from somewhere inside. I
crossed the street to a Korean market. There was a
public phone in the parking lot. From there, I
could watch the club.

An Asian answered in what I assumed to be Japanese.

"I'm from Carlton," I said. "I want to talk to the
old man."

The Asian tried to make me think I had a wrong
number.

"Get the old man," I repeated. "I'll call back in
five minutes."

I walked into the market and pretended to shop
for white rice.

Thirty seconds later, a teenager in loose white
cotton trousers and a belted judo jacket trotted out

the front door of the club and headed next door.
He went up a wooden outside stairway to the second floor and disappeared. A minute later the boy
reappeared and trotted down the stairs.

Thirty seconds after that, the old man came out.
He moved slowly but with a certain odd flat-footed
grace, the gait of a man used to walking barefoot
on rice mats. He was dressed in a shapeless black
suit and wore a white shirt buttoned to the throat.
He had straw sandals and white socks on his feet,
as another old man would have worn house slippers.

I let him get inside the club before I left the market and crossed the street. The entryway of the
club smelled old and damp, like the street. I
couldn't see around the screens that were just inside the door.

The door of the old Victorian building was heavy
but well oiled. I opened it slowly, slipped inside,
and closed it as softly as I could. The brass latch
worked as soundlessly as the day it was installed. I
unzipped my windbreaker, reached around to the
small of my back, and drew Uncle Jake's .45. As I
did, I remembered why I'd brought it north in the
first place. I had wanted Rory to polish the action
on it. Even Benny couldn't equal Rory's fine touch
with old weapons. Now that deft skill was gone, a
small loss among the many huge losses.

I took the chain flail from my pocket with my
right hand and looked around the screen into the
main room of the club. Two middle-aged Asians
were working out silently with long wooden staves
before a wall of mirrors. The staves were curved to
mimic the shape of swords like the one I had left in

the pawnbroker's vault. Each man judged his own technique in the mirror as he drew and parried and cut school figures in slow motion. The wooden swords moved like extensions of their bodies.

The stout old man stood beside the pay phone on the back wall, lost in his own thoughts. In repose, his face was hard and expressionless, but the skin of his jowls had begun to sag with age, and there were deep dark pouches under his eyes.

Despite its cheap construction, the flail had great balance. It would have landed where I threw it—at the old man's feet—had he not reached out and caught it in a flashing movement that reminded me of how I had gotten the bruises on my midsection and leg.

The old man's eyes cut to me like black marbles. He was neither surprised nor worried by my presence.

"You left that behind," I said as I stepped out from the screen's concealment.

The two men caught my movement in the mirror. It ruined their concentration. They spun and moved apart fast, opening a bigger space between them. They stared at me over the points of their workout weapons. Whether or not they had ever drawn blood, they would be formidable opponents.

I showed them my weapon of choice. They didn't back up.

"Tell them to join the twentieth century or get buried with the nineteenth," I said.

The old man said something in Japanese.

The two swordsmen glared at me a moment longer. Then, like well-programmed robots, they lowered their swords, bowed, and stepped backward. An instant later they marched off the mats, weapons in trail position, and disappeared into the dressing room.

The old man moved away from the phone and put his arms to his side. With a practiced twist of his wrist, he dropped the loose chain and let it hang from between the weights. He shook the chain gently to straighten it out, then picked it up with another flick of his wrist. The entire weapon disappeared into his hand, as though it had never existed.

"Clever," I said, "but not bulletproof."

He shook his head. "Clever is you to find me."

"Carlton made it easy," I said. "But then, you know how easy Carlton is, don't you?"

The old man nodded. He had what martial artists call restless eyes. Most men would have been riveted by the gun, but his glance traveled the room, touched my face, watched the middle of my chest and the bunched muscles of my arm. His eyes were like those of a hunting cat, everywhere at once, fearless. The mind behind the eyes was equally poised. He was perhaps the most dangerous man I've ever faced, precisely because he had no fear of death.

"I'm here to talk," I said, but I didn't put the gun away. It's my natural weapon, just as the flail seemed to be his.

"So," he said. "We talk."

He slipped the flail into a coat pocket, took the coat off, and hung it on a hook. He showed me his empty hands, then stepped out of his sandals and onto the mat in his stocking feet. He moved across the straw mats to a sword rest made of wood on the other side of the room.

"Yes?" he asked.

I nodded and flicked on the safety.

He knelt, lifted the metal sword from its cradle, and turned back toward me. His face was composed and his eyes were no longer as predatory. I followed him onto the mat, the pistol still in my hand.

"Know you much swords?" he asked.

"Enlighten me," I said. "I'm particularly interested in the one called the Thousand-Year Sword."

He looked at me for a moment, but his face betrayed no reaction. He shuffled onto the mat, caught up in the repetition of a familiar ceremony. When he reached the center, he broke his motion and looked at me.

"How you learn that name?"

I said nothing.

A flicker of a smile crossed his face. "Cairns," he said.

I still said nothing. You learn a lot more by listening.

"You are police?"

"No, but I could get a cop if you like. We have all flavors available, from local sheriffs to Seattle police and right on up to the FBI. I could even dredge up an immigration service investigator. I'll bet carrying a concealed weapon like your chain could get you deported."

"An old man's toy, nothing more," he said. He showed me the steel blade. "This is deadly weapon, if man has will."

He hitched the loose legs of his trousers, then

knelt slowly with the sword in his left hand, the edge toward himself. With slow, studied movements that seemed natural only because he understood them so well, he took the sword in both hands, held it perpendicular to the mat at chest height, and bowed over it.

"Come," he said. "Serious man must understand the blade. Is maker of civilization."

"Maybe at one time," I said, "but not anymore." I looked at the pistol that was still in my hand.

"Barbarian use gun," he said, but there was a faint self-mocking smile on his face.

"Barbarians won the last war," I pointed out.

His smile lost its self-mocking aspect. "War not over. Sword still sharp. Listen."

SEVENTEEN

Before I could ask a question, the old man withdrew into himself, gathering his thoughts, seeking the inner zone of his being. Without warning he tested the balance of the blade, using a long, graceful, one-handed slash that would have disemboweled an opponent. As he finished, he took the hilt in both hands, raised the weapon, and flicked the tip downward, pointing it toward the mat as he spoke.

"Thousand motions with sword. Each of twelve parts. That one is *chiburi*. Removes blood from blade."

His face was grave. Stylized violence was his religion, and he was an ardent disciple. Standing next to him, I suddenly felt clumsy with the gun in my hand. Perhaps the charisma of his ritual was intended to disarm me. Fiora tells me it's the greatest weakness of half the human race: the male fascination with ritual and violence, hierarchy and uniforms, the craving to be certain that you belong somewhere in the universe, on the masculine totem pole above some and below others.

In front of me, the old Japanese samurai executed a series of sweeping parries, hard thrusts, sharp cuts, and even a blow delivered with the end of the hilt. Each movement had its own foot and hand positions. Each had a prescribed breathing pattern. He concentrated like a ballet dancer at the barre. His eyes were closed, as though he were admiring the elegance of the perfect movement he could see in his mind, even as his arthritic feet and aging arms betrayed him.

I understood such concentration. I had always been able to hear Beethoven perfectly in my mind, even when my imperfect hands drove the violin's bow and fingered the strings.

Watching, I wondered how many times the old man had repeated this ritual. Too many to count, from the look of it. I knew a card mechanic who practiced five hours a day, five days a week, just to stay sharp. When he turned forty, he added an extra hour a day, just to compensate for the loss of his youth. He and the old Japanese samurai probably would have gotten along, each dedicated to a single one of all the many possibilities in life.

For a time the room was silent but for the soft whisper of sock feet on the mat and the faint Asian music in the back room. As I watched, I saw Roniko Call-me-Ron Nakamichi, flicking shells off prawns with precisely the same motions for each one. The Japanese turn everything into ceremony —business, tea, poetry, even violence. Repetition and ritual, individual safety ensured through loss of individuality.

Americans aren't much good at ritual and loss of self. We would rather discover a new and therefore better way to do things. Our way. Or, more precisely, *my* way. The miracle is that all the millions of *my* ways manage to hang together well enough for us to run a country.

From Japan's adhesion to tradition, its single-minded insularity, came great national strength . . . up to a point. From America's abhorrence of ritual, its single-minded individuality, came great national strength . . . up to a point.

One of the great shouldering matches of the twenty-first century will be Japanese ceremony against American chaos. The countries of the Pacific Rim are already watching the action build, taking bets, buying in on the sly, hoping to guess whether in the long run the island nation's insularity of thought will prove a better world model than the anything-goes mentality of the frontier nation that went farther faster than any other country in history.

The old Japanese swordsman wouldn't be around to see the end of the match, but he would be there in spirit, slicing the air with graceful rituals, preparing himself for a kind of war that hasn't been fought since the invention of guns.

After a few minutes, the old man concluded the fencing match against his invisible and perfect enemy. He bowed over his sword and stepped back. His eyes came open. He was calm, purged of whatever anger had driven him to step onto the mat and take up the ritual of violence and renewal.

Then he focused on me and remembered who he was and who I was and the Thousand-Year Sword that lay between us. He sheathed his sword and offered it to me, turning the edge toward himself as thought to demonstrate his peaceful intent.

"I am Eto," he said.

He waited as though he expected me to recognize the name. I looked at the sword without reaching for it. To take the sword would have required laying aside the pistol.

Eto smiled. "If I meant you pain, it would have come yesterday."

He was right. He probably could have killed me. For damn sure he could have made a better effort at it.

I nodded, slipped out of my windbreaker, and wrapped it around Uncle Jake's gun. I put the odd package on the floor just off the mat.

Mirroring Eto's posture, I reached for the sword with my right hand. Eto shifted it just out of my reach and looked at me disapprovingly.

"Insult? Threat?" he asked.

"I don't understand."

He grunted and pointed to my right hand. "Hand to fight. Hand to kill."

It took me a moment. "Strong hand or weak hand, that's what we call them. My left is my strong hand," I said.

He looked at the gun I had held in my left hand, bowed slightly in unspoken apology, then offered me the sword again. I took it in my right hand. Automatically I turned the edge toward myself, mirroring his care. He nodded his approval.

"Good," he said. "No edge, no insult."

"I learned to pass an open knife in the Boy Scouts," I said dryly.

If Eto knew about the Boy Scouts, he didn't say. Looking at my left hand he shook his head.

"Bad," he said.

"Don't bother trying to retrain me. People have been working at it all my life. No one has succeeded."

Eto grunted and guided me in the proper way to handle the sword. Under his light yet surprisingly powerful touch, the sword came to my right side, blade uppermost.

"Carry so," he said.

He took my right hand and wrapped it around the scabbard. "*Saya.*"

"*Saya,*" I repeated, trying the unfamiliar word.

"Hold all time. So."

I nodded.

He took my right thumb and curled it around the guard, to hold the sword in place. "*Tsuba,*" he said, tracing the guard as he spoke.

"*Tsuba,*" I repeated.

He grunted. Then he pushed my thumb outward. Instantly the blade came free from its seat in the scabbard.

Tradition and ritual have value. As I followed the old man's instruction, I discovered that the sword became easier to handle. After a few minutes it seemed quite natural at my right side. The awkwardness disappeared.

I slipped my thumb beneath the guard and lifted. The sword sprang from the sheath easily, like a well-oiled door latch. I drew it with my left hand and laid the scabbard aside. Curious, I tested the edge of the blade. Sharp enough, but nothing special.

"*Showa,*" the old man said, disdain in his tone. "Inferior."

"Not the Thousand-Year Sword," I agreed.

The sinuous temper line on the blade was faint and irregular, artless. I tested the sword's balance. The tip of the blade seemed heavy by comparison with Rory's sword. There was the same difference between a handmade split bamboo fly rod and a $23.95 fiberglass K mart special.

"Less edge," I said, "less balance, less everything."

Eto nodded curtly. "Machine make."

"*Showa* junk." I had heard the phrase from Oshima.

He grunted agreement. "Listen."

I nodded.

He touched the edge of the blade and said, "*Ha.*" Then he touched the back—"*mune*"—and the edge of the slanted tip—"*fukusa*"—and the back of the tip—"*kissaki.*"

The distinctions were small, the names utterly foreign. Eto drew an old warrior's pleasure from reciting them. Such men are materialists; they take their meanings, even their spirituality, from the objects of their craft. Rory had been like that. Benny is like that. I suppose I am that way myself. I need to know the name of an object and its proper use.

"*Katana,*" Eto said, indicating the whole blade.

"Why is it curved?"

He frowned, searching for the English word. "Forge. Forge bend."

"You mean the blade bends naturally while it is being forged?"

"Yes. Listen."

He ran his fingertip very lightly across the length of the edge, then stopped about seven inches from the tip.

"Monouchi." He hesitated. "Most death, here."

I looked at the part of the sword that killed most easily and nodded.

"Hamon," he said, indicating the cloud pattern that ran from tip to hilt. "Hard meet soft."

"The temper line," I said, looking at the place where two very different metals had been joined, the soft flexibility of iron mated with the hard brittleness of steel, each reinforcing and enhancing the best of the other.

"Man make good *hamon.* Machine cannot."

I nodded to show I understood that a fine *hamon* came only with handmade swords.

"Spirit here," he continued, touching the *hamon.* "Thousand-Year Sword is storm. Muramasa spirit is storm. Sameness."

"Muramasa made Rory's sword?"

Eto nodded. "Men say Muramasa mad."

"Was he?"

"No. He . . . knew blade. Death bring. Life bring. Storm. Sameness. All one."

I looked at him, inviting further explanation.

Eto smiled grimly. "Know you samurai?"

"I read Mishima's commentary on the samurai, long ago, after he staged his publicity stunt."

"No stunt. Mishima die."

I shrugged. "Then I guess I don't understand the mythic content of public suicide."

"Samurai code. You know?"

I started rummaging in my memory. I had known the code once, when such things had mattered to me, before Jake died and I threw my violin under the wheels of a passing Corvette.

"Samurai," Eto said slowly, choosing words from another language, another culture, alien sounds trying to describe that which was closer than life to him. "Samurai . . . death . . . must know. All time."

The halting words triggered a flood of memories in me. "'One who is samurai,'" I said, remembering Mishima and youth and pain, "'must before all things keep constantly in mind the fact that he has to die.'"

Eto nodded urgently. "Yes. Samurai duty is die. Sword duty is kill. Muramasa know. Forge blade . . . eager. Hungry."

"As eager for blood as a good samurai is for death."

"Yes!" Eto said explosively, nodding hard.

"But a good soldier lives to preserve peace, not to shed blood," I said. "Even in Japan."

"Death bring. Life bring." Eto touched the elusive, seething cloud line. *"Hamon."*

Abruptly Eto adjusted the position of my hands on the hilt, making me open my grip. The sword's balance improved ten times over, surprising me.

"What is Muramasa's curse, the one he supposedly built into the blade of his swords?" I asked.

Eto held up a finger. "One samurai. One death. Each time. All time."

I sorted it out with what Rory had told me.

"Each man who gets the sword has to feed it at least one person?"

Eto frowned, which told me I was missing some nuances. Then he shrugged, telling me my words were like *showa* swords—close enough, but not really sharp.

"And if you don't feed the blade, it kills you?" I asked, not bothering to hide my lack of belief.

Again, Eto grappled with English. "No feed sword, you no eat. Family no eat."

"You're saying that if I don't feed the sword, I starve to death and so does my family?"

He nodded vigorously. "Sword mine. Curse mine. You safe."

"But only if I give you the sword, right?"

Again he nodded.

"No sale," I said. "I'll keep the sword, and the curse."

"No!"

Eto burst into Japanese, realized he was getting nowhere with me, and switched to an English that was all the more urgent for its difficulty.

"Three sons. Me. All die before twenty year."

Eto looked away as though to hide his pain, then looked back at me. His eyes were as bleak as the sea under a cloudy sky.

"New son. Three year he live." He pointed a long wavering finger at himself. "Sword must have. Son not die!"

There was an aged father's madness in Eto's eyes; Abraham would have looked that way the day God asked him to sacrifice Isaac.

"Rory once told me about a man called Eto," I said. "He told me Eto was the warden of his camp, a war criminal, a butcher who tested his swords on Allied prisoners. Is that how the brave samurai owner of the Thousand-Year Sword avoided the curse?"

For an instant Eto's eyes burned with a young man's rage. "Father not criminal. Kill criminal, yes. Was law in camps."

"So that's how your father avoided the curse."

"No! Muramasa blade not use. *Showa* blade."

I raised my left eyebrow. "The blade demands not only blood but an honorable killing?"

Eto nodded.

I shrugged. "Fine. Then the curse should be on your father, not you."

"He die."

"And you inherited the sword."

"Yes. No." Eto made a frustrated sound. "Cairns take blade August six."

I thought for a moment, then felt the hair on my arms stir. "Hiroshima."

"Yes. War over. Parent choose seppuku. I stand behind, Muramasa blade ready, to finish kill."

"Wait."

I tried to shake off the eerie chill in my gut but could not. I had read about ritual suicide of the type Mishima committed. The suicide disembowels himself, inflicting a fatal wound with a short sword. But death most often comes at the hands of a second, who administers a quick coup de grâce with a long sword.

Eto had been appointed to deliver the coup de grâce to his own father.

"Did you do it?" I asked.

"No. Cairns break ritual. Take Muramasa. Parent

die bad. Plead for sword. Cairns listen. He refuse. He go. Take sword."

"Then wouldn't the curse be on Rory?"

"Muramasa mine. Curse mine. All time."

As he spoke, Eto's face sagged, showing his age. He was old and tired, worn out in ways that Rory had never been. Whether I believed in the curse or not, Eto did. It had ruled and ruined his life. I could see it in the tortured expression on his face and the tension in his body.

I thought about Rory. He had believed in the curse too. He had killed on the way out of the prison camp, and he had killed with the Muramasa blade. Then I thought about the sword's present owner.

Me. I wasn't ready to regard the weapon as cursed, but it had hardly been what you could call a blessing.

"It's difficult for me to believe in curses," I said finally. "There are too many other, simpler, explanations for evil."

"Believe. No believe." Eto shrugged. "Die same. Sword kill."

"The man who killed Rory will die sooner than most," I said flatly, "and to hell with any other curse."

Eto's eyes narrowed to black slits. "Eto no kill Cairns."

"Not even to save your fourth son's life?"

"No."

"If I kill you, will the curse pass on to your son?"

He thought it over and then smiled like a man finding the silver lining in a lifelong cloud. "No."

Cold pricked my spine.

"Curse go you, not he," Eto said. "Want revenge, you, yes?"

"Yes. I want to avenge Rory's death."

"So. Know you story, Forty-Seven Ronin?"

"No."

"Learn. Then give sword Eto."

He bowed, turned his back on me, and shuffled away. His white cotton socks made soft whispering noises on the straw mat.

eIGHTEEN

The elevator in Ron's building was stuck on the penthouse level. It was the proper cap on a wasted morning. I watched the indicator panel for three minutes, then used the lobby key to get into the stairwell. I could hear someone on the stairs far above me, heading up. It must have been Fiora, although I didn't realize it at the time. The eleventh-floor door slammed behind her while I was still on five.

I heard Fiora's scream when I was between ten and eleven. The scream was followed by a thumping, smashing sound.

A woman's scream is a powerful weapon. Fiora has developed a high-C shriek that sounds like a cross between tearing canvas and a turbocharged Formula One engine dialed to full boost. She lets anger, not fear, propel the scream. Fear tightens the vocal cords. Often as not, a frightened scream comes out as a peep. Anger triples the volume and quadruples the effect.

This scream was a corker, full-throated and ripping with rage. It worked, too. I came headlong out of the stairwell, Uncle Jake's .45 in my hand. To hell with style and ritual. When it comes to off-the-cuff mayhem, give me a good old-fashioned pistol anytime.

The atrium was filled with hard, white sunlight. The elevator door stood open. I ducked left, going one way around an air-conditioning shaft. Had I ducked the other way, I would have run headlong into the intruder. As it was, I got Fiora.

She stood in the doorway amid the ruins of a huge Chinese vase and pointed toward the other side of the shaft housing.

"Get him!" she said.

"You okay?"

"Yes! Get the bastard!"

"Gun?" I asked as I turned away.

"No." Then, "I don't know. Don't go. He could be armed."

"Get inside," I said. "Move!"

I ducked around the corner of the shaft housing. The open courtyard had been turned into a Japanese garden, complete with a gravel ocean and islands of boulders overgrown with carefully trimmed bonsai trees and ferns. The visual impression was disconcerting, like being thrown out of an airplane at ten thousand feet. I covered the garden with the muzzle of the gun, then examined each island big enough to hide a man.

It took too much time. I heard a faint metallic jingle from inside the elevator car, then a distant mechanical sigh. I dove past the far corner of the shaft housing just in time to see the doors of the elevator begin to shut.

An Asian in jeans and a long-tailed shirt flashed me a "Sayonara, sucker" grin and a single upraised finger. The grin died when he saw the pistol.

I could have fired, but with my luck I'd have hit him. In most states it's manslaughter to kill a burglar if he shows you his back. The law makes no allowances for the insult of his middle finger. As I cursed the rules of engagement of modern urban life, the smooth, stainless-steel doors slid shut and the intruder was gone.

The elevator was an express model. It would be in the downstairs lobby before I could run a half flight of stairs. So I did the next best thing: I watched through the window beside the elevator door. Eleven stories below, I caught a glimpse of the intruder as he left the lobby of the building, turned right, and went up Western Avenue. He disappeared among the concrete columns that supported the viaduct.

For once, Fiora had listened to me. The front door of the apartment was closed and locked. I rapped gently.

"It's me," I said.

The small round glass fish-eye of the peephole went dark as she studied me through it. I heard the dead bolt snap.

Fiora isn't fearless but she is calm under threat. Any woman who has lived alone learns to ration her fears, to stave them off until it's safe to let go. When Fiora saw me, she decided it was safe. She threw the door open and stood there, her face pale and her hands trembling.

"That didn't take long," she said. "What happened?"

"I think he heard his uncle calling," I said.

I kicked my way in through the bright shards of vase.

She gave me a distracted look. "Well, your timing is still great. I'm beginning to think you must lurk in the shrubs waiting for me to get into trouble."

"Don't tempt me. What happened?"

"I went over to Nakamichi Securities. It didn't go well, so I came back here to make some phone calls."

While Fiora talked, we went down the hallway into the bedroom. The place had been well and truly trashed. Blankets and pillows were strewn about, dresser doors and drawers were jerked open and left that way, and the mattress was askew.

"When I saw the elevator was stuck up here," Fiora said, "I took the stairs. I let myself into the apartment, dropped my purse on the sofa, and walked into the kitchen to get a glass of water. He must have been in the bedroom. I heard a noise; then I heard the front door latch. I had thrown the dead bolt, which slowed him down. He was fumbling with it when I came back into the hallway."

"Did he make a grab at you?"

She shook her head. "I started screaming, grabbed the vase in the hall, and slung it at him."

I blinked. The vase had been nearly four feet tall. Adrenaline, the overlooked, underappreciated wonder drug. From the size of the shards, the vase had been thrown with great force.

I glanced around the bedroom again. It was a shambles, yes, but an oddly orderly shambles. No hiding place smaller than the Thousand-Year Sword had been searched.

When I looked back to Fiora, her color was going from pale to paler. I took her in my arms and held her. After a few moments, the tremors began. Several shivers later she wrapped her arms around my middle and hung on tight. She's a tactile creature. She needs the closeness of another body. I always encourage that particular response. It makes me feel good too.

"I'm okay," Fiora said, her voice muffled against my chest. She pulled back and gave me a wobbly little smile. "I just don't like strangers invading my life like that."

I kissed her, released her, and went back to the front door. There were no scratches on the shiny brass faceplate of the dead bolt. It hadn't been worked over by a rake-and-pick artist, unless the guy was unbelievably good. That meant he had a key of some kind.

I sensed Fiora coming up behind me.

"Was the elevator on this floor when you got here?" I asked.

Fiora thought a moment, then nodded. "The doors were open."

"He had an elevator key too," I said.

"How do you know?"

"It's the only way to get the car to stay put without triggering the alarm."

"Then it was somebody from the building?" Fiora asked.

"Not necessarily. Lots of people have elevator keys. Custodians, the fire department, maybe even the local beat cop. Intelligence cops have keys, too. Black-bag guys."

Fiora blinked and asked instantly, "FBI?"

"Probably."

"I thought Hoover was dead," she muttered.

"He didn't invent dirty tricks, and they didn't die with him," I pointed out. "Claherty is a savvy guy. He has to prove I'm lying about the sword being stolen. He's not above having one of his Asian agents do a cold prowl for it."

Fiora's eyes narrowed angrily.

"It might even have been another of Oshima's pals," I added, "or one of Eto's. That's the problem. Too many players."

"Who's Eto?"

We went back to the bedroom and put things together while I told her how I had spent the morning. I expurgated the story a bit because Fiora's fey Scots nature predisposes her to worry about curses.

"Then there's always good old Call-me-Ron Nakamichi," I added.

Fiora flinched subtly, studied the Isfahan carpet on the floor, and said not one word.

"What happened to the deal?" I asked calmly. "Did Ron want the sword thrown in?"

Her shoulders were rounded and her arms were folded stiffly across her breasts. She wouldn't meet my eyes. Her entire body radiated deep anger and bulldog resistance. She was well and truly bunkered in.

"I'd be surprised if he didn't," I said. "If the sword is important enough to interest the Ministry for Culture, there would probably be a lot of positive press for Nakamichi if he got his hands on it."

Fiora said nothing.

"Look at the Mitsubishi thing," I continued. "They drag home a Renoir, and Japan goes nuts. Imagine how much fun it would be to bring home not some western painting but a genuine Japanese national treasure."

I could have been talking to myself. When Fiora finally looked at me, her face was so expressionless it almost broke my heart. Misery flashed in her eyes, reflected by the tears that glittered and clung to her lower lids.

It was one of those times I'd much rather have been wrong than right. I thought of Rory, dead in ambush. The Muramasa sword was the only thing I had to lure his murderer into the light. Without that sword, Rory's killer was free and the world was the worse for it in some small but meaningful way.

Then I thought of Fiora, with her dream of making the world a better place for the people who weren't born with her brains, skill, and drive. Perhaps the Nakamichi deal and its University of Tokyo chair was a small thing, but if it freed just one woman to blaze a trail for another woman, then the world would be better in a small but real way.

I couldn't say which way might be better in the long run. I might possibly find another way to

Rory's killer. I doubted that Fiora would ever find another way past Japan's tempered steel façade.

"Give Ron the sword," I said.

"No. I'd never ask that of you."

"I know you wouldn't. Give it to him. The sword won't bring Rory back."

"No one thought it would." Fiora unwrapped her arms and brushed her fingertip over my mustache. "It's all right. The Nakamichi deal is off."

"What?"

"I told Ron the sword won't be part of it."

"Tell him you changed your mind," I said.

"No. He withdrew his offer in its entirety. It won't be reinstated, with or without the sword. The deal is as dead as Rory."

Fiora's arms locked over her breasts again. The shutter came down behind her eyes, telling me she was thinking hard and she didn't like her thoughts. Her eyes were turned to the carpet again so I wouldn't see her pain. I put my arms all the way around her rigid body and drew her close. After a moment she leaned against me, her forehead on my chest like a rock.

"Let me call Ron," I said.

"No. It's over, finished. DOA."

I tried another angle. "What are you going to do?"

"I've been on the phone, seeing if I can't rev up some of the buyers who dropped out after Ron jumped in last month. Wall Street and Century City are both watching like vultures. If word gets out that Ron has backed away, they'll pick me apart. I'll be lucky to get out with a nickel."

"Why did he back out?"

"I don't know. His lawyers gave me some cods-wallop about not dealing with someone who refused to repatriate national treasures."

"When did Ron ask that you make the sword part of the deal?" I asked, afraid that I already knew.

"Last night."

"Damn! Why didn't you tell me? I'd have given you anything, you know that."

Fiora nodded a little and whispered, "That's why I couldn't ask."

Her breathing was shallow, as though she were only using the top of her lungs.

"Take a deep breath, love," I said. "Let go."

She shook her head. "Can't."

"Why not?"

"I can't let down," she said, pushing me away gently. "Too much to do."

When she looked up at me, the vulnerable, hunted look was gone from her eyes. Just that suddenly she was back in money-shuffling mode, and she was back with a vengeance. I hadn't seen her like that in a long, long time.

Anger and frustration and something else jolted me like a cattle prod. After a moment I recognized the third emotion. It was bone-deep disappointment.

We had been so close. So close to freedom.

At that moment I realized Fiora's decision to sell her business meant as much to me as it did to her. She had looked at cashing out as validation. I had looked at it as liberation. Either way, it would have been a watershed for both of us.

And now I was on one side of the watershed and Fiora was on the other.

"Don't look so worried," she said. "The Nakamichi deal would have been nice. Hell, it would have been fantastic. Pacific Rim would have gone on, just like before. My people would have been taken care of."

Fiora shrugged and stepped out of the circle of my arms.

"But I put one deal together. I can do it again. Or at least I could, if you'd just get out of my way and let me get busy on the phone."

"Fiora . . ."

She sealed my lips with her finger and started talking. "Maybe Rory had the right of it. He told me long ago that nobody quits winners. Maybe the best thing we can do is to get elected the new King and Queen of Nothing." She smiled oddly. "I'll have to work on that for a while."

Without another word, Fiora turned away, went to the phone, and started punching in numbers from the memory bank behind her sad green eyes.

I picked up one of the decorative pillows that had been tossed onto the floor and fired it toward the bed. The pillow bounced once, slammed against the wall, and fell back onto the bed. I headed for the front door.

Fiora put her hand on the receiver. "Where are you going?"

All I said was, "Lock the door behind me."

NINETEEN

There are seven long flights of stairs between the waterfront and the market. I did them at a trot without drawing a deep breath, trying to put my adrenaline to good use. The market was packed with tourists. Beneath the flash and color of the display goods, I noticed for the first time just how worn and shabby the place really was.

Adrenaline is a potent drug. It lets you see right through illusion.

The sign in Oshima's gallery window still read CLOSED, but the front door stood wide open. A burly Seattle patrol cop blocked the entrance. Francis Xavier Claherty was just inside, talking to a dark-haired man in a suit. The patrol cop looked up as I approached, then turned to face me fully. His chest was the size of a keg of Olympia. He filled the doorway.

"Don't you see the sign, sir?" he said, putting up

his hand to warn me off. "The gallery is closed to the public."

Claherty spotted me and intervened. "Let him in, officer. He was next on my list anyway."

The cop shrugged and stood aside.

Before Claherty could start talking, I did. "I'm from the Equal Employment Opportunity Commission. How many Asian agents do you have in the Seattle field office?"

Claherty shook his head as though I'd thrown a glass of water in his face.

"Consider this a formal warning, then," I said. "You'll be short one on your quota if the black-bag artist you sent down to our condo shows up again."

"I'm supposed to know what that means?" Claherty asked.

"If you don't know, forget it. If you do know, keep that little prick out of Fiora's life. Got it?"

The dark-haired guy in the suit looked at me. His attitude said he owned the place. "Who is this clown, anyway?" he asked.

"It's okay, Rudy. This is the swordsman I was telling you about," Claherty said, without looking away from me.

"The swordsman? Well, well, isn't that convenient."

The man slid his hand back on his belt, showing me the badge on its holder. It was just in front of the high-pockets holster that held a four-inch .357 Magnum.

"Morning," he said to me. "My name is Rudy Ahrens. I'm with the Seattle Police Department, and I wonder if I might ask you a couple questions."

It wasn't a request, exactly. This was a real take-charge guy. I tried to read the unit written across the face of the badge. My best guess was HOMOCIDE INVESTIGATION.

It would explain the smell. The odor of blood and human waste was faint but very real.

Just past the Seattle cop, several other men and one woman were gathered in the doorway that led toward Oshima's office. When the beaded curtain was drawn back, I saw one investigator bent over, examining something—or someone —on the floor of the short, narrow hallway.

"I hope you're better at homicide investigations than the sheriff of Malahat," I said.

All Ahrens said was, "Come over here out of the way where we can talk."

Again, it wasn't quite a request. As soon as we reached the far wall, he turned to me. Claherty was stepping on our heels.

"Suppose you could break out some ID?" Ahrens asked casually.

I took my driver's license out of my wallet.

He laid the license atop a glass display case and pulled a fresh notebook out of his coat pocket. Homicide investigators tend to be very methodical. Ahrens had already gotten a case number and a victim's name. He had entered them on the cover of the fresh pad.

Oshima, #170.

"You mean they killed a hundred and sixty-nine folks in Seattle before they got around to that green suede snake?" I asked. "Things are really going to hell in the Pacific Northwest. I would have thought Oshima would make the top thirty.''

Ahrens and Claherty both followed my glance to the front of the writing pad. Ahrens frowned. Investigators like to control information the way a good bridge player controls trump.

"I warned you, he's got enough mouth for another row of teeth," Claherty said.

"We could fix that, I suppose," Ahrens said thoughtfully.

"Chalk it up to too much experience with country cops," I said. Then I glanced at Ahrens and added, "Present company excluded, of course."

It's not always bright to bait a cop, but the run up the steps hadn't taken much of the edge off my adrenaline high. Too much clarity when dealing with cops can get you into real trouble.

Ahrens ran me through a bunch of questions to establish what Claherty had already told him about me. I'll give Ahrens this—he was a hell of a lot more efficient than Malahat.

"Describe your morning," Ahrens said finally. "Where'd you eat? Who saw you?"

"How recently?"

"Last hour or so."

I looked at Claherty and smiled. "How about it, Frank? Establish my alibi, and I won't beef to the Inspector General about your black-bag job."

Ahrens got real quiet.

Claherty looked at me for what seemed like ten minutes, his eyes as blank as those of a gutted rockfish. Then he turned and walked out the front door. At least he was smart enough not to use the phone in the gallery until it had been dusted for prints.

Ahrens was no dope. He moved on to another area of questioning, ignoring the alibi issue for the time being.

"All right. Tell me about your business with Oshima."

I described how the art dealer had lied to me and attempted to swindle me out of the sword.

"You strung him along anyway?" Ahrens asked.

"Yeah."

"Why?"

I weighed my answer. On one hand, it might have been construed as a motive. On the other, Ahrens hadn't read me my rights.

"I thought Oshima might have killed the man who used to own the sword," I said. "I established that Oshima was willing to be a thief, but that's as far as I got."

"Would you have killed him if you had gotten any farther?"

It was a "How-long-have-you-been-beating-your-wife?" kind of question, but they sometimes have their uses. I grinned, just to show him I knew the game. He stared back for about ten seconds, sighed, and flipped to a new page.

Claherty came back in, his hands thrust in his pants pockets—or, rather, his fists. He wasn't happy. His face was empty. He gave Ahrens a slight nod.

Ahrens sighed again. Homicide cops always like quick arrests. I wasn't going to be his gold star for the month.

"How about this kid Carlton, the one who works for Oshima?" Ahrens asked.

"We've never been formally introduced."

It wasn't a lie but it wasn't the truth, either.

"You're the free-lance troubleshooter, but you didn't bother to run Carlton down?" Claherty asked sarcastically.

"I lost interest when I found out he was a doper with barely enough brains to fill a sake cup. How was Oshima killed?"

Claherty nodded toward the back room. "Go ahead, take a look—"

His smile said, If you think you're man enough.

I walked back to where the investigators were gathered, surveying the crime scene and mapping it out on a sheet of grid paper. They must have mistaken me for another fed. They stepped aside to give me a clear view. I tasted breakfast in the back of my throat.

Oshima lay on his back in the hallway. He had been cut in half, lengthwise, from crown halfway to crotch. There was remarkably little blood, considering. Instantaneous heart stoppage reduces exsanguination. The murder weapon must have had a hell of an edge.

I remembered the focus point of deadly force that Eto had shown me. The old man's sword dance and ritual had seemed so stylized as to be bloodless. In a chilling way, it almost was. But the true purpose of the dance was here on the floor. Death.

Ahrens and Claherty said nothing when I walked back up to them.

"Well, I don't think it was a street junkie with a

switchblade," I said. "Can you do a ballistics match on a samurai sword?"

Ahrens shook his head, but he almost smiled.

"You through with me?" I asked Claherty.

He looked at Ahrens.

"Where you staying in town?" Ahrens asked.

I gave him the condo's address. "Oshima said he had a customer for the sword in Japan," I added. "You might check his overseas phone tolls."

Ahrens gave Claherty a look of overdone surprise. "You're right, Frank. He's a regular Sherlock, he is." Ahrens looked at me. "You got any more bright ideas?"

I thought about giving him Eto, but didn't. The old man was the only one in the world who knew I had the sword. It wasn't something I wanted let out of the bag yet.

"Talk to the Malahat sheriff," I suggested. "He might surprise us yet by turning up some evidence. Personally, I doubt it. I've caught smarter *fish* than him."

Claherty followed me out into the street.

"Hold it just a second," he said. There was a federal-agent edge to his voice.

I stopped and drew a deep breath, still riding the adrenaline high. "Don't push me," I said. "I'll let the black-bag trick go, but that son of a bitch scared the hell out of Fiora."

"Could have fooled him," Claherty muttered. "Said he'd sooner cold-prowl a tiger cage than take her on again."

"He was lucky. I could have shot him in the left eye, no sweat."

Claherty grunted. "You still carrying?"

"I've got all the right papers."

He shrugged. "You could have plugged him. You didn't, which means you've got enough brains to come in out of the rain, even here in Seattle." He looked up at the overcast, then shoved his hands in his pockets again. "You got any idea where the sword might be?"

The set of his body told me this was the question he had followed me out to the street to ask. I felt a sudden twinge when I remembered that pawnshops in some towns have to report all transactions to the police.

"At this instant, I would give a great deal to know where the damn thing is," I said truthfully.

Claherty smiled, reached into his breast pocket, and produced a legal-sized envelope, good twenty-pound bond, with my name typed across the front. It was too late to duck, though I gave it a thought.

"Tag, you've been served," Claherty said, shoving the envelope into my hands. "I really appreciate your making it so easy."

There was nothing to gain by dropping the envelope, so I took it. The return address said it was from the Federal District Court for the District of Western Washington.

"Think of it as a little memory jogger," Claherty said. "U.S. District Judge Gerrard Tomlinson would like you to repeat your story about the theft. Under oath. Next Tuesday, ten o'clock."

"With the threat of contempt hanging over my head if I can't remember. Nice work. I should have shot your smart-ass agent."

Claherty shrugged. "Why complicate your life? Just turn the damn sword over to the State Department. I'll get it checked for bloodstains, just to keep Ahrens happy. When the sword comes back clean, I'll put it on the next JAL flight to Tokyo."

I didn't bother to look at the subpoena. I just folded the envelope and stuck it in my hip pocket.

"Think about it," Claherty offered. "The judge can't make you talk, but if he thinks you're holding out on him, he can throw you in jail until you produce the damn pigsticker."

I thought about Eto.

"Tuesday, huh?" I asked. It might be enough time.

"Why wait?" Claherty said instantly. "Federal judges are funny. They really think they're God. Last guy who pissed off Judge Tomlinson did seven months. The federal lockup here is a real pigsty."

"You ever get tired of being a hard-ass, Francis Xavier?"

"Nope."

He turned and walked off toward the market. There was a spring in his step that said he was delighted to be fighting the good fight.

I kept moving, turning squares until I was sure I was alone. Then I found an empty phone booth beside the bus depot on Fifth. Fiora must have been working the wires hard. It took me three tries to get through.

"Did you lock the door?" I asked.

"Yes, dear," she said patiently.

"Well, you can relax. The prowler was an FBI agent."

"What?" Then, fast and hard, "Why?"

"Guess."

"Other than the fact that Japan underwrites the U.S. national debt, I can't think of a single reason."

"You don't have to. You just thought of trillions. How's old Ron? Any way you can hang him out to dry for breach of contract?"

"I talked to a lawyer a few minutes ago, but I don't think there's anything I can do legally. Ron had a shrewd man on the deal memo. I wasn't as sharp as I should have been. I thought we were proceeding in good faith."

That, more than anything else, told me how badly Fiora had wanted the deal with Nakamichi Securities to work. Normally the lady does *not* wear rose-colored glasses.

"Maybe we can reestablish that good faith," I said.

"Fiddler." She said it as a warning.

"What?"

"Forget Ron. I have."

"What's the name of the lawyer?" I asked.

"Why?"

"Some federal judge wants to take the sword, and I have the subpoena to prove it."

"Can they really take the sword away from you?"

"They'll make my life hell deciding," I said. "Cultural conservation is big right now. Unfortunately I need the sword. It's the only edge I've got, so to speak."

She made a pained sound and gave me the lawyer's number. I hung up and tried him. He was out until four. I left my number and headed downhill again for the International District.

As I walked, I wondered if Eto's practice sword was sharp enough to split a man in half so fast he didn't bleed.

tWENTY

Pike Place and First Avenue were both frenetic, too many warring psyches vying for space. To a country boy like me, cities have always been beautiful and powerful, sensual and rich, fascinating and subtly dangerous. Like Fiora. But sooner or later, cities begin to make me crazy. So would Fiora, if her wealth and power meant more to her than it does.

The International District was less crowded but there was tension in the air, like the smell of ozone around an electric motor. The western rim of the United States is a seething mélange of cultures and peoples. A new society will emerge eventually, but the road to that brave new world will be paved with the broken bones and hearts of people who preferred the old ways of living and dying.

The soaped windows of the sword emporium stared blankly at the Asian market across the street. Freeway noise from Interstate 5 all but drowned out the tinny music from the back room. I tried the front door. Locked.

Next door was the apartment building where Eto had come at the messenger's call. The building was made of old red brick, yet the lines were Asian. Most overseas Chinese are from Canton, in the south, where it's hot and muggy; they build second-floor verandas to catch the evening breeze, even in cold new places like Seattle.

An old Asian woman sat on the veranda now, letting the sunlight soak into her wrinkled face.

"Is Mr. Eto in his apartment?" I called up to her.

She shook her head, then pointed back at the sword emporium. "He went there."

Good functional English, probably the product of a lifetime in the U.S. I wondered what language was spoken in the old woman's dreams.

"When did he leave?" I asked.

"An hour ago."

She turned her face away from me to the sun.

A coldness welled up from the middle of my belly. I walked quickly down the alley between the two buildings, then around behind the old store. Tinny music overrode the freeway sounds. There was a deadness to the air, like summer just before a storm.

I pulled Jake's gun and tried the back door. The knob turned but the door didn't move. I pushed. The door yielded an inch. The smell of gunpowder and blood drifted out through the crack. I pushed harder. Nothing doing.

Someone groaned from the room beyond. A fast look around told me the alley was deserted. I laid the gun on the stoop and put my shoulder to the door, trying to roll the obstacle out of the way.

The top of the door gave, but the bottom didn't budge. I crouched, braced myself, and shoved against the bottom half of the door. Slowly it gave way until there was an opening barely large enough to squeeze through. I grabbed the gun, shoved through, and saw what my nose had told me to expect. I was glad I hadn't had lunch.

There were three bodies in the room. Two were the men who had been working out the last time I was here. The third was the teenager who had run over to fetch Eto when I called. All three of them had been shot. The teenager was lying against the door. He had been hit in the chest and thrown aside, as though no longer important.

I touched his neck and caught a carotid pulse. Children have enormous resilience. His heartbeat was steady, even though it looked as though half his blood had leaked from the wound in his chest. A quick check told me nothing I could do for him would make a difference either way.

The killers had been more thorough on the two men. They lay as they had worked, close together. Each had taken a couple of bullets in the body and a coup de grâce in the head. The tinny music played over their corpses like an alien dirge.

I breathed through my mouth and looked around. A handful of empty shell cases were strewn across the floor of the back room. Nine millimeter, straight-necked brass. One Uzi, maybe, but more likely two. I had seen both swordsmen work out. It was doubtful a lone gunman could have walked through the door and bagged both of them

before they had time to separate and counterat-
tack.

When I went into the exercise room Eto was still
on the mat. So was the heavily tattooed stranger
who must have been first through the door. The
dead man was Asian. He lay at Eto's feet. Once the
killer might have been tall. It was hard to be certain, though, because his head was lying beside his
body now.

Eto lay on his side, curled in death as he once
had been in his mother's womb. One of the practice swords he had so disdained lay on the straw
mat beside him, broken in half. The bloodstained
tip lay beside the dead attacker. The other half
shone clean and unblooded above the cheap, pig-
skin-wrapped haft.

Death had contorted Eto's stoic expression. Now
he grimaced, as though he was embarrassed at being caught with such an inferior weapon at hand.
There was no peace in his death, no sense of personal accomplishment. There should have been.
He had taken at least three slugs in the chest and
still delivered a death blow to one of his enemies.

Something about Eto reminded me of Rory. I
wanted to sit on the rough straw mat beside Eto as
men were meant to do with their dead. I hadn't
been able to do that with Rory. It would be the
same for Eto.

I closed my eyes and listened. Somewhere out
beyond the alien music was the sound of gulls, and
water slapping against the side of the boat, and the
shrill cry of the reel as a fifty-pound salmon tore
off line at a hundred yards a minute. Somewhere
out there Rory sat in a late-summer twilight, lis-

tening to the faint hum of the northern lights rippling overhead and whispering the secrets of the universe to the King of Nothing.

Eto had never heard the lights sing to him. He had spent his whole life in pursuit of a malevolent grail, the Thousand-Year Sword, which had come to me so easily and at such great cost. Eto had died knowing he would never reclaim it. He had died believing his failure would doom his children, and his children's children, for a thousand years.

I closed Eto's eyes and picked up the unblooded half of the practice sword. A groan came from the other room, where the teenager struggled to live. I wrapped the broken sword in my windbreaker, put it under my arm, and went out the front door to the street. The clean air was better than any wine on earth.

The old woman was still on the veranda, eyes closed, basking in what remained of her life.

"Did you see anyone else go in there?" I asked.

She nodded without opening her eyes. "Three men. Fifteen minutes ago. One still there, two left."

"Nobody's there," I said. "Everybody's dead except one boy. Call the police. It looks like some kind of gang war in there."

Her eyes opened. "Gang war?"

"*Yakuza*. Get an ambulance here, or the boy will die too."

I left, walking fast. It wasn't long before the first squad car came down First Avenue and made the left into the International District. Sixty seconds later, sirens started up all over Old Town—police cars and paramedic units and backups for everyone. That many dead bodies put a strain on the system.

Before the sirens quit howling, I had found a quiet pay phone. By pretending I was Carlton's parole officer, I talked my way to the nursing station on his floor at Harborview.

"How's Carlton doing?" I asked. "He up and around yet?"

"No," answered the nurse. "Probably not for a few more days."

"Too bad. Does he have a phone in his room?"

"No. Welfare won't pay for one, and he's broke."

"Visitors?"

"Just one, yesterday."

"Asian?"

"No, Caucasian. Big man, good-looking, dark hair and mustache, gray eyes. Brought Carlton some cigarettes."

I thanked her and hung up, knowing now who had killed Oshima and Eto.

I had.

The black clerk looked a little disappointed when I laid the pawn ticket and $325 on the counter.

"Nothing personal, but I was hoping never to see you again," he said. "That's a nice piece. I got to liking it better and better all the time."

"Be glad to see me. The sword would have brought you a thousand years of bad luck."

He gave me an odd look, then scrounged up a long cardboard carton that had been used to ship replacement gun barrels. It was big enough for both the Muramasa blade and the broken *showa* sword.

I walked out and turned up Spring Street. I could see Nakamichi's building five blocks up First Hill. There was a pay phone at the corner of Fifth and Spring streets, just inside the Freeway Park. Nakamichi's secretary tried to earn her $22,000 a year by lying politely.

"Mr. Nakamichi is not available at the moment. Perhaps someone else could help you?"

"Tell Ron he can hide from Fiora but not from me. Then tell him I know where the sword is."

The mention of a weapon seemed to make her nervous. "Is Mr. Nakamichi supposed to understand what that means?"

"He has thirty seconds to figure it out. Tell him."

"He is *not* available," she repeated.

I started counting off seconds aloud. I got to twenty before Nakamichi got on the line.

"What do you want?" he asked impatiently.

"To close a deal."

"There is no deal. My attorneys made that clear to Ms. Flynn."

"I'm the direct type," I said. "I want to hear it directly from you, in person."

"I have no interest in a meeting," he said.

"A meeting, no. But a Muramasa blade?"

His breath came in audibly.

"Yeah, that's what I thought," I said. "I'm at street level right now, at the phone booth in the park. If you look out your window, you can probably see me."

I stretched the metal-clad coaxial cable on the

receiver out to its full length, looked up toward the top of the office building, and held the box up.

Nakamichi was able to see me. He drew another deep breath.

"I'll meet you on that bench over there," I said, waving the box like a pointer. "Five minutes and I'm gone. Muramasa goes with me."

I hung up before Nakamichi could argue.

As I walked to the bench, a pair of street buskers tuned up a fiddle and an accordion. The fiddler was tall and skinny and had blond hair that hung to the middle of his back. He sawed with the reckless abandon of a country boy who had taught himself to play. His fiddle was a novelty—strings stretched along a toilet plunger. A naked woman was painted on the folded bellows of the accordion. When the bellows moved, she did a peep-show bump and grind.

The two buskers worked the noontime sidewalk crowds like cocktail-bar pianists, sizing up their marks with a glance and sliding from musical genre to musical genre, seeking the tunes that might draw a quarter or a buck. They were sharp enough to try Bob Dylan's "Billy the Kid" on me. I gave them a five and watched Nakamichi's building.

Four minutes later the revolving door spat out three men, Ron and two bodyguards. All three crossed against the light. I watched the two thugs long and hard and decided they had left their Uzis behind. I tried to forget that all three of them had probably listened in while Fiora and I made love the night before.

The buskers picked up the three new lords of the universe while they were still in the crosswalk. The fiddler tried a little "You Are My Sunshine," one of the cross-cultural hits in the Japanese singing bars. No reaction. He switched to "Japanese Lanterns," the only Asian song that ever made the Top Forty.

It worked. Nakamichi glanced at the musicians as he passed. One of the bodyguards dropped a ten on the blanket next to my five.

As I watched Nakamichi approach, I wondered why he wanted the Muramasa badly enough to kill for it. Maybe it was an icon of the good old days when men like him controlled the ultimate expression of power in their society—the samurai sword.

No wonder the rulers of Japan had so fiercely resisted the pistol. One revolver could wipe out ten centuries of ritual and ceremony in the time it took a hammer to fall on a firing pin. So godlike a power, the power of death, should be reserved for the ruling class.

Nakamichi, like lords of the universe throughout history, bought his deaths. He had killed three times by remote control. Not one of those dead men could be laid at his feet in a court of law.

But then, we weren't in a courtroom.

"Nice of you to drop by," I said, gesturing toward the vacant end of the bench.

Nakamichi glanced past me to the long box that rested against the back of the bench just beneath my arm.

"You found your sword, I see," he said as he sat down.

The two goons took up posts a respectful twenty-five feet away—close enough to protect, but not so close they became part of the conversation.

"One of Oshima's employees had the sword," I said, watching him. "I'll have a word about it with Oshima later, but I thought I'd give you first bid."

If Nakamichi knew Oshima was dead, it didn't show. Nakamichi's eyes had less emotion than a cue ball. I reached over and pulled the Thousand-Year Sword out of the box, being careful not to show him the broken blade that was now wrapped in the sword bag.

"Here it is," I said.

I handled the sword carelessly, offering it to Nakamichi edge outward. He shouldn't have reached for it so quickly and he knew it, but his fingers weren't under as much control as his face.

"You should have told me at lunch you wanted it," I said. "Fiora has this thing about being self-sufficient. She never told me about your new demand."

That surprised him.

I smiled. "The problem is, you just don't understand American women. Fiora can be as independent as a hog on ice."

Ignoring me, Nakamichi took the sword and turned it in his hands, demonstrating a competence with it he hadn't shown before. He inspected the scabbard carefully, then pulled a few inches of blade. Noontime sunlight glinted on the polished steel and made the *hamon* seethe.

The two bodyguards stared at the sword, transfixed. Nakamichi was a better actor. He glanced casually at the blade, then slid it into the scabbard with an easy motion. When he handed the sword back to me, he also presented it edge first. There was a small smile on his face, as though he enjoyed giving the insult even if I was too ignorant to recognize it.

"How much?" I said, taking the sword.

"It's a very valuable piece," he said. "If offered at auction in Japan, my experts tell me it probably would fetch three hundred million yen—say, two million dollars, more or less."

"What's a few yen among friends, right? I'll settle for a million bucks, American, plus Fiora's deal."

Nakamichi's mouth drew back in what only an optimist would call a smile.

"The situation is more complex than your direct American logic allows you to understand," he said. "That is why I withdrew my offer for Ms. Flynn's modest little firm. It is also why I'm not interested in your back-channel offer of a Japanese national treasure. I doubt that any other Japanese will be interested either," he added.

I made a sound that said I wasn't impressed.

"Japanese are very proud people," Nakamichi said. "It would be a great loss of face for any son of Nippon to traffic with cultural pirates."

He was sure enough of his power to let a touch of smugness contaminate his smile. His attitude told me how the FBI and the culture police had gotten onto me so fast. He must have been on the phone to Tokyo five minutes after he left the restaurant.

That's the problem with real, integrated, pervasive corporate power. It has a hell of a long reach. Japan, Inc., Benny and Fiora call it. I'd seen nothing to make me disagree. Government and industry are one and the same, a single coordinated force that operates with the sort of autonomic collaboration that makes American monopoly capitalists look like Keystone Kops.

I might have played it the same way, if I had held Nakamichi's cards. Then again, maybe not. My taste has always run more to kicking over hives than building them.

"You want the Thousand-Year Sword for nothing? Is that it?" I asked.

"I don't want it at all." Nakamichi's smile was definitely smug this time. "The sword has become tainted by barbaric money squabbles. If the United States government offered to return the sword with abject apologies, the Emperor might accept. Short of that—" He shrugged.

I waited for the other shoe to land on the bottom line.

"You must understand," Nakamichi said. "There are still many wounds left over from the last war."

"Too bad Rory isn't alive," I said sardonically. "You two could compare war wounds, psychic and otherwise."

Nakamichi shook his head unhappily. "You take this entire matter too personally, Fiddler. It is not a personal contest. It is impersonal, as all business ought to be. We are simply acting in our own best interests, as a nation and as a corporation."

"That's always been my problem," I agreed. "I take things personally."

"In that, you have contaminated your woman's thinking as well," Nakamichi said coolly. "I was told she had a strong business sense, but my experience in the past few days suggests otherwise."

"Business has always been personal with Fiora. That's why she stayed in it as long as she did."

The fiddler on the sidewalk went to work on a Scots lament. For an instant I thought I saw Rory from the corner of my eye, but when I looked, I realized I had been mistaken.

I put the sword back in the box and stood. Nakamichi watched the box in my hands with too much interest for his own comfort.

"What do you intend to do?" he asked.

"What do you care? You had your chance. You passed. Sayonara."

Nakamichi came to his feet with a speed that revealed the anger just beneath his control. He walked away without a backward glance. The two bodyguards gave me one last inspection, memorizing me, then fell in step behind their boss.

I had no doubt Nakamichi was planning my death with every step he took.

That was only fair. I was planning his.

tWENTY-ONE

On the way back to the condo, I stopped long enough to get a coffee at Starbuck's. It gave me an excuse to cadge a felt-tip pen and a blank sheet of paper from the girl behind the bar. The note didn't take long to write.

When I let myself into the condo, Fiora had already changed out of her business armor and was sprawled on the couch in jeans and a cotton shirt, talking on the telephone. She was fully alert, her body fairly crackling with intensity.

I checked the kitchen to make sure Nakamichi's maid wasn't lurking. Fiora saw me and held up three fingers, indicating she wouldn't be long. I sat on the couch beside her and waited impatiently for the conversation to end. The bits and scraps I heard told me she was butting heads with some Wall Street bull. She didn't seem to mind the exercise.

"Of course I know it doesn't make sense, Chris," she said. ". . . Yes, I know the firm is worth a lot more if I remain on as a consultant, but I want your best offer right now, for the deal as I outlined it: the portfolios, the existing staff, and the physical space in Newport Beach. Everything but me."

Whatever Chris said irritated Fiora.

"I came into business with a spotless reputation," she said flatly. "I'll go out with that reputation intact. Everything is just as I've represented it to you. Pacific Rim is sound and solvent and, no, we have not lost any major clients in the last week."

Her eyes shifted as she talked from hazel green to apple jade. They do that when she's angry.

Chris mumbled something that might have been an apology.

"I'm sure you didn't," Fiora said in a clipped voice. Then, more gently, "Look, I know this offer to sell is unusual, but there's nothing hidden—no trapdoors, no deadfalls, and no padding of the books. We made a good profit last year, and we'll make an even better one this year, whether you take the deal or not."

She paused, listened, and said, "Personal reasons."

My palms suddenly tingled. I get the same reaction when the tip of a trolling rod suddenly dips as a salmon mouths the bait. I had about given up hope of separating Fiora from Pacific Rim.

I settled back in the couch. The corners of the folded note were sharp against my fingers, but I didn't show it to her for fear of distracting her.

"I said cash and I meant cash. They don't let you fund a university chair like a leveraged buy-out. Education requires real money, not junk bonds."

Abruptly Fiora sat up and grabbed the pen that had been resting on a legal pad on the coffee table. The top sheet of paper was covered with her precise, angular numerals. I looked at them long enough to recognize revised projections of start-up and long-term funding costs for her business-school endowment. The bottom line had seven figures in front of the decimal.

Fiora scribbled a number on the sheet that I assumed was Chris's offer. It was a hundred thousand dollars less than her bottom line.

"I said I wanted out for personal reasons, but insanity wasn't one of them," she said dryly. "You're not even in the ballpark."

The tone told me this was a friendly negotiation again, the kind based on mutual respect between two well-matched parties. I was intrigued to notice that the frown lines on Fiora's face were less pronounced than they had been when Nakamichi was on the other end of the line. She had loathed the man but never showed it, not once.

There was a silence while Chris talked. Fiora masked the receiver with her hand and whispered, "Can it wait a few more minutes, or should I tell Chris I'll call back?"

The woman is scary. She's lip-deep in the negotiation of her life and she has enough brainpower left over to notice that I've had a rough morning.

"An hour more or less won't matter," I said softly. "Get it done right."

She flashed me a quick, searching look, then focused fully once more on the deal Chris was offering.

Chris must have been figuring on his own tablet.

Finally he said something. Fiora drew a line through the first offer and wrote down a new, higher one. It didn't take the frown lines from her face.

"It won't fly," she said with genuine regret, the voice of someone walking away from a deal and not looking back. "My salary this year is more than the profit I'd make if I took your offer."

I bit down hard on my disappointment. Pacific Rim was Fiora's to keep, to sell, or to give away. It had nothing to do with me.

And if I said it often enough, I might even believe it.

Chris must have been bright enough to know that Fiora had one foot out the door. He talked fast. She drew a line through the second offer and wrote down a new one.

"Closer, but . . ." she said.

The offer was less than half the one Nakamichi had made.

I laid the folded note on the table and motioned for Fiora to turn around. As soon as she did, I went to work on her shoulders. The muscles and tendons were tight, but nothing like the slab steel and braided cables I had encountered the previous evening. She reached over her shoulder with her free hand and touched my fingers, moving them to a particularly knotted spot. Her eyes closed and her lips curved with pleasure when I found the trigger point and dug into it gently.

"Look, what about this?" she said. "For a year I'll do a few hours a month of teleconferencing with you and your executive committee. No formal consulting contract, no exclusive employment rider, no nothing except my promise to be as candid as possible in my analyses.''

Whoever Chris was, he had a firm grasp of his priorities. His counteroffer came quickly. Fiora sat with pen poised, listening but not writing anything down.

''Make that one day a month—additional hours at my option—for a year,'' she said.

Despite the calmness of her voice, the flesh beneath my hands fairly vibrated while Fiora waited for an answer.

''Two days a month for two years,'' she countered. ''Any more and there's no incentive to sell.''

I felt Chris's agreement radiating up through Fiora's body before she turned and gave me a smile that told me we were going fishing after all.

''You've got a deal, Chris. Start the paperwork and fax it to the number I gave you.'' Fiora paused. ''Yeah, me too. Talk to you soon.''

She hung up the phone. I stopped rubbing her back.

''Keep going,'' Fiora said. ''I've got to sit here and think for a minute. Jesus, what a head rush. I'm dizzy. But the employment clause is going to be tricky. . . .''

I went to work on the trigger point under her right shoulder blade. Strangely, the muscle seemed to have unknotted itself. I ran my thumbs along her spine, digging a bit deeper, probing. The tension seemed to have dissipated from one moment to the next.

''Old Chris must be a real smooth talker,'' I said.

"I'm not sure whether to take lessons or shoot the son of a bitch."

Fiora sat with a faraway look on her face for a moment, savoring the sensations of the back rub and the successful negotiation. I didn't disturb her. I meant what I had said—an hour more or less wouldn't matter to anyone, least of all to Rory and Eto.

She let out a long sigh. "I really thought it wasn't going to fly unless I stayed on, half time."

"That wouldn't have worked. You don't do anything halfway."

"I know."

Sighing again, she leaned across my lap and looked at me. Her eyes were clear, intent, very green.

"Can you handle that?" she asked, her face suddenly serious. "I mean, I know how important freedom is to you, but a few days a month won't cramp your style too much, will it?"

For an instant I felt like an ogre. And like a king at the same time.

I kissed the nape of her neck and went to work on the front of her shoulders, loosening muscles and at the same time tracing the rise of her breasts, marveling at the gift of trust that is involved in physical intimacy.

"I'll try to spare you for a couple of hours a month," I said against Fiora's neck. "I need a little recovery time, once in a while, anyway."

She cupped her hands over mine and held them where I could feel the growing tightness of her nipples through her shirt. Beneath the cloth she wore nothing but a subtle perfume.

"Have I ever complained about your recovery time?" Fiora asked.

She turned slowly, letting me enjoy every bit of it, then gave me the kind of kiss that would have ended with her on her back on the couch, except that we weren't really alone. Reluctantly I pulled away and held a finger up to my lips.

Fiora reads me very well. The sensuality vanished from her expression, as did the underlying triumph of having sold Pacific Rim. She sat up and waited with the air of someone expecting bad news.

It wasn't long in coming. I picked up the folded note, opened it, and showed it to her: THIS CONDO IS BUGGED.

An instant of rage flashed in Fiora's eyes. She looked around the room reflexively, as though seeking the hidden microphone. When she looked back at me, no trace of her emotions showed. She was in full money-shuffling mode, except that there was nothing on the table to shuffle. For a few seconds, we stared at one another without speaking.

"Since you're not in the mood for a quick toss, how about a walk on the waterfront?" Fiora asked calmly. "I feel like I've been cooped up forever."

"I've had a hell of a day myself. I saw Nakamichi."

"What on earth for?"

The surprise in Fiora's voice was genuine.

"Simple. I offered him the sword if he'd put the Pacific Rim deal back on track."

"Judas priest!"

"Don't worry," I said, smiling at Fiora's astonishment. "He turned me down flat."

She looked stunned. "Did he? Why?"

"He wants the sword for free. Wrapped in gold ribbon and with profound apologies for not thinking of it sooner. From the State Department, no less."

"Gee, I'd like to walk on water, but I don't go around advertising the fact," Fiora said caustically. "What did you tell the odious little dildo?"

"Sayonara. It's the only Nip word I know."

Fiora laughed, the way only a woman can laugh over a pompous man's discomfiture.

"Yeah, that's kind of how I felt about it," I said.

"What are you going to do with the sword?" she asked.

"Take it fishing off Twelve Mile Banks."

"Fishing," she repeated carefully.

"Yeah. The bank was one of Rory's favorite places. I'm going to fish there. When I catch a salmon, I'm going to turn it loose and then scatter Rory's ashes. Then I'm going to the deep trench off the southeast end, tie a cannonball to that damned sword, and drop it over the side."

Fiora gave me a long look.

"You have some problem with that?" I asked.

"Only your use of the first person singular pronoun," she said. "*You* aren't going to do it. *We* are."

"No," I said, fast and hard.

"This relationship, this new freedom, is only going to work if we share experiences like the Twelve Mile Banks equally," she said.

"We have different talents. We can't share everything equally."

"Not everything has to be shared," she agreed. "Just some things. Rory's funeral is one of them."

Fiora's eyes had turned to apple green again. She moved a little closer to the floral display on the low, lacquered table. It was the best spot in the room to hide a microphone. She looked from it to me and waited.

Suddenly I knew what that Wall Street entrepreneur had gone through a few minutes before on the phone. I wondered if he had been any happier with the final deal than I was.

"Done," I said curtly.

It took us five minutes to pack and vacate the bugged condo. We were on the ferry to Bainbridge Island before either of us said another word. Then I told Fiora everything I knew and most of what I guessed. I also laid down a few ground rules for the next few days. I couldn't be looking over my shoulder every minute, worrying about her.

"Are you carrying the Beretta?" I asked.

"Yes."

She opened her shoulder bag. The gun was in a small pocket inside.

"Loaded?" I asked.

"Yes."

"Keep it that way and keep it within reach."

"Yes."

Three in a row. I was on a roll.

"Okay," I said. "You'll stand guard at the house while I—"

"No."

I glared at her. She glared right back. It got very quiet for a few minutes.

"Fiddler." Fiora's voice was a lot softer than her eyes. They were bleak. "You're going to need me."

A cool finger traced my spine. "I'll call Benny."

She shook her head. "Even if he could get up here by then, *The King of Nothing* isn't rigged for a wheelchair."

"What can you do that I can't do better alone?" I asked bluntly.

"Pilot the boat. I'm better at it than you are, and you know it."

She had me there. I could drive the fire-breathing, made-to-be-manhandled Cobra without a hitch, but the boat's soft, sluggish steering was a real bitch for me to get a handle on. Fiora had taken to it immediately, delighting Rory by freeing him to fish instead of steer.

"I'm not planning on fishing," I said.

"No. You're going after much rougher game."

I hissed through my teeth. *"Shit."*

"Happens."

She looked at me and waited. I thought fast, but I knew it was useless. She was right. Alone on a rowdy sea, I'd have my hands full and then some. There had been real greed in Nakamichi's eyes. That greed gave my trap a chance. Unfortunately, I had no way of predicting when the trap might be triggered.

"If you got hurt . . ." I couldn't finish.

"I feel the same way about you," she said. "I always have. That's why I walked away from you or drove you away. I couldn't bear loving you and waiting for you to die."

"And now?" I asked, wondering how Fiora had reconciled the irreconcilable.

"I'm older. I know we're all waiting to die."

tWENTY-TWO

Fiora was silent all the way back to Malahat. As we drove slowly down the winding driveway toward the cottage she had inherited, her face was unguarded, haunted by memories and regrets. When I got out and went around to her side to open the door, she was so lost in thought I had to touch her cheek to get her attention.

"Don't think too much about what might have been," I said. "Rory refused to sell the sword because I had admired it. He wanted me to have it. That's on my head, not yours. So is Eto. I should have figured Nakamichi for the kind of slime who would bug his guest accommodations."

"It's not that," Fiora said, stepping down out of the truck with unconscious grace. "It's the curse."

"You don't really believe in that crap?"

Foolish question. Of course Fiora believed in that crap. She was hair-raisingly pragmatic about business, but the druids in her ancestry—and in her dreams—still worried about my safety.

"Let me worry about the curse," I said quickly. "Muramasa and I have an understanding."

"I know. That's what scares me."

She slipped under my arm and curled against my chest, hiding from the cold wind off the water. I leaned behind the seat and pulled out my Gore-Tex jacket. It was much too big for her, hanging below her knees and knuckles, but it kept the wind at bay.

We walked across the road to retrieve Kwame from Marley's wildlife station. He was ecstatic. He had languished most of the time in a vacant flight cage because Marley's resident bald eagle, Tyrone, had spent the past three days trying to pluck his Rhodesian rope of a tail bald.

The instant Kwame scented us, he danced and barked and generally threatened to tear his chicken-wire cage apart. When I let him out, he forgot his manners and tried to deck me with a flying leap. Then he tore around the yard, chasing the eagle from pole to pole and generally acting the fool.

After ten minutes, Kwame came back with his tongue lolling, and the three of us headed across the road. Somewhere between Marley's place and the cottage, Kwame picked up on our mood. When I gave him the hand signal for Search, he vetted the yard with impressive speed and silence. It was the same at Rory's house; he went through it like a fanged, tawny shadow. I took him to the boathouse and then to the cottage. His keen nose pronounced the place free of strange scents.

Together Fiora and I assembled a cold dinner: garden tomatoes, salmon salad, and sourdough bread. We drank sun tea instead of chardonnay. Outside, the last of the day's rich light made every pebble and bough stand out in high relief.

The long summer days were falling away quickly. By the time we'd cleared the table and taken care of the dishes, the long twilight had begun. We took Kwame for a long sentry-go through the woods, just to refresh him—and me—on the lie of the land. He found nothing more threatening than a squirrel.

Waiting is the hardest part of setting a trap.

Back at the cabin, I tore down Jake's .45, cleaned it, oiled it, and reloaded the clip with bright new brass. Fiora's Beretta had been in her luggage most of the time. The barrel was factory clean, but I shucked the rounds out of the clip and reloaded them, just to make sure the salt air hadn't corroded the cartridge cases.

About nine I made a pot of strong coffee and poured myself a big cup.

"They'll expect us to put out about five-thirty," I said. "I'm going to be up and down all night. You want me to sleep on the couch?"

Fiora shook her head. "What I really want is a little time with you."

The old bed recognized our bodies and made a place for us. I toed off my moccasins, turned out the lights, and lay on top of the covers, fully dressed. Fiora took off her shoes and socks and crawled under the covers in her clothes. She curled up inside my arm and rested her hand on my belly possessively. We listened to the sounds of the house settling down and the gentle rattling of the leaves and the whisper of needles when the wind moved.

After a few minutes I heard the click of nails on the wooden floor. The moonlight was just bright enough for me to make out Kwame in the doorway. I heard his foot pads on the old rug, then felt the deft, pleading pressure of his head on the far end of the mattress.

"No Rhodesian Ridgebacks in my bed," Fiora said.

"He says he's really just a Chihuahua."

"He lies."

"You heard the lady, Kwame. On guard."

He heaved a deep, heartfelt sigh. Then I heard his foot pads and toenails on the wooden floor as he returned to sentry-go around the cabin.

My mental alarm was set for four, but Kwame awoke me well before then. The moon was nearly overhead. Its light cast pale silver squares on the bedroom floor. In the distance I heard the sound of a diesel engine running at full throttle, a long-liner or a purse seiner passing on the strait. A barn owl hooted softly, asking questions the night never answered. Kwame paced back to the bedroom doorway, stared in for a moment, then methodically quartered every inch of the cottage.

The dog's restlessness was infectious. I began to disengage myself from Fiora's arms. She awakened instantly.

"What's that sound?" she said after a moment.

She had good ears. The revving marine diesel was almost too far away for me to hear now.

"Just a commercial fisherman heading for the banks," I said.

"No," she said very softly. "Not the distant sound. That one."

I heard a faint, furtive, scrabbling sound. Claws on a hard surface. Could have been a rat in the cellar or a raccoon on top of the boathouse or Marley's crazy eagle, Tyrone, who loved to perch on Rory's chimney.

"I don't know," I said, as softly as Fiora had.

Quietly, I rolled out of bed, picked up Jake's gun, and padded barefoot into the front room. Kwame stood expectantly beside the door. He had heard the sound too, and he didn't much like it.

I moved to the window and looked out, careful not to disturb the white curtain. The moonlight cast deep shadows in the woods at the edge of the lawn and gave detail to the landscape in the clearings. The scrabbling sounds had stopped, but now they started again.

A movement on top of Rory's house caught my eye. I had seen Tyrone roost on the chimney just before dark, apparently hoping Kwame might come out to play. The eagle was still there but he was awake now, spreading his wings repeatedly, restlessly. He hopped awkwardly down to the roof-line and waddled a few feet on talons made for grasping prey rather than for walking. Abruptly the eagle leaped into the moonlight, heading back across the road.

Eagles aren't famous for nighttime flying. Something had disturbed the bird badly enough that he was seeking another roost.

"Kwame," I said very quietly. "Heel."

He materialized like a black shadow at my left heel. I slipped his choke chain off. Dog licenses and ID tags make too much noise in the stillness after midnight. Kwame's ruff was spiky, like a closely clipped Mohawk. He stared intently at the closed door, then at me, then at the door, obviously amazed that I hadn't read his mind yet.

"Stay."

I slipped back into the bedroom and pulled on my mocs. The Beretta contrasted blackly with the paleness of bedcovers and Fiora's hand. I had left her training to Benny; he has the properly dispassionate ruthlessness when it comes to her, and he had done his job well.

"What is it?" Fiora asked, her voice so soft I barely heard it.

"It looks quiet," I said casually, "but I'm going to take a quick look around with Kwame. If we don't make a lot of noise coming back, shoot, because it won't be us."

She didn't even argue.

I took Kwame's braided leather leash from a peg in the hall, fashioned a slip loop, and put it over his head. He shivered with cold eagerness as he waited for my signal.

"Quiet."

He was.

"Heel."

He did. I shortened the leash, holding him close. While the two of us work with reasonable regularity, I'm too unstructured myself to require robotic responses from my dog. It was a long time since we had hunted real game. I wasn't sure he would call off, once his blood was up. Normally I wouldn't have minded if Kwame made a midnight snack out of a prowler, but I wanted evidence that would lead back to Nakamichi—living, breathing, talking evidence.

Kwame and I went out the kitchen door and into the shadowed woods without a sound. He slid into the lead, sniffing the night air, moving lightly on the dirt path, silent without even trying to be.

After a time I began to think we were both hearing enemies that didn't exist. Then I remembered the way Eto had moved and concealed himself and moved again in the underworld beneath Pioneer Square. Ninjas are like cursed swords, ridiculous until one slices you to the bone.

The night breeze came up. The sounds of the trees masked our movements . . . and other movements, as well. We circled halfway around the clearing, stopping every few steps to listen and look and let Kwame work the scents. When I touched him to silently get his attention, his neck was taut, electric, radiating a predator's focus. He was fulfilling his genetic destiny with the kind of passionate intensity that would be called insanity in humans.

A flickering movement caught my eye. It came from across the clearing, in the little clump of yew trees on the bank above the boathouse. An owl had left its hunting perch and flown into the moonlight, its wingbeats absolutely soundless. Once out of the trees, the owl flew straight toward the water. It wasn't hunting. It too had been disturbed enough to alter its normal nocturnal patterns.

I tugged lightly on the leash, slowing Kwame. He strained against me, then stopped. His ears came up. He cocked his head to one side, then the other, trying to identify a sound I couldn't even hear. He tested the night air. Then his teeth gleamed as his lips came back in a near-silent snarl.

It was a primitive signal: Prepare to fight or flee. I felt my own senses heighten and clarify. I wrapped my hand briefly around Kwame's muzzle, demanding silence. He was quiet, but he took two steps toward the boathouse. I tightened the leash to remind him he had a hunting partner.

Together we stepped out of the trees and into the moonlight. I could feel Fiora's eyes on me from the cottage. I showed her the palm of my hand, telling her to stay put. Kwame and I went across the lawn toward the yew trees.

At first I thought the sound was the river itself, lapping against the planks of the floating dock beside the boathouse. The banks were overhung with trees that cast inky shadows. The river current gave a rippling suggestion of motion to the surface of the water, which distracted me for a second. Then there was a faint, muffled splash and a dark shape that seemed to be moving against the flow of the water.

Some kind of animal, perhaps an otter, was swimming just in front of the boathouse. Another muffled splash was followed by a faint bump. Another jolt of adrenaline went through me; otters didn't go bump in the night.

Kwame was straining against the leash, ignoring

my tugs in the opposite direction. I grabbed him by the scruff of his neck and shook him the way a mother would a pup. He stayed quiet, but his eyes never left the boathouse. Scruff firmly in hand, I turned Kwame back toward the cottage. He didn't want to go, but I was bigger than he was.

The door opened. Fiora's face and blond hair were pale in the moonlight.

"I think there's somebody down by the boat-house," I said softly. "Keep Kwame here."

"Let Kwame take him."

"I want the bastard alive."

"And I'd rather have *you* alive."

But she took the leash and scruffed Kwame firmly. He barely noticed. Every atom in his body was pointed toward the boathouse, where his prey bumped and splashed softly in the dark.

Attack dogs are like samurai, bred to forge straight ahead, to take the bullet intended for their handler, if it comes to that. I understood guns and could avoid them better than Kwame could.

I went back to the top of the bluff and looked down on the river again. The shadowy swimmer was still in the water. Light glowed dimly, as though at a great distance. At first I thought I was seeing the moon's reflection on the water. Then I realized I was looking at some kind of hooded diving light.

The light went out, returning the river to darkness. Gradually I made out two dark shapes glistening wetly on the sun-bleached wood of the dock. The two shapes looked suspiciously like long guns. As I watched, the swimmer surfaced and deposited another long gun on the dock. Then he disappeared underwater again.

I went to the head of the stairway where Rory had first fallen. There the boathouse and the trees screened me from the man in the water. I went down the steps two at a time, on the balls of my feet.

The boathouse was the size of a single-car garage, built on a big U-shaped float with three feet of dock on either side. There was a door at the front and an overhead garage-type door at the back that was wide enough for the boat. The front door of the boathouse was ajar. The overhead door had been raised. The swimmer was back in the water, searching for more guns.

I stepped from solid ground onto the float and felt it settle a little beneath my weight. Though sun-bleached, the wood was solid; it took my movements without creaking. Then the whole float shifted. I heard the quiet thump of another gun being deposited on the dock. I stole a fast look through the front door but couldn't see much.

The float shifted again. Either the guy was doing chin-ups or he was pulling himself out of the water onto the float. The wet slap of a swim fin told me he was on the float.

Walking flat-footed, I went to the far corner and looked around. The swimmer was thirty feet away. He wore a dark wet suit. As I watched, he took off his fins and dropped them into a small Zodiac he had tied off on the river side of the boathouse.

The man was so close I could hear him pant. All the ninjas were getting old.

He reeled in the Zodiac and began loading the five long guns. It didn't take any particular genius to figure out that the guns were the ones taken from Rory's case the night he was attacked. They had been stolen to cover an outright execution, but that was no reason to let them go to waste. The Purdey shotgun alone was worth a couple grand. Even if it hadn't been protected, a few days in fresh water wouldn't destroy its value.

The guns would be a nice little bonus for the hit man.

Muffled sounds told me he was busy loading his booty into the Zodiac. I eased along the dock on the bank side of the float, trying to get closer. Night vision doesn't allow for finesse, and I wanted this one alive.

He finished loading the guns just as I reached the open end of the boathouse. He was in a hurry now, eager to cast off and let the current carry him down the river into the salt water. I heard the sound of movement and risked a waist-high peek around the corner. He had vaulted from the dock onto the transom of *The King of Nothing*.

Satisfaction and anticipation went through me. He was inside the boathouse, aboard the boat, just about where I wanted him.

Then I heard scrapings and rustlings from the enclosed pilothouse, as though the prowler was tampering with something there.

Rigging a bomb, perhaps?

Not a happy thought. Maybe Nakamichi had panicked. Maybe he was going to settle for closing down the trails that could lead back to him—beginning with Fiora and me. A dawn salmon raid, an explosion in the boat—too bad, how sad, and when will those damned Californians learn to pump the gas out of their bilges?

Very quietly I moved toward the open overhead door. There was a light switch just inside. My hand was groping for it when the dock dipped suddenly as another weight hit it. A low savage snarl ripped through the darkness as a hundred and twenty pounds of Rhodesian Ridgeback blew past me and landed on the boat.

I reached frantically for the light switch. Too late. The report of a heavy pistol was deafening, yet not loud enough to drown out Kwame's sharp cry of pain. The strobe light of the muzzle flash froze the scene for me—a dark figure rising up out of the cockpit, gun in hand, aiming at the glowing eyes of the dog who stalked him.

Just as I found the light switch, another shot slammed through the darkness. Three unshielded one-hundred-watt bulbs burned brightly, blinding the man in the wet suit as he thrust a .357 Magnum toward Kwame's face. Even with his eyes closed, the man couldn't miss; the dog's jaws were locked on the swimmer's neoprene-covered forearm.

"Drop it!" I said, stepping into the light, dividing his attention.

Jake's gun was in my hand but I was deliberately careless about aiming it. I wanted the attacker to think he had a chance to beat me.

I watched the muzzle of his gun. Adrenaline slowed time so much I was able to discern the Day-Glo orange dot on the sight blade. The weapon looked oddly familiar. It twitched in my direction.

Gotcha!

Then he realized his mistake. Maybe Kwame's teeth got through the suit. Maybe he just decided the dog was the more dangerous threat. The dot swung back toward Kwame's bloody muzzle.

I fired. There was no thought, no mind, no aiming, no anxiety, nothing but my metal finger pointing.

All the drill paid off. The bullet caught him in the head and slammed him against the console inside the pilothouse. It was a great shot, an inspired shot. All I could think of was that it had cost me a chance to avenge Rory.

Kwame's jaws were still locked on the dead man's forearm when I reached them.

"Of all the stupid, goddam stunts!" I yelled. "Drop, Kwame. He's dead. Drop him!"

There was too much blood, fresh, still coming. Kwame's muzzle was covered with it. A glistening stain was spreading down his tawny chest.

"Dammit, you ill-trained, ill-mannered blockhead—"

I couldn't say any more. I knelt beside him and tried to prize his jaws open. Reluctantly he surrendered his trophy.

Fiora appeared in the doorway, gun in hand. Her face was a hard Kabuki mask, a blond demon. She spares no sympathy for those who threaten what she loves. Her eyes went over me like hands: no blood, no injury. She looked at the intruder. He was dressed in dark rubber as though he had known of his death in advance and brought his own body bag.

Then she saw Kwame and the blood. In an instant she was transformed from avenging angel to angel of mercy. She knelt next to Kwame.

"Easy, boy," she crooned. "Let me see." Then, in the same gentle voice, she asked, "What happened?"

"I must have made some sound that gave me away. He was waiting in the dark boat, gun in hand. If Kwame hadn't gotten loose and jumped him, he would have nailed me as soon as I turned on the light."

Fiora's face turned chalky but she continued to make soothing noises. Kwame weighed more than Fiora, his eyes were fully dilated, he was shivering with adrenaline and the taste of blood . . . yet he let himself be held by a gentle touch and a soft voice. Fiora crooned some more to him, talking him down, bringing him back.

When I touched Kwame's shoulder, blood ran red across my fingers. I took the little penlight from my hip pocket and flashed it across him. There was a slash, like a sword cut, in the short golden fur on his shoulder. Blood welled up in the cut, but I could see no tendon, no bone.

Kwame's face was smeared with gore. He kept working his washcloth-size tongue, trying to clear his mouth. When I flashed the light on his muzzle, I saw a deep cut at the corner of his mouth.

"How bad?" Fiora asked.

"Can't tell. Looks like he tried to take a bite out of the business end of the revolver." I bent over for a better look. "Hold still, boy. Let me see."

Kwame wagged his tail and grinned at me, fangs all bloody. The wound was so deep I could see into his mouth. The slug had sheared off a molar just above the gum line, then had ripped through the fleshy part of his mouth and cut the slash across his chest.

I let out a long breath. "Bloody, but he'll live unless I decide to beat him to death myself for insubordination."

Fiora made a sound of relief, stroked Kwame's broad head, and told him what a fine, foolish, beautiful dog he was.

"He's going to have a smile as wide as a used car salesman." I released Kwame and stepped back. "Hold him while I search the frogman."

This time Kwame stayed with Fiora. I rolled the body over. The man's face was framed by the rubber balaclava and concealed by a diving mask. I peeled the mask back and flashed the light on his face.

Lindstrom.

"Son of a bitch," I said.

"What?"

"I just killed a Malahat County deputy sheriff."

tWENTY-THREE

Fiora followed me out onto the floating dock where the little Zodiac bumped in the current of the river. I played the flashlight on the guns in the well at the front of the flat-bottomed boat.

"Are those Rory's missing guns?" Fiora asked.

"Yeah. The mysterious burglar's loot, except that the investigating officer was also the burglar." I stood up. "Lindstrom knew where to find the evidence even in the dark, because he knew where he had dumped it."

"So it was a cheap burglary after all," Fiora said unhappily. "And he was the cheap burglar."

"You're half right. Come on, let's get Kwame over to Marley."

Kwame was moving easily enough, so we hiked across the road in the dark. The stars were cold sparks, clear and sharp. Out over the water, the faint outline of Vancouver Island had been swallowed up by clouds. A front was coming in, silently eating the night. The blue-white patches of snow on Hurricane Ridge were gone too.

The wind picked up. It smelled like the Northwest—evergreens and rain. The air had an edge to it that told me winter was coming down from the north.

The chilly wind got to Kwame, stiffening his chest wound. He started limping. I picked him up like a calf and kept walking. The pressure must have burned across his chest, but he didn't even whimper.

"I'd say 'I told you so,'" I muttered to Kwame, "but you wouldn't know what I was talking about."

He licked my chin, leaving a bloody mark.

"Now you know what I go through all the time," Fiora said.

"I wasn't talking to you."

"Too bad. I was talking to you."

She knocked on Marley's door. Marley came down in a flannel nightshirt and carpet slippers.

"Car?" she asked, seeing the blood on Kwame.

"No. Bullet."

"Damned hunters. I don't mind when they shoot each other." Marley turned away. "Come on in the kitchen. Light's better there."

Kwame was hardly the first gunshot animal Marley had ever seen. She gave his chest a look, saw that the wound was shallow, and turned to his muzzle. Gently she peeled back his lip and exposed the shattered molar. Kwame didn't flinch.

Fiora did. She drew a sharp breath between clenched teeth. Marley took a pair of pliers from a drawer, reached into Kwame's mouth, and removed the remainder of the tooth with a quick jerk. Kwame looked a little startled for a moment, then nuzzled Marley's hand as though to see what it was that smelled so bloody interesting.

"Their teeth aren't wired to the same alarm systems yours and mine are," Marley said to Fiora.

"I'm going back to clean up," I said to no one in particular.

Fiora looked up. "Don't go fishing without me."

"You sure? What with all the excitement, I thought you might want to sleep in."

"If you go fishing without me, you can do everything else without me too."

Her voice told me she meant it. I'd expected as much, but that didn't mean I liked it.

"I'll wait for you," I said, "but make it quick."

"Fishermen are fools." Marley said. She shook her head. "It'll be raining and rough out there."

"The fish won't care," I said.

Marley's acid comment about the mental capacities of fishermen followed me out the door. I didn't argue, because she was right.

The wind gusted. Evergreen needles combed the air with a sound like rushing water. No moon, no stars, only clouds and darkness and wind. It wasn't raining yet, but it wouldn't be long.

It would be a bitch beyond the strait, out on the open water.

The wind followed me while I looked around Rory's place. Lindstrom's Jeep and a two-wheel trailer were stashed at the end of a little logging road that stubbed off at the water's edge a mile east of the house. The trailer's tires were still wet from backing down into the salt chuck to launch the

Zodiac. There was only one set of footprints in the damp sand at the water's edge.

A man alone, trolling for salmon from a Zodiac in the middle of the night, without a rod and dressed in a wet suit. Lindstrom's exposure would have been minimal—maybe fifteen minutes on the river and a few minutes in the boat-house. Five hundred bucks for half an hour of work. Not bad wages for a back-country deputy.

But Lindstrom hadn't revisited the scene of the crime just for the guns. Even he wasn't that stupid or arrogant. He had been after something aboard *The King of Nothing.* The only question was whether he had been taking something . . . or leaving it.

I drove back and parked a hundred yards short of Rory's. A fine rain had started falling. There was no hint of light in the east. The woods were quiet. The damp ground took and held tracks very well. None were there but those of the local animals, myself included.

The boathouse was a tomb with a garage door. Lindstrom lay where he had fallen, his face still twisted in surprise and fear. I knelt and searched him. He had carried his gun in a sealed dive bag. I shook out the rest of the bag's contents: handcuffs, nippers, a wire stripper, and a roll of black electrician's tape.

No way was I going to start the boat's engine until I had checked it for add-ons.

Lindstrom had been in the pilothouse when Kwame leaped aboard, so I started there. My Mag-Lite lit up slices of the darkness inside. Rory's god was the salmon, and this was his chapel; Lucky

Louies and Stingzildas, pink squid and Day-Glo green Hot Spots dangled like carnival prizes from the pegboard mounted beside the wheel. Nearby were carefully coiled hand-tied leaders, bright red Deep-Six planers, silver flashers and dodgers—all the paraphernalia Rory had loved and understood so well.

The long thin wire looked like another piece of stainless-steel leader to be used as terminal tackle for halibut or dogfish. The wire ran off the colorful display of lures and terminal tackle and disappeared under the dashboard. Had I not been Rory's acolyte for so many years, had I not studied in his chapel, I probably would have missed what Lindstrom had done.

I squirmed down between the pilot seat and the wheel and flashed the light into the jungle of ignition wires and fuel lines under the dash.

Bingo.

Taped in the shadow of a mahogany boat rib was a bright, shiny, flat aluminum box the size of a cigarette case, with the wire antenna jacked into one end. The wire was tied into the ignition circuit. It could have been a solenoid or a junction box for the electronic fish finder, except that salt air hadn't corroded the metal of the box.

Rory would have spotted the wire two seconds after he walked into the pilothouse, but Rory was dead. Lindstrom must have figured I was too green about boats to notice an extra wire here or there.

I wiggled around under the dashboard for several minutes, examining the box from all angles and analyzing the wiring pattern. The only identifying marks on the box were partially obscured by the black tape the deputy had used to hold it in place. Very carefully I peeled a strip. Beneath it was the word CESSNA and a parts number.

For three breaths I stayed put and tried to guess why Lindstrom had wired an airplane part into a boat. When nothing came to me, I put the tape back in place, crawled out, and jogged up the steps to the main house.

Benny answered on the first ring. I was so surprised I nearly dropped the phone.

"There's a bogie on my screen," I said.

"Get a classier brand of playmates."

"I'll keep it in mind. Kwame nearly bought it when he jumped into the middle of the game to save my life."

"Is he all right?" Benny demanded.

Kwame stays with Benny when I'm out of town. They play Sergeant Preston and Yukon King in Benny's wheelchair. They are close.

"He had a tooth extracted by a three-fifty-seven slug but he's okay otherwise," I said.

"You?"

"All teeth intact."

Benny grunted. "So tell me about this bogie."

I described the box, the antenna, the wiring harness, and the Cessna part number.

"Anything that looks like a laveliere or nailhead microphone?" he asked.

"No, just the long braided cable jacked into one end."

"Where in the ignition circuit is it wired? Before or after the switch."

I thought for a moment. "Before the switch, on the hot lead from the battery."

I must have sounded tentative. "Make sure, mate," Benny growled. "If it's on the hot wire from the battery, it's a transmitter that needs external power. If it's on the cold side, it's probably a bomb set to go off when you turn the key."

Silence.

"It's on the hot side," I said finally. "Besides, if it's a bomb, it's a damn small one."

"Then I'd say it's a beacon, a bird dog. Wait a minute. What was the part number on the box?"

After I repeated the number, he left me on hold. I watched the patterns of rain on the window. Benny came back within two minutes.

"I called Cessna's eight-hundred parts line," he said. "That thing's a radar transponder, the kind that squawks an identifying radar code. Put it on a salmon and you could follow him up the Columbia River all the way to Coeur d'Alene."

I felt a tickle of excitement. "The nice thing about electronic leashes is that they have two ends."

"Right. Be bloody careful how you jerk the leash on this one. As they say in the old country, Nakamichi is as dirty as a clam."

"A lot of corporate types are."

"Not like this," Benny said flatly. "Ever since yesterday, I've been crunching his numbers in my spare time."

"And?"

"I just found out he's in deep sushi with the *yakuza*."

"Why?"

"The *yakuza* in Japan are like assholes," Benny said, "everyone has one, and nobody talks about them in polite society. But recently the connection between *yakuza* crooks and corporate Japan has been making headlines back home."

"Has Nakamichi's name come up?"

"Not in public. Not yet. He appears in some interesting computer files, though. Seems our boy is real ambitious. He was serving as an international investment broker for the two biggest *yakuza* organizations in Japan, and he had the bad taste to get caught at it."

"He's still running loose," I said.

"He gave up one of the *yakuza* gangs, but he's trying to save his corrupt ass by placating the head of the other one, a thug named Taoka."

"So?"

"So Taoka has only one passion: collecting ancient samurai swords. A friend of mine from Saigon days, who's working now at the embassy in Tokyo, thinks Taoka might be planning to add a new prize to his collection real soon."

"Not if I can help it."

Benny grunted. "You may not be able to, boyo. The *yakuzas* are nasty."

"And I'm not?"

"With them, good isn't enough. You have to be lucky too. What are you planning?" Benny asked.

"I'm going fishing."

"Who's guarding Fiora?"

"Good question. Why don't you ask her?"

"Ouch," Benny said. "You two not speaking again?"

"Oh, we're speaking all right. We're just not saying anything the other one wants to hear."

For once, I hung up first.

I was sawing on the barrels of the Purdey shotgun when Fiora appeared in the doorway of Rory's workshop. I had field-stripped the other guns and dumped the parts in a tub of fresh water to keep the air off them until I could clean them up. I didn't have the luxury of waiting for the shotgun. I had broken it down and mounted the twin barrels in a cloth-padded vise.

Fiora winced when she saw the hacksaw and realized what I was doing. I was already most of the way through the lovely old blued steel, midway between the front bead sight and the breech, turning a beautiful field gun into a short-barreled street sweeper.

It was slow going. The metal was as hard as Eto's sword. I stopped long enough to wipe the sweat from my eyes and twist a new blade into the hacksaw.

"That was Rory's favorite gun, wasn't it?" Fiora asked.

"This is a serviceable twelve-gauge double-barreled shotgun," I said through gritted teeth. "That's all it is. It is not a work of art. It is not a collectible weapon worth a few thousand bucks. It sure as hell isn't a symbol of lost imperial vigor and feudal hierarchy."

I leaned on the hacksaw. "This is a tool and it's meant to be used. It's too long to use aboard the boat the way it is, so I'm taking off a few inches."

I laid down the hacksaw, picked up the Purdey's stock and receiver, and looked at Fiora. "Here. Try it on for size."

Fiora raised the gun to her shoulder and laid her cheek along it, like she was plinking clay pigeons at the South Coast Gun Club. The stock was a little long. I undid the screws that held the recoil pad, cutting the length by an inch. The adjustment made the stock easier for Fiora to handle, both at the shoulder and at the hip.

It was a relief to know I wouldn't have to put the saw to the lustrous, silver-inlaid walnut stock. I could always have Purdey replace the barrels, but the wood was a work of art.

Silently I resumed, hacking my way through the last quarter inch of cold-rolled English steel.

"If you find yourself on the trigger end of this," I said, "shoot from the hip. Without a shock absorber, the recoil won't do your shoulder any good."

She nodded. "Anything else?"

"Try not to shoot holes in the bottom of the boat. And make sure you know where I am before you pull the trigger. At fifteen feet the spread pattern from these barrels would cover the broad side of your average barn."

"And if you're in the way?" Fiora asked coolly, picking up the stock again and throwing it to her shoulder, as though she relished the idea.

"Tell me to duck." I went back to work. "How's Kwame?"

"He's still trying to figure out whose blood he's tasting. Marley put a few stitches in the corner of his mouth."

"I suppose she wants someone to stay with him . . . ?"

I glanced at Fiora, hoping she'd volunteer to stay home and tend to the dog.

Silently she looked back at me.

I went back to sawing. The steel would give before Fiora did.

"You need me," she said. "You can't do it all by yourself. And even if you could, I can't bear the waiting."

The front eighteen inches of the twin barrels fell off onto the concrete floor. The steel rang like a good bell. I chose a file from the case at the back of the work counter and smoothed out the shiny burred steel on the new ends of the barrels.

I didn't answer Fiora. There was no point. We had conducted more than our share of discussions about old-fashioned men and modern women and the rights and responsibilities of each.

"Fiddler?"

I looked at her. "Galahad never had to put up with this kind of shit."

"Galahad never had it this good," she said.

And waited.

I put down the file and reached for her. We held one another for a long time.

As I untied the bowline on *The King of Nothing*, light was seeping into the east very gradually, as though the sun were on an infinite rheostat. The first gulls rose from the water and started to complain about the rain and their empty bellies while they winged downriver toward the sea.

Fiora threw the clutch lever into reverse. I stepped onto the foredeck with my light as she backed out into the river.

The Douglas firs were faint shapes against the sky, but by the time we got near the mouth of the river, the old snag that was our guide mark was clearly visible. Fiora took our heading from the tree, feeling for the channel in the low water of slack tide. At the mouth, the channel was only ten yards wide, and we didn't want to ruin the prop on the river-bottom rocks.

Crouching on the foredeck in the darkness while the boat tiptoed down the channel before dawn was a familiar ritual, except that Fiora was behind the wheel instead of Rory. She knew the drill. She had watched me play lookout for Rory often enough and had done it herself a time or two under his calm guidance.

The dash lights were off but the running lights on the bow glowed red and green against the pale marine paint. The inboard engine throbbed a deep steady 700 rpm, more for steerage than for propulsion. It was the force of the river flowing down to the sea that carried us toward the open salt chuck.

The scent, the taste, the very feel of the experience was so familiar . . . except that Rory wasn't there. I thought I had suspended my grief, but now it carved a hole in my heart.

The shadow of an underwater boulder loomed ahead.

''Port,'' I said softly.

Fiora didn't have Rory's decades of experience, but her response was smooth and precise, with none of my tendency to oversteer. As always, the boat obeyed sluggishly, like the Cobra on a lightly greased skid pad. No front-wheel discs and back-wheel drums to stop you, no low-profile radials to change your direction. Boats respond in slow motion. Fiora was better at negotiating that kind of dreamscape than I was.

The bulky rock shadow fell away to the side. Ahead there was nothing but the dark transparency of the river before dawn. I wished I could see through time half as well as I could see through the clear water.

I had the trigger man, but not his controller, not the man who had wound him up and sent him out to kill Rory. I had no guarantee of getting him, either. He was too smart, too powerful, too well insulated. Other men died for him, samurai whose loyalty transcended their own animal drive for self-preservation.

All I could hope for was one samurai who was slow, undertrained, or overeager to survive.

The Thousand-Year Sword lay next to the mutilated Purdey, wrapped in its silk bag and covered with plastic sheeting against the salt air. I could sense Muramasa's malevolence humming through the steel blade and the eelskin wrapping of the handle. It didn't bother me. There is a time and a place for everything under the sun.

The King of Nothing's exhaust burbled softly, telling of power held in check. I flashed the light into the water one last time. All I saw was water and more water, fathoms of water under the keel. Rain dappled the surface like baitfish feeding.

"We're clear," I told Fiora.

She responded by killing the running lights and sending the throttle up a notch while I scrambled into the cockpit.

"Coffee?" I asked.

Fiora nodded without taking her eyes off the water. She looked at her watch, then at the course chart, and turned the wheel.

"Next stop, Cape Flattery," she said.

Her voice surprised me. It was her money-shuffling voice, clipped, precise, and unemotional. Or nearly so. A thinness to the tone told me she was humming inside like an over-stressed E-string.

I poured both of us a cup of coffee before I slid in beside her on the little banquette seat behind the wheel. She sipped silently. Then she looked at me, her face a pale blur in the slowly condensing dawn.

"Look," I said. "I know you'd prefer it if I turned this whole thing over to Claherty or—"

"I didn't say anything," Fiora interrupted.

"You didn't have to. And I'm not going to. Claherty would have to work through Washington, and Washington would have to work through Tokyo, and the government in Tokyo—"

"Is hand in glove with the *yakuza* in a way that gives our Mafia something to shoot for," Fiora finished crisply. "I understand that better than you do. From Washington, state of; to Washington, D.C.; to Tokyo; back to Washington, state of. A closed circle, and we're on the outside."

Nobody ever accused Fiora of being stupid. Stubborn, maybe, but not stupid.

We sat and listened to the rain against the windshield. It was harder now, but the wind had gotten no worse. I settled in. It was going to be a long unpleasant ride. The only silver lining in this particular cloud was that whoever was following us was having a long unpleasant ride too.

tWENTY-FOUR

There was a big navigation light on Tatoosh Island, a mile off Cape Flattery. A yeoman with a good pair of field glasses could probably have seen me wrestling with Lindstrom's body, had it not been for the rain and the fact that lighthouses are automated now.

Fiora held the wheel and watched the sheer rock cliffs of the point fifty yards away. They loomed out of the water like the dripping dark wall of Alcatraz. There were no boats nearby. No one else wanted to risk the wind that was running against the cliffs.

"Close enough. Come about," I said.

"Thank God." She watched me uneasily as I handled the corpse. Part of me took a malicious pleasure in her discomfort. Maybe next time she'd stay home.

"Depth?" I said.

"Fifty feet."

"Good. Lots of nice little dentalia down there."

"Dentalia?"

"Yeah." I fastened Lindstrom's wrists together with the handcuffs I'd found in his diving bag. The wet suit he wore was cold and clammy. "The dentalium is a deep-water worm with a tube shaped like a tusk."

I ran a fifteen-foot length of anchor chain through the cuffs and wound it around the body. Chain rattled and clanked coldly.

"The Makahs and the Malahats," I continued, talking as I worked, "used the shells for money, back in the bad old days. This was one of their favorite places to get the little beggars."

With a grunt, I propped the body in sitting position against the coaming and began wrapping more chain.

"There's a point to this story, right?" Fiora asked loudly, as if the sound of the chain had chilled her.

I snapped a heavy padlock on the loose end of the chain and hooked it to the cuffs. The other end was bolted to a seventy-five-pound plow anchor. Steel would last a lot longer than flesh and bone. It was heavier, too. What went down wasn't going to come up.

Ever.

"The Indians had an interesting way of collecting dentalia," I said, resting the anchor on the rail and watching the reddish light of the depth finder in the cockpit. "They'd tie an anchor to one end of a worn-out slave and throw him off those cliffs over there."

Fiora grimaced.

"After a while," I continued, heaving the corpse into a better position, "they'd reel in the remains, which were by that time well encrusted with hard currency. Instant money. Sort of a Native-American ATM."

Fiora glanced at me unhappily. She was not amused.

"Look, love," I said, "this son of a bitch killed the man who was closer to me than my own father. If Lindstrom can't take a joke, fuck him."

The depth finder found the shelf that dropped off to two hundred feet. I chucked the anchor into the water and let its weight help me lift the dead man over the side. Anchor, wet suit, chain, and corpse disappeared with very little splash, and even that was muffled by the soft, vast sound of the rain.

One down.

The open ocean hit us like a runaway train the moment we left the shelter of Cape Flattery. The swells came out of the west, preparing for their first landfall since Japan. They lifted the boat high in the air and dropped us deep in the troughs as casually as gravity. The immensity of the ocean's power made you understand where people got the idea for one God, omnipotent, omniscient, omnipresent.

As I watched a rainswept wave rise a full ten feet above the level of *The King of Nothing's* flying bridge, I cursed whoever had first called in the FBI, which had called in the federal judge, who had made it impossible for me to bide my time and set a careful trap on land.

Die or fly.

Being on that boat was a little of both. Land was a memory shrouded in rain. We were eight miles offshore, heading for the Twelve Mile Bank, and I could only hope that whoever was following the transponder under the dashboard was a better navigator than I was.

While Fiora watched the instruments and peered into the heaving, slate-gray mountains that were bearing down on us, I read the loran numbers to her, watched for deadhead logs, and tracked the boat traffic around us. The North Pacific shipping lanes and the best late-season salmon fishing in the world sort of collide west of Flattery. Outbound freighters from Seattle, southbound supertankers loaded with Prudhoe Bay crude, and every adventuresome fisherman in Washington and British Columbia all end up within a few loran digits of the same spot on the ocean.

We weren't the only fools out in "pleasure" craft on the water. It's amazing how many sportsmen have fifteen thousand bucks to invest in the good hulls, down riggers, quick-release terminal gear, and stubby single-action rods that can drag salmon out of those depths. A regular morning commuter crowd was strung out behind us when we began to close on the banks, everything from seventy-two-foot cabin cruisers to Boston Whalers driven by hundred-pound outboards with madmen in yellow raincoats hanging onto the gunwales as their boats bounced from crest to trough to crest.

A dozen commercial long-liners were already at work when I called out the two three-digit coordinates that designated the southern tip of the banks, plus or minus forty-two feet.

I headed out to rig the rods. A fishing boat that wasn't fishing would draw attention. I was so busy I missed the passage of the mammoth freighter until we were struck by its four-foot wake. I grabbed the cabin frame and hung on while everything that hadn't already been shaken loose by the huge rollers got its chance to bounce free. The gaff damn near came out of its clips. The two heavy cannonball sinkers jumped up and crashed back down into their places beneath the gunwale.

I wiped rain and sweat off my face and began picking up stray pieces of fishing gear. I pushed the gleaming metal gaff back and looked in the cabin. At least the Purdey had stayed put. It was riding across Fiora's lap.

By seven o'clock, more than fifty boats had gathered to troll at the loran junction, cutting roughly parallel wakes through the rain. We all ducked and wobbled to avoid the various freighters and commercial fishermen.

"How will he come at us," Fiora asked, "over the side, like Bluebeard?"

"How he does it is his problem. Mine is making him believe he can get away with it. Take us farther west of the twelve-mile line. I don't want to make anyone nervous about working inside territorial waters."

I set up three rods, one on each side and one off the stern. The stern rod had its line clipped to the down rigger. The other two lines were on their own, with nothing more than a special planer to hold them under the water. The hooks all had something in common. They had been nipped off below the barb.

The last thing I wanted was to be distracted by a fish when the bigger bait of the sword was taken.

If it was taken.

I hate waiting.

Over the next half hour, the entire fleet trolled off slowly in different directions through the rain, looking for action. Fiora let us drift to the west, waiting for something—anything—to happen. We kept the boat at the outside edge of the flotilla, idling slowly, trying to look like a wounded herring, hoping to encourage a strike. I had Rory's big yellow marine binoculars in my hands. Even through the persistent rain, the glasses brought in a surprising amount of detail.

We were four hundred yards from the nearest boat, with the rest of the fleet scattered among the wave troughs and veils of rain. The wind had dropped, leaving nothing to relieve the tedium of the weather. From just inside the cabin door, I examined every boat in sight, looking for anything out of place. The most dangerous thing I saw was some long-liner's shark gun on the bulkhead just inside his cabin door.

"Take us a bit closer to the other boats," I said, "but not inside the twelve-mile limit."

Fiora cocked the wheel on a new course, trolling back on a tangent. We were walking a tricky tightrope, trying to use the flotilla of pleasure boats as a cover but still look vulnerable enough to attract an attacker.

So far, nobody seemed interested.

"Anything?" called Fiora.

"No."

She didn't say another word. She didn't have to. Her face said it all.

If I'm bad at waiting, Fiora is worse. It's the only real weakness I've found in her. Her favorite cartoon shows a pair of disgruntled buzzards sitting on a tree limb surveying a barren landscape. One is saying to the other, "Patience, my ass. I'm going to go out and kill something."

I lowered the glasses and went to Fiora. When I wrapped my hands around her upper arms, she felt as hard as the barrels of the Purdey across her lap.

"Let go," I said softly.

She sagged against me and let me rotate her shoulders. Tension. Anger. Disappointment. Fear. She's no more immune to them than I am.

"Let it go," I said quietly. "You're the Queen of Nothing and I'm the King. Nothing to worry about. Nothing to rule."

"But what if he doesn't take the bait?"

"Then I'll try a new lure," I said. "There's no hurry. My memory is as long as my life."

I squeezed her arms, picked up the binoculars again, and headed for the cabin door. Before I got there, the tip of the rod in the left rod holder suddenly dove toward the water. The reel screamed like a small brass siren as monofilament ripped off.

Purely by reflex I grabbed the rod, wondering what had impaled itself on a barbless hook. The rod's action felt heavy and sluggish.

"A shark," I said, disgusted. "That's what we get for trolling so slow."

I cranked in a few yards of line.

I peered into the bottomless gray water, trying to follow the line to see what I'd hooked, when the boat dipped and something wet hit the deck.

Fiora screamed, "Behind you!"

I whirled to face a man in a dark blue dive suit. He was coming out of the water in one smooth motion. I've seen the motion before. It takes a great deal of strength and the kind of training a SEAL gets at Coronado.

He had one leg over the rail on the port side of the boat and was just swinging the other leg abroad. His left hand was on the rail. His right hand clawed at the watertight flap of a holster, revealing a quick glimpse of blued steel.

Jake's .45 was in the small of my back, under my jacket, too far away. The gaff was closer. I grabbed it with my left hand and lashed out. The needle tip of the gaff sank into the wet suit just above his right wrist. I jerked hard, setting the hook and pulling his hand away from the butt of his pistol at the same time.

He made a guttural sound as he twisted his hand and caught the tip of the gaff handle. I jerked again, trying to free the gaff to whack at a more vulnerable part of his body. He knew what I had planned for him and hung on to the gaff with both hands.

The .45 was still in my belt but its handle was positioned for a left-hand draw, and my left hand had too much to do already. I grabbed the butt end of the gaff with both hands just as he reached with his left hand across his body, going for his own gun. I jerked hard. He countered and tried to knock my feet out from under me with a sweeping round kick.

The gaff transmitted the energy of the fight like a graphite trolling rod. I had the diver well and truly hooked. I yanked viciously, trying to punish him so much he would give up. He hissed in pain and showed me bared teeth instead.

Suddenly he shoved back on the gaff, catching me off balance, throwing me against Rory's carefully stocked pegboard display of colorful plugs and treble-barbed hooks. Steel talons raked my back. As I braced myself against falling, I felt the smooth length of an eight-ounce Stingzilda beneath my palm.

The diver reached for the knife strapped to his left calf. I tore the heavy lure free of the board and swung the snelled treble hook at his face. The dive mask ripped away, leaving his eyes vulnerable. I lashed out at them, raking lines of blood across his face. He freed the knife but used it to parry, not to attack. I flung the lure at his face again and caught his knife wrist with my right hand.

We were locked together in deadly symmetry when I saw Fiora in the doorway of the pilothouse. She stood with the Purdey at shoulder level. Its barrels seemed to point more at me than at the man I was fighting.

"There's another one! Duck!"

I went down to the deck, taking my man with me. An instant later Fiora fired both barrels. The hot breath of the shotgun's muzzle blast seared past. I heard a groan and a heavy splash, as though the charge of shot had carried its target over the side. Then there was nothing but the falling rain and the harsh sounds of my own struggle.

The diver fought to gain control of me. He was well-trained and had muscles like rebar. If I hadn't crippled him with the gaff, he would have taken me apart. But the advantage was slim. I head-butted, kneed, and twisted the gaff every chance I got.

Somehow we ended up back on our feet again. Finally I began to turn his knife back on him. He was losing blood and starting to weaken. It was just a matter of time before he gave up or I killed him. He couldn't win, and he knew it. I saw the knowledge in his eyes. Yet he never quit: another samurai who had already made his peace with death.

I didn't want to kill him. I wasn't going to let him kill me. He wasn't going to give up short of death.

He twisted away in one last effort. His knife hand wavered. Then he let himself collapse, hoping to sideslip me and bury the sharp blade in my neck. I felt the move coming and tried to turn his hand at the last second, wanting to inflict less serious damage.

We both ended up on the deck. He broke free of my grasp and rolled to one side. His good hand clawed at the flap of his holster. The boat wallowed and rolled in the waves. I let go of the gaff and pulled Jake's .45. He watched my gun come up, looked into the muzzle, lashed out with his foot, and kept on reaching for his own gun.

His hand was on the gun butt. The angle was awkward, impossible. He was a dead man unless he stopped. He didn't stop. I shot him once, a shoulder wound. He drew the gun. I shot him again and my luck ran out.

He flopped back onto the deck and didn't twitch again.

tWENTY-FIVE

Fiora knelt beside me. I noticed she didn't croon over me as she had over Kwame. I didn't know whether to be hurt or pleased. When she moved unsteadily, I reached for her. She groaned at my touch.

"My shoulder," she cried in protest.

Then I remembered she had held the shotgun at her shoulder instead of her hip. I touched her right shoulder lightly. She flinched and hissed between her teeth.

"I told you to shoot from the hip," I said.

"I don't even remember grabbing the gun," she said. "He was coming over the transom." Her eyes looked a little shocky.

"Hey, I'm not complaining."

Keeping low, I stripped out of the yellow slicker, pulled off my flannel shirt, and rigged a sling for Fiora. Once I thought she was going to faint and so did she, but she held on. She was pale green and woozy before I was done, but she didn't say a word.

"That's it," I said. "We're going home."

"No."

"You've separated your shoulder," I said, "maybe even broken it."

"Those two frogmen had to come from somewhere," she said, ignoring me. "If we keep the bait in the water, we may get another bite. I can drive the boat with one hand."

"Pretty lady," I said angrily, "if you think that shoulder hurts now, just wait until the adrenaline wears off and the pain messages get through to your brain. We're outa here."

"Don't do this to me," Fiora said through her teeth. "You aren't responsible for my choices or the consequences of my choices."

I looked into Fiora's level eyes, more gray than green at the moment, dilated with pain.

"Crawl into the cabin," I said curtly. "Don't show yourself. Someone could be watching us."

I lay in the rain and finished catching my breath while Fiora got to the cabin. She braced herself against a bulkhead, looking pale.

"Now get the binoculars and check the boats," I ordered. "Don't silhouette yourself against the glass."

She crawled to the padded bench that was beneath one of the windows and eased the binoculars into position. Twice she fumbled and nearly dropped them. Finally she picked them up in her left hand and propped them on the ledge that ran around the cabin at the base of the window.

"Anyone coming our way?" I asked.

Pause; then, "No."

"Any boats have a diving platform over the stern?"

Another pause. Another "No."

The *yakuzas* must have done it the hard way, ass over teakettle off the side.

"Anyone even watching us?" I asked.

A longer pause, but the answer was still "No."

"Keep looking."

While she did, I checked the frogman for anything that might tell us where he came from. Nothing but a body full of tattoos. He was samurai, cannon fodder. No individual identity necessary.

"Fiddler, there's something . . . damn the rain and waves! I lost it."

Fiora's voice was strained. It sounded like she was crying. Maybe she was. She'd never shot a man before. She'd never steered a boat with her shoulder dislocated. She damn well should have stayed on shore.

I crawled into the cabin, grabbed a spool of 40-pound test monofilament line, and began making real tight figure-eights around the dead man's ankles. When I had enough to hold a bull elephant, I fished the spare cannonball sinker out of the bin and tied it on securely.

Then I crawled to the stern, tripped the down rigger, wound up the other cannonball sinker, and dragged it over the side. When I finished fastening it to his ankles too, I cut all the trolling lines so that nothing would get in the way.

"What's going on?" I called to Fiora.

"A power cruiser is angling our way."

"How close?"

"Too far to see anything important," Fiora said.

"Let me know when that changes."

Silence then, "The man I shot . . ." Her voice died.

"Floating?" I asked bluntly.

"Swimming."

I looked up sharply. "Where?"

"Toward the cruiser."

"Can we get to him first?" I asked.

"No."

"Can you read the name on the cruiser?"

"No," she said. "The angle is wrong."

"Have they seen him?"

There was a pause. "They must have. They're heading toward him."

"*Shit.* How much water is underneath us?" I asked.

"Enough to bury the Sears Tower," she said curtly. "We're over the trench."

Her tone was still strained and harsh, a stranger's voice. My own wasn't any better.

"Anyone looking our way?" I asked.

"They're too busy rescuing him."

I slid the dead man over the coaming, then pitched the cannonballs after him. The lead sinkers made a bigger splash than he did.

"They're picking the swimmer up," Fiora said. "They're dragging him on board. He's got blood all over his wet suit, but he seems to be—oh, God, someone just stabbed him in the back!"

I went into the cabin in a long lunge. "Give me those glasses!"

The cruiser started up again and began turning

away from us. The boat's name was emblazoned on the stern: *Rising Sun*.

Either I said it aloud or Fiora's getting too damn good at reading my mind.

"The *Rising Sun* is Nakamichi's boat," she said.

"Keep us over the trench."

I grabbed the microphone of the CB radio and punched the transmit button. "Ron, this is the thousand-year man. I can see you, Ron. Do you see me?"

Through the glasses I watched the cruiser as I repeated the message. There was a flurry of movement as the cruiser stopped. The man on the flying bridge drew my eye.

"Gotcha," I muttered.

Nakamichi picked up binoculars and looked toward our boat. A moment later the radio crackled to life.

"What do you want?"

"It's not what I want," I said. "It's what I've got. A thousand years, Roniko. It's all yours. Just come and get it."

He laughed. "I am a patient man. I will wait."

"There won't be anything to wait for," I said. "The sword's going over the side."

I looked at him through the binoculars. He looked back at me the same way. We were close enough so that I could see the color of his foul-weather gear.

I handed the glasses to Fiora. "Watch. If you see anything that looks like a rifle, let me know."

I grabbed the Thousand-Year Sword from its hiding place in the cabinet beneath the pilot's seat and stepped out into the open cockpit. A length of chain was wrapped around the scabbard.

"What are they doing?" I asked.

"Staying put and watching us through three pairs of binoculars."

"Tell me if that changes."

The rain was cold on my skin. I faced the *Rising Sun,* held the scabbard blade outward, and pulled the sword.

It seemed to draw light the way a magnet draws iron. The temper line rippled as though alive. It felt too good in my hand, almost warm. I wondered whether it was truly cursed or simply unusually blessed, and then I realized there was no difference between the two.

"Any activity?" I asked.

"Ron's arguing with one of his bodyguards."

I felt real hope for the first time since I had realized who was ultimately responsible for Rory's death.

"Make your move, you bastard," I prayed.

"They're still arguing."

In slow motion I sheathed the sword and held the chain-wrapped scabbard out over the water.

The *Rising Sun's* engines ripped to life. The cruiser turned away from us.

"Is he still watching?" I asked.

"Yes."

I remembered the greed I had seen in his eyes for the sword. Nakamichi would have to watch while it slipped forever beyond his reach.

It wasn't much to lay on Rory's grave, but it was all I had.

"Take a good look, you bastard."

I opened my hands and let Muramasa's blade slide deeply into the sea.

Sometimes a little vengeance is all you get.

ePILOGUE

A few days later I sat at the kitchen table, listening to the rain and reading all about a local tragedy in the *Malahat News*. Seems a local deputy apparently drowned while diving alone. His body hadn't been recovered, but his Zodiac washed ashore about seven miles down the strait from Cape Flattery.

I was reflecting on the wages of sin when somebody hammered on the door. I opened it and wasn't surprised to see Francis X. Claherty.

He looked unhappy. That made two of us. I had been hearing Nakamichi roar off in his damned fancy cruiser for days.

"What do you want?" I asked. "Judge Tomlinson kicked me loose."

"Yeah. What did you give that creep Carlton to testify that he stole the sword and gave it to Eto?"

"It was the truth. You should know. You're the

one who hooked Carlton to the lie box and watched the needles say he was rock solid."

Claherty grunted. "Where's the goddam sword, Fiddler?"

"Ask Eto."

"He's dead."

I shrugged. "There's a lot of that going around lately."

"You have any coffee?" Claherty asked.

"There's a café back in town."

"This isn't official. I just thought you might want to talk shop about Roniko Nakamichi."

"What about him?"

"What about that coffee?"

I stopped blocking the door and stepped back. "Keep your voice down. Fiora's still sleeping."

"Yeah, it's hard to get your rest with a broken shoulder. Next time you won't go fishing in such rough weather." Claherty sat at the table and watched me out of shrewd dark eyes. "Did you catch anything for all your trouble?"

"Nobody did. That's why you're here."

I poured coffee into a clean mug and set it in front of him.

"You wanted to talk," I said. "Talk."

"Did you know Nakamichi was involved with the *yakuza*?"

"Does it matter?"

Claherty took a sip of coffee. "He was. Then he got in deep crap with them. He really pissed off his patron saint, a guy called Taoka."

"So?"

"Nakamichi was being set up for the high jump

when word of a samurai sword came. Did I tell you that Taoka was a collector of old swords?"

"Get to the point."

"The point is simple. Nakamichi wanted the sword to get Taoka off his ass, but Cairns wouldn't sell it. Nakamichi got someone to burgle Cairns's house but they didn't find it. Cairns was killed in the process. Am I right so far?"

"It's your story. You tell me."

Claherty looked disappointed, but he kept on talking. "Somehow Nakamichi knew you were Cairns's heir. He approached you. You set up a meet somewhere out of sight and killed him."

"Get real. No one comes close to that guy but his bodyguards."

"Yeah? Well, the authorities over on Vancouver Island just came up with a body. He hadn't been in the water too long, and he's a dead ringer for Nakamichi. A very dead ringer."

"*What?*"

Claherty looked at me like he wished I was attached to a little black truth box. "You heard me. Nakamichi's dead."

I couldn't believe it and didn't bother to hide it.

"You really didn't know, did you?" Claherty asked, disappointed.

"No, but don't expect me to cry at his funeral. All I regret is that I wasn't there to watch him die. Who did it?"

"One of his bodyguards. He's back in Japan now, Taoka's right-hand man. Nakamichi is dead. You figure it."

I laughed.

Then I laughed some more, feeling better than I

had in days. It had been a long shot, a parting shot, the only shot I'd had. And it had landed dead center.

Sometimes you only get a little vengeance.

And sometimes you get lucky.

I was still laughing when Claherty stood up in disgust and left.

107